MORE RAVES FOR
RUNNING WITH LIONS

"A warm, funny, smart and poignant debut, full of heart and full of hope. I loved the adorably cute relationship that emerges between Sebastian and Emir, I loved the humour, and I loved being reminded what it's like to be a teenager during a long, hot, messy summer, when everything is new and exciting, anything seems possible, and the world is opening out in front of you. I throughly enjoyed it and hope it gets all the accolades and praise it deserves."

—Simon James Green, author of *Noah Can't Even*

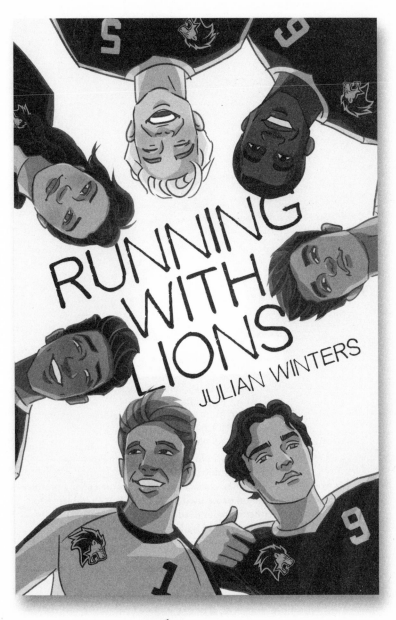

RUNNING WITH LIONS

JULIAN WINTERS

interlude press • new york

To every LGBTQIA+ person who has questioned their place in life: You're strong. You're important. You're a lion. Let the world hear you roar.

Some readers may find some of the scenes in this book difficult to read. We have compiled a list of content warnings, which you can access at www.interludepress.com/content-warnings

 1

"ARE YOU CERTAIN YOU'VE PACKED everything?"

Sebastian grins at his mom from the bottom step outside their modest two-story house. "Of course, Mom," he replies. The faded paint on the cedar fence behind her catches his eye. A streak of bright sun gives the fresh dew on the grass a glitter effect. Summer is in full bloom, weaving a heavy blanket of heat around them.

"I just don't want you to forget anything," she whispers. Sunlight accentuates the soft wrinkles around her eyes and her graying blonde hair. Lily Hughes's smile still has a hint of youth when she fixes the zippers of his duffel—for the fifth time this morning.

"I won't."

"Like a toothbrush, or a sweater in case it gets cold."

The growth spurt Sebastian experienced in freshman year makes him a giant when he's facing her. Three years later, he has a good six inches on her. She stands on her tiptoes to hug him, for the third time in ten minutes.

Sebastian rolls his pale brown eyes but squeezes her tight.

"Did you pack lots of underwear? I can't have you going butt naked for a month—"

Sebastian groans, unable to hide how mortified he is.

"I've got it all, Mom," he insists.

"Extra pairs of socks? Your shorts for the lake?"

"We won't have time—"

"Hush, now," she says, swatting at his chest. "Every year you swear you won't have time for fun. But then you come home with a gorgeous tan. You grow all these muscles and recite every lyric from the *Dirty Dancing* soundtrack."

"That's not true."

Sebastian only knows the words to those songs because of his older sister Carly's obsession with corny '80s movies.

"And you're at that age where—" Lily pauses with a perceptive expression. "If you need condoms…"

He chokes; his features immediately morph into that mortified look that comes with talks about sex with your parents.

Who invented sex talks with parents, anyway? Sebastian thinks. *They should be burned, buried, dug up, and lit on fire again.*

"Jesus, Mom." Sebastian drags the toe of his scuffed Converse on the sidewalk. He's suffocating from humiliation, his hot neck, and his tight collar.

"Don't start with me, Bastian."

Sebastian tenses when she squints accusingly at him. It's as bad as that time she caught him kissing Julie Hammonds in eighth grade. He won't win this argument.

Avoid, avoid, avoid.

His fingers comb through his hair; it's usually a tree-bark-brown, but hours of mowing the lawn in the sun have brightened it to a tawny hue, like a lion's mane. "Mom," he says with a sigh. She smirks back. "I'm not going off to the *war*. It's just soccer camp. Me and the team and lots of practicing."

It's more than that. Ever since Willie dragged him to soccer tryouts their freshman year, it's been so much more.

Every summer, after making the team, he skipped the teenage glory days promised to him in every punk song since the existence of Blink-182. Year after year, he traveled to the school's training camp just north of Bloomington. He learned to love the sweet stain of green on everything he owns and a second skin made of pure sweat.

Sebastian honestly loves it: a month away from family and existence and freedom, sore muscles after hours of running drills, his skin baking under the haloing sun, smelly socks and unwashed practice jerseys, the *symbolism* of being with his boys for weeks.

"Of course, Bastian. You have no time for girls, right?" Lily's not condescending. "It's all soccer and homework, ever since Samantha left for college."

Sebastian tries not to flinch. *Sam*, not Samantha. She liked when boys called her that. Sam was spunky and gorgeous and an *almost* happily-ever-after for him—an "almost" that came with an asterisk and a footnote and a pile of disappointment when she left for college last year. Two months in, she ditched him for a physics teaching assistant. She was majoring in dance. Go figure.

"Sure, Mom." He grins, but he's dying to get away from this conversation.

He didn't love Sam. Sebastian isn't sure what love looks, feels, or sounds like. Lately, he's been imagining it's something stupid, ridiculous, and utterly confusing—like Katy Perry songs. He's not ready to venture to the dark side of comparing his feelings to Katy Perry music.

What happened with Sam is another talk he hasn't had with his parents, along with: "Hey, Mom and Dad, I like boys, too" and "I get a chubby watching Chris Evans in anything," though he's pretty sure he's gonna keep that last one to himself—not that *who* he is or *whom* he falls in love with matters lately. Sebastian Hughes is nothing but soccer and pleasing everyone else, and not always in that order.

Lily stares as if she's already read his mind. Before he can get the courage to say anything, a cheap sound system blaring the synth-heavy, raucous drumming of Imagine Dragons grabs their attention.

Mason pulls to the curb in a vintage Ford Mustang painted a flaking candy apple red. Its bumper is rusted. The canvas roof is peeled back, the white leather seats age-stained.

"Well, Mrs. Hughes!" Mason's mouth curls mischievously. Leaning over Willie in the passenger seat, he cuts off the radio. "You're looking lovely this morning," he says. His coffee-brown hair falls into blue-green eyes.

"Oh, Mason, be quiet," she says with a giggle. "You're such a tease."

"Loser," Sebastian coughs into his knuckles.

Willie doubles over laughing. He has cool blue eyes, pale skin, and white-blond hair. He seems exotic and intimidating, but he's always happy, and that, of course, makes him Sebastian's favorite. Willie's cheap neon sunglasses fall down his nose as he croons, "Smooth," at Mason.

Mason's too busy wiggling his eyebrows at Lily to notice.

"I've told you a dozen times to *please*, call me Lily," she tells Mason.

He grins. "Lily."

Sebastian prefers Mason Riley as an ally rather than an enemy. It's been that way since they were twelve, after Mason's dad left his mom. Mason never admitted it, but he needed a friend. Enter Sebastian Hughes. They were two complete opposites that clicked.

"Ready, Hughes?" Mason asks, sinking back into the driver's seat. He drums his fingers on the steering wheel. "The road is calling."

Sebastian nods. He tosses his duffel bag into the back seat where Willie has crawled. It's a privilege if Willie offers you the passenger seat.

"Boys," Lily says in the overprotective voice Sebastian's heard for three summers now, "Please take care of my sweet Bumble—"

"*Mom*," Sebastian whines.

Lily snorts, ruffling his hair. Usually, Sebastian wears his hair in a buzz cut, but he's grown it out into a faux-hawk. He thinks it's epic. Mason calls it a douchebag 'do, but Mason's worn the same longish, constantly-pushing-hair-out-of-his-face style since middle school, so whatever.

Sam used to love his buzzed hair. That was the best reason for a change.

"Sorry." Lily's nervous smile reminds him of being a five-year-old, marching off to his first day of kindergarten. "You know I worry."

"I know," he mumbles and flashes her his best "I'll be good" grin.

"Call me every day."

"Every weekend," Sebastian says.

"Every other day. And FaceTime us on Sundays."

"Three times a week and a quick text after practices," Sebastian bargains. She concedes with a small nod and a motherly kiss to his forehead.

"Oh, my heart," Mason teases under his breath.

Sebastian waits until Lily is distracted by Willie promising to call too before punching Mason in the shoulder. "Asshole."

Mason cranks the radio; Fall Out Boy's pop-punk-chanting blares from the speakers as the car edges from the curb. He says, "Ready, boys?"

Sebastian grins as though he can taste it—*freedom*. Nothing stands in the way of a perfect summer getaway with his team-mates, nothing except that gnarly little rumor from a few days ago: "Did you hear? Emir Shah joined the soccer team. The coaches gave him an invite to the training camp."

He has no idea how that's going to go. Will Emir speak to him? Punch him? Violence has never been Emir's thing, but Sebastian doesn't *know* him anymore. It's not as if he's hung around Emir, not since they were kids.

If there's one person who can turn his summer upside down, it's an ex-best friend Sebastian hasn't gotten over.

Sebastian slouches, concealing his scrunched face from Mason and Willie. Perfect summer? No such thing exists for Sebastian Hughes.

Sebastian takes in the dirt roads and greenery on the drive. It's an hour from Bloomington to Oakville. He rolls his eyes when Mason complains, "I'm gonna hurl," with a cigarette hanging from his lips. Mason fails to appreciate nature. He's a city guy, a lover of tall buildings, muggy weather, and the smell of ozone.

"You'll be fine."

"Whatever," Mason grumbles. He takes another drag, savoring it. Oakville has only one decent market, so they stopped for supplies. Mason used a fake ID to buy his favorite brand of cigarettes and bought cheese puffs for Willie. A short stretch of road awaits. "It's our last year, boys!"

Willie howls into the wind. His hands drum against Sebastian's headrest to Mason's latest addiction, The 1975.

Sebastian taps his foot along with the muted bass. It's better than the constant hum of club beats and Bruno Mars songs they've heard too many times. Ahead, pools of dandelions drift by; clouds tumble in a cornflower sky. "Still thinking about traveling?" he asks over whipping winds.

Mason nods before he says, "How about it, Will? Next summer, overseas?" He checks Willie out in the rearview mirror. "Catch a few Real Madrid games?"

Willie laughs. "Hook up with a few babes over in Barcelona."

Smoke fogs around Mason's mouth when he says, "Damn right!"

"You two will never score," Sebastian jokes.

Mason rolls his eyes. "We could bum around Greece, right, Will?"

"Live it up like kings?"

"Hell, yeah!"

"More like peasants," Sebastian mumbles, but his smirk belies his words.

"What about you, Bastian?" Mason asks. "Still gonna stick around the city? Work for your pops?"

Sebastian shrugs. Oliver Hughes works in construction. It's not exactly Sebastian's dream career. He slumps, closes his eyes, and kicks a foot up on the dash. "Haven't thought about it," he replies, but it's a lie.

Life after high school is every teenager's dream, Sebastian's too: being out of his parents' house, doing things his way. And this big world is ready to swallow him whole.

"Is it the money?" Willie asks.

"Not exactly," he says.

Sebastian's parents can't afford an Ivy League school with a good athletic program where he can strengthen his soccer skills. And Sebastian isn't the best in the field; that's Mason, by far. Athletic scholarships don't come easy. It's not as if talent scouts pack the stands to take notes on him. All those hopes of playing in the Premier League and wearing the jersey of Manchester United, Oliver's favorite team, are just pipe dreams. Those are the fantasies you have as a kid, not when you're a goalie in a small city. The headlines of the school newspaper never asked: "Who is Sebastian Hughes?"

"I hear Sebastian's getting captain this year."

Sebastian elbows Willie. "It's not happening, dude."

"It's true, bro," Mason says; the corners of his mouth lift while smoke seeps out. "I've overheard people talking—"

"*No one* talks about me."

"—and they say that *you*, Hughes, are going to be—"

"They'll pick you," Sebastian interrupts quickly.

"No way." Mason flicks his head to get hair out of his eyes. It falls right back. "The coaches love you, man. I'm reckless."

He *is*, but Sebastian says, "You're not," to humor him.

"Dude, I've got a rep." Mason chuckles.

"You'd have better focus if you'd stop chasing all those girls."

"Hey!" Mason scowls. "I've expanded my horizons. The guys on the swim team…"

Okay, so Mason flirted and got *one* guy on the swim team's number.

"And Willie's friend—"

"Miguel." Willie sighs, nose wrinkling.

"Miguel!" Mason releases a pleased grin. "I hooked up with him at Carl's last party."

Willie tosses cheese puffs in Mason's hair. They bicker like kid brothers constantly; Sebastian plays mediator. In less than a year, he won't be pulling them apart anymore.

When Mason veers the car down a long stretch of familiar road, giddiness thrums inside of Sebastian. Clean countryside air fills his lungs. He can't wait to fall into his cabin bed, run around the pitch, and hang with his teammates.

But this Emir rumor is a zombie feasting on his brains. The chance of Emir Shah turning up at *his* training camp in any alternate universe is zero. Why would he? Emir is a loner who doesn't play any sport, including soccer.

"You haven't thought about it?" Willie asks.

Sebastian startles. Haven't thought about what? Emir being at camp? The fact that their childhood friendship was unceremoniously flushed down the drain when they became teenagers?

"Being captain," Willie says, face contorted.

He has. Sometimes he daydreams about being the leader who gets the team a trophy. It'd be incredible. But it's an awesome responsibility too. It's like floating on the ocean, being weightless and consumed at the same time. "I don't know," he finally says.

Sebastian closes his eyes. The sun burns pretty colors behind his eyelids: the cornflower of the sky mixes with the pink in Willie's cheeks and a wash of green from the passing grass. The easiness of summer drowns out everything else.

 2

Oakville isn't officially a *town*. It's a short stretch of narrow road with one gas station, a single traffic light, and a few attractions for summer tourists, like a cheesy '50s-style diner with wonky air conditioning but the best burgers Sebastian's ever had. The ice cream shop has outdoor seating, and an old drive-in at the edge of town brings in a handful of townies at night. But the rest is mostly old shops selling "Greetings from Oakville!" postcards or antiques, owned by lifers who refuse to move out.

"Here it is, kids!" Mason says in a corny TV announcer voice.

A mile and a half off the main road, a summer camp has been renovated into their training facility. An ancient wooden sign hangs at the entrance bridge: "Camp Haven." It used to be Camp Heaven, a Christian youth camp, but one of the E's fell off a decade ago.

"Welcome to hell," Mason says as they pass over the bridge.

Willie chuckles from the back seat while Sebastian takes it all in once again.

The modernized cabins fit two boys, a stupid rule according to Willie, but that's because he wants all three of them to bunk together. Behind the cabins sits a massive lake that shines like black diamonds after sunset. Nearby is the old main lodge, now a cafeteria. Guys use the picnic area to sneak cigarettes at night.

Around the bend is a huge shed used for equipment storage, affectionately called "the Hot Box" because there's no ventilation, a hard lesson Sebastian learned his first year. The locker room is bathed in an eternal stench of sweat and jockstraps, but the water pressure in the showers is amazing.

The vibe reminds Sebastian of Jason Voorhees, Camp Crystal Lake, and all those lame '80s horror movies Willie loves.

Mason grins and hops out of the car. "And look, most of the hellions have already arrived!"

Willie says, "Quit it, Mace," as he pulls on his backpack. "This place is a sanctuary," he announces. "A no-man's-land, dude. *Sacred.*"

Sebastian snorts, dropping an arm around Willie's shoulders and a hand in his sweaty hair.

"Very poetic, Will," Mason mocks. "Keep waxing sweet haikus like that and I'm gonna marry you." Clearly, Mason has no idea *what* a haiku is.

"Not because I'm a good kisser?"

Mason scrunches his face. "Dude, I'll take your word on it."

"You should." Willie grins wryly. "I suck face better than I cook."

Yep, these are Sebastian's best friends.

NOT TOO MUCH LATER, THE rest of the team pulls in. Sebastian's eyes scan the usual faces along with rookies who trained with them during the spring. He's not searching for anyone...

Captain Obvious, front and center.

High-fives and fist bumps are passed around. The bigger guys roughhouse, give noogies and headlocks, talk smack for the hell of it.

Mason chuckles and says, "They have no idea," to Willie.

"Better call the ambulances now."

The thing about soccer is, it's a rough sport where the primary objective isn't just getting the ball in the goal. It's about maneuvering the ball toward the posts without being slaughtered on the way. All of them have racked up some harsh injuries over the years. It's all worth it.

The brotherhood within the team is what attracted Sebastian and Willie. This team broke all the rules. He remembers Coach Patrick's speech that first day: "No exclusions around here, boys! Be who you are! Be proud! Treat each other like family."

Rumor was, Coach's nephew Xander went to one of those blazer-and-tie Catholic schools and got kicked off the baseball team when he came out. Coach decided to change the system: Sexuality in sports became a nonfactor. Whom you were attracted to off the field didn't matter. If you could get the ball to the goal without falling, you were in.

"At the end of the day, you're a bunch of lost boys with big dreams, anyway. Screw the other BS!"

And that was that. No one cared when Willie came out, because he was the best defensive player they had. Mason's make-out session with Miguel was forgotten the following Monday. Acceptance was huge for Sebastian. He had a place where he was safe and wanted. There was no turning back.

"Fresh blood!" Mason howls like a starved wolf.

"No hazing," Willie warns.

"And no pranks," Sebastian says, eyebrows knit together. "Remember what happened last year?"

Mason cackles; pride flashes in his eyes at the memory. *The Great Riley Flood*, capitalized, italicized, and overemphasized, nearly got Mason kicked off the team. A few of the returning players are still raw about it.

"That was kids' stuff, Hughes. They were all overdramatic."

"You flooded half the cabins, and our parents had to pay the bill for us to stay off-site for a week afterward," Sebastian says.

Mason shrugs, like "no big deal." He cocks his head to eye the smaller guys. "Are you done making noise?"

Sebastian elbows him, then sizes up their teammates.

Zach, Robbie, and Giovanni stand together, cracking jokes. Jack is trying to worm his way into their group while Charlie practices keepie-uppies with his new ball. And then there's—

"Is that *Shah*?" Mason hisses.

Yep! *Emir.*

Maybe Sebastian should've brought this up on the ride to Oakville? He's been tight with Willie and Mason for years. They would've understood Sebastian's concerns. Secrets aren't allowed in their little circle. But Sebastian hasn't had the guts to discuss Emir with his friends, not yet.

"I heard…" Willie starts. Sebastian misses everything after "He signed up for tryouts a few months back" because he's staring at Emir while his heart sinks into the acidic abyss of his stomach.

It's been years since Sebastian and Emir Shah said more than five words to each other, not since they were scrawny ten-year-olds playing video games and reading comic books—when Sebastian only had one friend.

Emir stands off to the side. He still chews his lip nervously. Sebastian remembers the cheekbones, soft and distinct, but the stubble on his jaw is new, as is the knit beanie covering his dark hair. He's wearing an oversized Bloomington Lions sweatshirt that swallows his skinny frame, athletic shorts, and tube socks that almost touch his knobby knees.

Christ, he's wearing cleats!

Mason snorts. "This is some awful joke, man." It comes out a little harsh. Sebastian suspects this isn't because Mason has a thing against newbies, but because Emir isn't exactly friends with anyone on the team. "Shah's trying to be one of us?"

Sebastian hisses, "Shit," under his breath when, in a very awkward, electric moment, Emir's eyes meet his.

"It's true, dude." Willie's mouth curls into a partial grin. "The coaches say he has potential."

"Yeah, the potential to wreck our entire last season, bro." Mason wrenches Willie into a headlock. They wrestle. Emir is momentarily forgotten, but not for Sebastian. And then his overthinking leads to one of the worst ideas ever conceived.

Sebastian tries to play it off when he jogs over to the other players. He gives out quick high-fives or chest bumps, leveling the frosh players with the evil eye just to rile them. "Chill, I won't bite," he teases. They laugh warily. "Watch out for Riley, though."

One kid, peering at Mason, goes ghost-white, so Sebastian says, "Just feed his ego and you'll be fine."

When Sebastian reaches the end of the line, his jerky heart slams against his ribs. Where's the off-switch for all these damn childhood memories that flood his mind? Emir's "what the hell, dude!" glare quickly remedies that problem.

"Hey." Sebastian grins nervously. "Emir?"

Emir scowls at him. His eyes are hypnotic—storm-cloud gray. Up close, moss green surrounds his irises.

"I mean, I know it's you!" Sebastian laughs nervously, but Emir does nothing more than raise an exasperated brow. "It's—it's *you*. Here, at camp. And I wasn't expecting that." He sizes Emir up. Last year, Emir was a skateboard punk with tall, waxy hair and ripped jeans, a fan of band T-shirts and Vans. This isn't *that* guy.

"Yeah," Emir deadpans.

With sweaty palms, Sebastian tries another tactic: smiling like a psychopath. He's taken aback by Emir. He's used to hanging out with meatheads: guys who watch, play, and breathe the game. Stereotypes suck, but most of Sebastian's teammates fit the mold.

"It's good to see you?" It's not supposed to come out as a question. "I remember, um, when we were younger—"

"We practically potty-trained together. Glad you remembered," says Emir, dryly. His eyes flit around as if he wants to make sure no one catches them interacting.

Is being seen with me that awful?

"Yeah," Sebastian says. "We've known each other that long, haven't we?"

"Mmhm."

Sebastian is distracted by the way rays of sunlight spread over Emir, highlighting the smoothness of his brown skin. His matured appearance is different in a good way. But his scowl gut-punches Sebastian back to reality.

"Your parents—from Yorkshire, right?" Sebastian winces. Making useless conversation isn't a good icebreaker, but he just wants Emir to lighten up. "Your family moved over here when you were four. Our moms would have lunch together."

Emir nods but doesn't say much else.

Sebastian tries again. "My dad is from—"

"Sheffield," Emir interrupts.

Sebastian's mouth nearly splits his face—*Emir remembers*—but his delight dissolves at Emir's annoyed expression.

"So, you're here. At camp. And, um, why?"

Smooth move, douchebag, Sebastian thinks.

"What's up with you, mate?" Emir hisses. His jaw tightens. "Should I not be here? You don't want me getting in the way of your little team? Mucking things up, right?"

Sebastian gasps, adding to the utter embarrassment he's accumulated. "Wait, *what?*"

"Don't worry," Emir says while shaking his head. "I won't be in the way for long. I'm not any good. The coaches will either bench me or just kick me off the team. You don't have to pretend like I'm one of the boys." He stomps off toward the cabins, muttering "I thought you were better than that" just loud enough for Sebastian to hear.

A little supernova explodes in Sebastian's brain, leaving him lightheaded. *Did that just happen?*

Willie and Mason flank him with sympathetic smiles. They had a clear view of Sebastian the Idiot. Like all his previous failures, he's never living this one down.

"That guy has being an asshole down to a science," Mason mumbles. He hooks an arm around Sebastian's extremely tight shoulders.

"He's just new," Willie says.

"Whatever."

"Give him a chance."

Mason groans. "No, seriously, Will. We all know Shah's a loner who never wanted to hang with any of us. This isn't his crowd."

When he was friends with Emir, this wasn't Sebastian's crowd either. Back then the guys in the neighborhood teased him for being short, chubby, and too clumsy to play street ball. "Bastian the Trashcan" was their favorite chant, everywhere he went. The nickname stuck for too long and haunted him in his bedroom mirror. His mom let him stay inside to play FIFA on his Xbox instead of being taunted. That put a target on his back at school. Bullies love to terrorize kids who isolate themselves; Sebastian was no exception.

"I'm sure he'll come around," Willie says. His optimism reminds Sebastian how sports brought him out of his shell. He played basketball, swam, and then dove headfirst into soccer.

"Or he'll go away, whichever." Mason changes the subject. "I'm rooming with Charlie this year."

"Again," Sebastian and Willie say, synchronized, then laugh at themselves.

Mason says, with a grunt and zero anger, "Get a life." He leads the way toward their cabins.

Willie, a favorite among the coaches, scored their usual cabin for the summer. He's proud and embarrassed when Sebastian says, "Sweet, Willster."

"Here's to a killer summer, right?"

Sebastian nudges Willie. "Our last summer here."

"Our *best* summer!" shouts Mason, and Sebastian puts on his best fake grin. So far, it sure as hell doesn't feel like their best summer.

 3

"It's good to be back." Memories hit Sebastian the second he steps into the cabin.

Sunlight spills in from the nearby window; tall pine trees frame a sweet view of their practice pitch. He walks to a twin bed that's angled awkwardly in a corner. A tattered poster of Keira Knightly has hung over it since their first summer.

"Still stinks, though," Sebastian scoffs; the stench of dirt and sweat wrinkles his nose. He flops on the bed. Dust glitters in the air like the aftermath of a pixie war. "Smells like you, Willster."

"Whatever," Willie says from the other side of the room.

Sebastian runs his fingers along his initials carved into the wall above his headboard. He grabs his jersey from freshman year out of his bag and stuffs it under his pillow the way he does every summer.

"It sucks they won't get us a TV," Willie says. Only Coach Patrick's and the rec room, where they scrutinize film footage, have televisions. Sebastian doesn't mind. He and Willie can watch *The Walking Dead* marathons on his laptop.

"How long before the first practice?"

"Half an hour?" Willie is already unpacking. He smiles slyly, making a suggestive motion with his hand. "Do you need a little alone time?"

"No!" Sebastian laughs until his eyes tear up. "And I better not catch you!"

Willie has his practice clothes laid out. He flips Sebastian off and says, "You know the rules." His jeans are pulled low, providing Sebastian a glimpse of pale ass he really didn't need to see. "Sock on the door."

Sebastian gazes at the ceiling rather than Willie's shameless nudity.

"What's up with Mace and what's-her-name?"

"Valerie," Sebastian tells him.

"Yeah. Val!" Willie grins lewdly. For a gay guy, Willie's maintained a ridiculous crush on Mason's ex-girlfriend.

Wait—is she an ex? Sebastian doesn't know. Mason's love life is very confusing, which Willie's decided needs immediate attention.

"I don't get them," he says, pulling on a snapback. He's a typical frat-boy-in-training, and Sebastian can't decide if he likes it or not. "They're always breaking up. Is he gonna cool it off before college?"

"You never know with Mace," Sebastian replies, turning on his side. He stares at scuff marks from their cleats on the hardwood floor. "It's never a clean break. Period."

His experiences with romance have been like boxing Floyd Mayweather, Jr.—you never win.

"She's a sweet girl," Willie says.

"That's why Mason fell for her."

It might not be the *only* reason, since Val is gorgeous too. She walked into Mason's life wearing denim shorts, wavy brown hair in a ponytail, and a cherry lollipop between her pouty pink lips.

She was supposed to be a summer crush, but turned into four years of confusion.

Why doesn't anyone ever get over a summer crush?

Willie daydreams while Sebastian pulls out a change of clothes. Silence with Willie is never awkward. Mason talks a lot, but Willie coolly observes the rest of the world.

"Can't wait for the weekends around here," Willie says.

Yeah, the weekends are great. Almost forty-eight hours of freedom from soccer, discipline, and all of Coach Patrick's movie quotes about teamwork. Is there a universal coaching rule that every life lesson must come from *Rudy* or *Hoosiers* or *Remember the Titans*?

Sebastian anticipates swims at the lake, and crackling bonfires where they'll talk about how the team will finally earn a "W" over all their opponents this season. Bloomington High's a middle-of-the-road school when it comes to sports: Football sucks. Basketball is hot and cold. The swim team is good when they're on. Soccer draws the biggest crowd, being the only sport that's come close to putting a trophy in the barren case in the entrance hall of the school. "What about you?" Sebastian turns the topic back to Willie. "Gonna finally land a boyfriend?"

Of the three of them, Willie avoids relationships the most. He hasn't given a real reason. Bloomington isn't the easiest place to be an out-of-the-closet teen.

"You mean besides my hand?" Willie says, his lips teased by a smile.

Sebastian rolls his eyes. "Yeah, dude. Though that's been a pretty solid relationship, right?"

Willie wiggles his eyebrows. "I dunno. With you and Mace around, I'm good. Right?"

"Yeah, you've got us, man. Who needs anything else?"

"Exactly!" Willie walks toward the door. "Now get your lazy ass up before we're late," he says as he goes.

He's right; they can't be late for practice. Sebastian gets off the bed and stretches his arms over his head until he hears something crack satisfyingly. He changes clothes, missing the softness of his old uniform that's been stuffed in his closet at home for too long.

When they step outside, sun haloes the entire camp, making it a golden dream. Willie mumbles, "Time to die," and that means one thing: Practice is going to suck.

AFTER THIRTY MINUTES OF PRACTICE, Sebastian's muscles throb, and his skin drips layers of sweat. He hasn't ached with this much life since spring training. The dizzying sun pounds on him as the team jogs laps. Their feet dragged during basic foot drills. This is their punishment.

"How does one pack of lions suck this bad?" Coach Patrick barks. He has a perpetual love for hats. They hide some of his face, but Sebastian can imagine those thoughtful, deep-brown eyes staring them down. Summer sun has given him a slight tan, but his cheeks are red with frustration. He's menacing enough at nearly six-foot-five with a brawny build, but the stiffness of his round jaw adds to the effect. "What did you all do during the off-season?"

"Well, I didn't *suck* anyone." Mason's been wheezing for air since halfway into practice.

"Dude, uncalled for." Sebastian uses his collar to hide a grin from the coaches.

"Another one down!" Zach announces, cackling as a green-faced freshman runs past him to bend over a trashcan. Most of the frosh players barely survived the first hour, either collapsing on the sidelines or puking Gatorade behind the bleachers. The upperclassmen pick them apart like scavengers and earn extra laps for their lack of sympathy.

"Patético," Gio says. He's developed a habit of switching between languages since his parents, originally from Puebla, speak exclusively in Spanish at home. His insult draws Coach Patrick's attention. Gio scrambles to catch the rest of the pack.

"Don't think I don't know what that means, Sanchez!" Coach yells.

Sebastian has studied every player; he can predict the survivors. Gio will make it. Hunter, a defender whose skin tone is mellow ochre, like an acorn, will too. He's not sure about Charlie, who's more out of shape than anyone, or Smith, whose sweaty, tie-dyed hair lies flat against his forehead.

"Kyle," Sebastian says, huffing. "Try harder."

Kyle's blond hair flops into oceanic blue eyes. His fatigue diminishes his all-American build; his creamy skin has been replaced by a blistering sunburn. Still, he pushes himself a little more.

All of them are lumps of hard clay, waiting to be softened, then molded.

"You'll suffer later, Hughes!" Mason cries as Sebastian passes him for the second time today. He's balancing a ball between his feet, never missing a beat, even when Mason flips him off.

"Bite me!"

"You're a prick."

Sebastian shrugs. He says, "You taught me," before going for another lap.

During cooldowns, Willie steals a ball from Zach. He parades around the pitch like an MVP. "Bro, you make it too easy!" Willie guffaws. Drills are a joke to Willie; he claims it's the Irish half of his lineage. For three seasons, he's played sweeper, the last line of defense between an attacker and the goalie.

"All-star moves, Willster!" Sebastian shouts.

"Don't encourage the idiot." Mason is doubled over, hands on his knees. When he can inhale, he says, "I'm the only one who can have an ego around here."

"Of course," replies Sebastian, bouncing a ball from the toe of his shoe to his knee, then his chest. Rinse and repeat. "No one can out-Mason you." He ignores Mason's sarcastic response to focus. Like Mason, he wants to be the best. Soccer is his life; it's where he belongs.

Zach waves at him, shouting, "Heads up!" while he waits for Sebastian to pass him the ball.

Sebastian says, "Keep up this time, okay?" before head-butting the ball to Zach.

"Watch out!" Zach calls. He dodges the coaches carrying Tom off the field.

"Another one down." Mason sighs. "Amateurs."

"Just give them a chance, Mace," Willie whines.

"For what?"

"Because we need them. They're trying."

"Seriously, this is you using your brain right now?" Mason asks.

Willie mouths something back.

Eventually, Sebastian will step in before it gets out of hand. He's not their *captain*, but Sebastian has spent most of his life being called "Super-Dad" and "The Responsible One." This particular trait was inherited from his dad, the middle child of six, who looked after his younger siblings while also covering for his older sisters when they snuck out to parties with their boyfriends. Despite being the youngest child, Sebastian has an urge to protect his friends and teammates.

"A good heart doesn't need a reason; take care of people the way you'd want them to take care of you," his mom always says.

Yeah, he's doubled down on the responsible thing, and this is Sebastian Hughes: first guy to take care of a sick teammate, ensure everyone does their studies, and prevent the wilder ones, mainly Zach and Mason, from getting arrested. He's the peacemaker. This pack of misfits is *his misfits*.

"It's okay if they suck right now. You did too," Willie tells Mason.

Mason was a disaster his first few games. He missed passes more than he came close to scoring, and a bad case of nervous upchuck sidelined him for the second half of a big game. Now, Mason is their best attacker, justifiable ego included.

Swiping off sweat, Sebastian drags his wrist over his forehead. "We're gonna be champions this year, remember?"

"You're gonna make a great captain."

Sebastian flinches and sputters when he says, "I'm just a decent goalie, man."

"Get a life, loser."

"You first."

Laughing, they fake like they're going to punch each other.

"Why am I friends with you two?" Willie asks, limping away.

A skateboarding injury screwed up Willie's knee a few years ago. It flares up every season, but Willie refuses to sit out, no matter how much Coach Patrick begs him. Willie believes soccer is his one great contribution in life, a thought all the players share. None of them are super-scholars, ruling out law or medicine. This is what they can offer this world: kicking ass at soccer. No one wants to pass up that opportunity.

"Is that it? Is that all you've got?" Jack taunts someone from the penalty box.

It's Emir.

Jack is their second string goalie. He's adequate at best. Emir's lack of skill is clear when he struggles to get around Jack's shitty defense.

With his beanie pushed back and his dark fringe catching in his eyelashes, Emir says, "Shut up." His formless kick sends the ball sailing wide.

Jack crows.

Emir's eyebrows furrow. Exhausted, he scrunches his face. Tension keeps his shoulders tight as a wire hanger. He sets up the next ball. He scowls, breathing hard. He tries again. And misses.

Jack doesn't put much effort into blocking because the ball never comes close. "Should I just take a nap?" he asks.

Sebastian folds his arms over his chest and tilts his head. Emir has too much force in his kicks. He's way too focused; his motions are unnatural and erratic.

He's got potential, Sebastian says to himself, as Emir grumbles at the next ball. "C'mon! Go *in* this time."

"Is this kid for real?" Smith asks.

"He's gonna need a lot of help," Hunter mumbles after a mouthful of water. "Any volunteers?"

"Count me out," Zach says, long sweaty hair falling like a curtain over his eyes. "He acts like a jerk at school. We never got along."

"Have you tried *talking* to him?" Hunter asks. "Or is that something you're just sorry at, like picking up women?"

Zach drags Hunter into a headlock. Zach's not a born asshole. His mom ditched him and his dad years ago. Since then, he doesn't play nice with anyone he can't guarantee will stick around.

Playing nice isn't Emir's thing either. He swears while stomping away.

"Hey! Shah! We're not done." Coach O'Brien's voice booms like a megaphone. He's the defensive coach and a stern, stocky man. He spent three years in a professional league before too many injuries sidelined him for good.

"I am."

"Shah!"

Emir strides off like a man on a mission.

Sebastian ignores Mason's whispered, "He kinda looks like he doesn't want to be here, Bastian," turns away, and gets in another lap. He tells himself it's to loosen his muscles, but the truth is he wants a better view of Emir before he marches off to his cabin.

Emir's "screw you" attitude simmers in defeat.

Sebastian quits halfway into his run. It's merely first-day fatigue, that's all. It has *nothing* to do with Emir.

 4

"TRADE YOU PEAS FOR GARLIC bread," Willie offers.

"Sure," Sebastian says, passing the bread while Willie spoons his peas onto Sebastian's plate. The peas are mushy, but the garlic bread is overbaked and greasy, so it's a fair exchange. The food in the dining hall is either dry pieces of grilled chicken or pasta drenched in debatable "tomato sauce," but it's better than school cafeteria food.

Everyone sticks to the same people they talk to during school. Sebastian shares a table with Willie and Mason; usually Zach or Hunter or Charlie joins them. Spread around like lighthouses across the shore is the rest of the team. The coaching staff takes a table in the corner, where they talk between bites of food about strategy, their opponents, and the professional leagues.

"What about Montreal this year? Will they be any good?"

"Probably," Kyle says to Charlie after swallowing a mouthful of chicken.

The guys always banter about the same things: their favorite teams, inappropriate jokes, and girls. Usually the last two go hand in hand. Sometimes, discussions turn to their first game of every season—a match against their rivals, St. Catherine's.

"Dumb Spartans," someone will say, and the whole team will grunt.

Tonight, the team is fairly quiet; their asses were handed to them during practice. Heads lowered, they mumble through their meal.

Charlie tosses Smith a dinner roll. He asks, "Who's going to win the Western Conference?" and hoots when Smith catches the roll one-handed.

"My money's on Seattle."

"That's 'cause you're an idiot." Zach grins smugly at Jack. They fist-bump across the table.

Gio flips them off. "Vete al infierno." He loves to tell the others to go to hell during their fantasy league tournaments. This year, he's stuck with a bunch of Seattle's injury-plagued players.

Sebastian looks out of a window. The sun's a heavy flare dropping behind the trees.

Zach goes on about a pretty girl he's dating. It sounds promising, according to Zach's standards. He jostles Sebastian with an elbow, then says, "She's got a friend for you, bro. Remember Amelia?"

Sebastian shrugs. He vaguely recalls sharing a class, not that they talked. He scoops peas into his mouth to avoid responding.

"She's pretty," Willie mentions.

Yeah, thanks, Will!

"See," Zach says, pointing his fork at Sebastian, "the gays approve." His voice isn't mocking, and Willie sits tall as if he's accomplished something. He's a traitor, and Sebastian considers stealing back his garlic bread.

"Who has time for dramatic romances?" Mason drums his hands on the table. "Definitely not me."

Sebastian is thankful the attention is off of him and his nonexistent romantic life.

This time, Zach derides Mason, asking, "So you and Val aren't hooking up this year?" When Mason hesitates, Zach lifts his eyebrows. He chugs his Red Bull.

Mason argues, "I didn't say that—"

"Slow down, Zach," Carl, another defenseman with jackal eyes and a blond crewcut, sneers. "He's saving himself for Coach's daughter, remember?"

Zach and half the team laugh. He snaps his fingers; his eyes are lit. "That's right! You and Grey?"

Mason scowls, scratching his nose. "Knock it off, dude. I have no interest in—"

"Where is the brat, anyway?" Smith asks Mason.

"How am I supposed to know?" Mason nearly shouts, but his throat tightens around the last word. He glares at Willie, who chokes and laughs simultaneously. Mason probably isn't against burying Willie's body somewhere in the woods at this point.

Sebastian's about to interfere, but—

"I'm here! I'm here! Sorry I'm late!"

Well, there goes saving Mason's ass.

A girl with floppy bronze curls, pink cheeks, and bright emerald eyes runs breathlessly to the coaches' table. She's wearing a wrinkled BHS Lions T-shirt, denim shorts, and dirty Chuck Taylor All Stars.

Coach Patrick gazes at her with a smile. "It's okay," he says gruffly.

"Hi, Coach," she says with a wink. She pecks a kiss to his cheek. He gives her one of those one-armed half-hugs. When she pulls back, Sebastian can see that the entire team is watching.

Sebastian can't control his own grin when he sizes her up. Grace *freaking* Patrick, the Coach's stepdaughter, doesn't look much different than the twelve-year-old soccer fan who used to follow the team from match to match. Back then, she carried a mini-clipboard in her skinny arms, trying to play field general like her stepfather.

"You've got an audience, Grace," Coach Patrick says with a chuckle.

She wrinkles her nose. No one calls her Grace but Coach. The last guy who did got kneed in the balls. She goes by Grey. "Grace is for princesses," she told Sebastian once, "and I'm a soccer brat, through and through. No pink dresses and tiaras for me."

Sebastian respected her wishes because, besides being a wannabe coach, Grey is a phenomenal soccer player. But she's not interested in playing. Grey prefers observing from the sidelines, and carrying a pretty gnarly crush on Mason.

"Grey," she mumbles under her breath.

Coach gives her a meaningful look and pats her hip.

When she sees Sebastian, her dimples show. She's taller, more statuesque, than when she was twelve. Then she finds Mason, who is noticeably tense.

"Love is in the air," Zach sings softly.

"Screw you," Mason whispers.

"Okay fellas, let's welcome Grace—" Coach snorts when Grey smacks his shoulder. "I mean, *Grey*, to camp."

"More like welcome to my hell," Mason says to Sebastian.

"You know the rules," Coach says.

They all do. It's soccer suicide to give Grey any shit, which a few of their best players learned the hard way. But Grey is a good kid, so there's no real reason to mess with her.

Grey, still pink and shy, sucks in a deep breath before shouting, "Let's kill it this year, Lions!"

The team echoes their approval, but something else follows. A few players hum under their breath. The sound builds and builds like a bee in Sebastian's ear, until they're all staring directly at Mason.

Their first year at camp, when Grey made her crush too apparent by wearing Mason's jersey number to every scrimmage, the seniors taunted Mason. In the showers, a chorus of "Build Me Up, Buttercup" and kissy faces broke out daily. It's an historic tradition now.

"Knock it off," grumbles Mason, unable to meet anyone's eyes.

"Bro, she's been in love with you since she was twelve," Zach says, cackling as he shoves Mason's shoulder.

Mason flips him the middle finger and pushes his plate of food away. He slouches in his chair. "She's a pain in my ass."

Sebastian lets Zach and Charlie give Mason a hard time, partly because Mason will prank them all before the summer is over. Sebastian gets distracted observing his surroundings. He's not actively *searching* for anyone...

Which is a total douchebag lie, so he can't blame his eyes when they zone in on a table in the corner.

Head lowered, Emir sits alone, forking his food around his plate. He's without his beanie; his mussed dark hair matches the color of his thick eyelashes. His jaw protrudes as he grinds his teeth. One of his legs shakes under the table. Quickly, he scans the room. He's painfully out of place, a square piece for a round hole. Everyone else has a spot, including the freshmen piled together at one table.

"Someone's gonna have to help that guy fit in," Charlie says, shaking Sebastian out of his guilty stare. He's lost track of how long he's been watching, but most of the guys have finished their food and filed out of the hall.

"Not me," Mason says, holding up both hands as if he's surrendering. "We're not friends."

Willie rolls his eyes. "He's not friends with anyone, Mace. That's not the point."

"That's not my fault."

"Maybe he's not interested in friends?" Zach suggests, scratching at his five o'clock shadow. Zach's built more like a college freshman than a high school senior. He's always been mature, physically.

"Or he doesn't like any of us," says Charlie.

"I doubt that," Hunter says with an easy tone. "Whether he likes us or not, someone has to help him improve on the pitch, or we're all screwed if we need him to play."

Sebastian, in a vain attempt to become invisible, leans on the table and covers his face with his hands. This will only go one way. Someone—Willie—will suggest Sebastian convince Emir to let them help, and then Sebastian—the perpetually whipped guy he is—will be the hero by bringing the team together for Emir.

Aren't there already enough Disney teen movies like that?

But while Sebastian waits for the inevitable, Mason says, "Let's just leave him alone. His bad attitude won't do us any good."

No one argues with him. It's as if they've all already given up on Emir. Sebastian wants to tell them how messed up that is. It's a team, not a clique. They don't leave anyone to figure it out on their own.

By the time he gets the balls up to confront anyone, the guys have cleared out, including Emir. It's just Sebastian, half-eaten pasta going cold on his plate, thoughts stewing in his head. He pushes the plate away and thumps his head on the table.

Yep, he's going to make one awful captain.

⚽

When Sebastian finally steps outside, the sky is streaked the colors of a circus tent: red, canary yellow, and swirls of blue. Behind the trees, the sun's setting. The summer air is quiet, not far from muggy.

Sweat shines on Sebastian's skin as he lugs equipment across the lawn toward the shed. Traditionally, it's the team's job to maintain the grounds. Sebastian doesn't mind, because he gets a sweet view of the pinprick stars over the lake.

"Christ," he hisses, mopping at the sweat on his brow with his T-shirt. He shoves the shirt into the back pocket of his jeans. He'd walk around in just his damn boxer-briefs if he dared, but he's self-conscious just being shirtless. Lately, familiar words keep looping in his head: *Bastian the Trashcan*. After months of skipping his workout routine, he's not rocking a Hollister model's body. His confidence is shot. The bags of cheese puffs while streaming Netflix didn't help either.

He glares at his stomach's post-dinner pudge. "You'll get it back, eventually," he says with a sigh. Muscles straining against the load of bricks-heavy bag of equipment, he starts his walk again.

"Want help with that?" Grey asks. The black sports car she leans against is sleek. Sebastian can't identify the make and model, but the paint is glossy, so it must be new.

"Looks like you've got enough to carry." Sebastian grins, nodding his head toward the bags at Grey's feet.

"Possibly," she says, smiling. "Maybe you can help me?"

Sebastian pokes his lips out. "Now Grey, you haven't turned into a spoiled rich girl who expects big, strong guys like me to rescue you, have you?"

Grey rolls her eyes. Besides the team, Grey is all Coach has, so maybe she's a tiny bit spoiled. But Grey is too cool and goofy to adopt a diva attitude.

She points at the car and says, "It was a sweet sixteen gift from Coach." She never calls him Dad. Sebastian isn't sure if it's because Coach married her mom when Grey was old enough to know the truth or because she's stuck in a sports headspace all the time. "I told him not to."

Sebastian whistles, impressed. "Too flashy?"

"Too girly." She sticks her tongue out. "I wanted a muscle car."

Sebastian snorts. *Welcome back, twelve-year-old Grey!*

"Coach is trying to bribe me into joining the girls' soccer team," she says dryly, blowing upward to get the curls out of her face. They fall right back. "I'm not interested, though."

"Why not?"

"Just *because*," she whines, pouting. At least that hasn't changed either. She digs the toes of her Chuck Taylors in the dirt. She asks, cheeks crimson, "So, um, how's Mace doing?" Curls curtain her face as she stares at her shoes.

"Still hung up on that crush?"

"Nope."

Sebastian doesn't believe her, but whatever. He gets it. He hasn't crushed on anyone since he was like, eleven? He met Sam at a party, they exchanged numbers and made out at a movie, and that was it. The unrequited infatuation phase never happened.

"Look at you!" He adjusts the balance of equipment on his shoulders. "He has you lovesick right now, doesn't he?"

"Shut the hell up, I don't like—" She pauses, more abashed than angry. Her eyes meet Sebastian's, and he levels her with his best disbelieving stare. "Mace is just a good guy, okay?" she says. "Awesome player. That's all."

"That's all?"

"That's it."

Sebastian expects her to stomp her foot. When she doesn't, he considers her a little more carefully. "He treats you like garbage, Gee."

Her shoulders slump. "Not all of the time."

It's a weak effort, but Sebastian empathizes. Sam wasn't the best at feeding his own superhero confidence.

"Okay," he finally says. "Then ask him out already."

Grey freezes, tension gripping her mouth. In a hushed voice, she pleads, "I can't. You know how Coach is about anyone trying to date me. He'd kick Mace off the team."

Yeah, that would suck. Being in love sucks, actually! How does anyone do it?

"Plus," Grey sighs, tucking curls behind her ear, "Mace wouldn't be interested, anyway." She's trying to smile through the words, but all the cracks in her usually hardcore armor are visible.

Sebastian says, "You're Grace-freaking-Patrick, dude. I've never seen you back down from a fight." He once witnessed Grey get in the face of a defenseman twice her size for an illegal tackle against Mason. She didn't blink when he growled at her. "Work it out, okay?"

Grey beams as if Sebastian's a victorious gladiator. Any time she smiles, he's as overwhelmed as if he's just slain Godzilla.

"Love you, Bastian."

"Love you too, you spoiled princess." The corner of his mouth lifts when she scrunches her nose. He readjusts the equipment. "Now carry your own bags. I've got to finish this up and hit the sack because your dad—"

"*Step*dad," she corrects.

"—is going to go General Zod on our asses tomorrow if we don't get it together."

"General who?"

"Oh, my God." Sebastian groans at the sky. "Never speak to me again. *Ever.*"

Grey's cackling fades as he walks away. Leave it to her to get his mind off everything. As far as friends go, most days Grey is ranked right next to Willie. He forgets the weight of the equipment and the sweat dripping off his nose as he treks toward the Hot Box.

THE FEW TREES THAT SURROUND the practice field allow an excellent view of blossoming stars. Sebastian's found a spot near the edge of the field. The city's smog and lights hide the stars in

Bloomington. But out here? Stars are giant ivory beacons, casting their glow in a smear of indigo.

Sitting with his knees pulled to his chest, Sebastian gulps a healthy amount of borrowed Gatorade. Okay, he *stole* it, but he's earned it. Besides, no one will miss it. After moving the equipment, Sebastian's muscles are numb. He has to wiggle his fingers and toes just to ensure they work. But mostly, his mind drains him.

When Sebastian first started playing, he pushed himself just to survive. Extra hours on the pitch before and after practice were a necessity. He did more reps in the weight room than anyone else. Cardio became his enemy and his friend. Whatever was needed to stay competitive, Sebastian did.

Sebastian's determined to make this year memorable. It's a craving, an *addiction*. He carries the weight of being an anchor for the team, on and off the field. Who wants to have that responsibility at seventeen? It's messed up, but the truth isn't always a pretty, dreamy montage. Sometimes, Sebastian would rather life sold him a lie about his purpose.

Crawling out of his thoughts, he downs more Gatorade. His eyes focus straight ahead to the pitch. At this hour, it should be empty, but it isn't. Sebastian has a clear view of drooping shoulders, a knit beanie, and a perpetual scowl.

It's *him*.

Emir lines himself up before running toward one soccer ball in a row of them. His foot smashes a ball toward one of the posts. It misses, and Emir shouts, "Are you kidding me?" while marching to his next ball. Emir kicks up a clump of grass and misses the ball. His head bows as he says, "Stupid piece of…"

Sebastian winces.

Emir walks himself through all the steps, reciting tips the coaches give amateur players: "One foot in front of the other... See your target..." It doesn't work, though. Emir stalks the balls as if he's starring in a *National Geographic* special on caged beasts let into the wild.

Sebastian says, "Calm down," so softly he can hardly hear himself.

Emir chants, "Pull it together, Shah," but all his motions are stiff.

"You've got it," Sebastian says. Wait—this is a total out-of-body experience. Is he actually *rooting* for Emir?

Emir's fingers curl into fists by his sides as he glares at another ball. His beanie is pushed back, exposing sweaty hair stuck to his forehead. "Go in or die," he growls at his mortal enemy: the ball. He races forward, catching the ball with the wrong side of his foot. It sails over the posts. "Bloody idiot!" he howls at the sky.

This is a massacre, and not in a hilarious way like *Funny or Die* videos on YouTube. But Sebastian can't avert his eyes. Maybe it's empathy? He's not too sure.

Emir's rubs his fists over his eyes. He stutters, "Can't you do any better?" Smeared tears shine on his cheeks. He wipes them away. "Abbu would be so..." His words die in his throat.

"Shit." Guilt sits heavy on Sebastian's chest. Everyone's hero, right?

Emir collapses in a pile of ragged exhaustion in the middle of the field near his discarded sweatshirt. Has he been out here since after dinner? He's stretched out like a dead starfish, reciting, "Just give up, mate, this was a mistake," to the stars.

Sebastian's seen enough. He pushes to his feet and dusts prickly grass from his clothes. His stomach drops when Emir crosses his vision again; that voice in the back of his head needs to shut up. The point it's trying to make is simple. They don't quit on this team. Sebastian doesn't quit at anything. "I wish I got a cool cape for this," he grumbles, turning away. He walks toward his cabin. Briefly, he wishes he had Mason's ability to walk away from people without guilt.

THE LAST THING SEBASTIAN NEEDS is insomnia. *Great, now my safe place is ruined!*

Willie's snoring roars like a jacked-up lawn mower, but that's not what keeps Sebastian awake. Sweat clings to his brow, but it's not the heat either. Nope, it's his thoughts—and Emir's defeated voice in his head, to be exact.

"Can't you do any better?"

Sebastian's quite intimate with that voice and those words. They're the same words Sebastian heard when he was younger and the world gave up on him, back when he wasn't good at anything, until soccer came along.

Maybe he can do for Emir what soccer did for him?

Sebastian turns on his side. The alarm clock's bleeding red numbers assault his vision. 3:36 a.m. *Crap.* He needs to sleep and to stop silly thoughts of saving someone else's ass when he's still not sure how to save himself.

 5

"Are you happy?" Sebastian asks his phone when the alarm screams at him. He aches like twice-run-over roadkill, but that's okay. The sky has cracked open for an epic sunrise, and that means one glorious thing: Time for a morning jog.

"You're annoying," Sebastian tells his phone. He groans when his phone responds by going back to sleep mode. After a yawn and stretch, Sebastian makes quick work of pulling on a comfy hoodie and a pair of loose shorts. He steals Willie's iPod from the desk between their beds.

Willie's snoring away, dead to the world.

"Lucky you," Sebastian grumbles, and Willie answers by snuffling his pillow.

Sebastian grabs his sneakers. He runs to the pantry for bottled water before hitting the hiking trail.

Bloomington is pretty cool, but Oakville is a different version of awesome. It's the nature vibe he likes: glittery dew on green leaves, heady, clean air, everything gold and ivy instead of gray and dull.

He jogs around the edge of camp, down by the lake, following a winding dirt path that leads to town. None of the other guys want any part of waking up before the ass-crack-of-dawn to join him. Mornings are his private sanctuary.

"Hello, Mr. Walsh!" Sebastian shouts when he's passing an auto shop in town. The owner, a husky man, stands in the parking lot surveying his muscle cars and used tires.

Mr. Walsh waves back, grinning in his gruff, kind way. "Back for another summer, Bastian?"

"Always!"

Sebastian likes checking out the small shops. Their "SALE" signs are hung in the windows and the owners sweep the sidewalks in front of their doors, preparing for another day of boring small-town life. Never slowing, he nods at all of them. He likes to run a few miles in under an hour, keeping pace to Willie's truly *suck* playlists. How many acoustic covers can one person download?

Daft Punk comes on, and Sebastian says, "Finally," before sprinting back to camp for breakfast.

Mason grunts, then says, "You stink," when Sebastian flops into a chair at their table. Mason's useless without caffeine in the morning. He's already sipping coffee from a paper cup.

"Good morning, Mace," Sebastian says in a singsong voice rather than flipping him off.

A tray of food is pushed toward him. "The usual?" Willie offers. His mellowness in the morning reminds Sebastian that life is good.

On the tray is everything Sebastian loves: wheat toast slathered in Nutella, fresh fruit, chopped bananas in Greek yogurt. These are three reasons Willie is lightyears ahead of Mason in the friendship department.

"Wicked. Thanks, Willster."

Waving as if it's nothing, Willie turns pink and ducks his head. But Sebastian is curious. *When has Willie ever been bashful?*

"Kiss-ass." Mason pokes Willie with a plastic spoon. "You never get me breakfast."

Willie replies, indignant, "Because you don't eat breakfast."

"Coffee—"

"Is *not* breakfast," Willie tells him.

Mason sips loudly at his coffee in rebuttal. Willie rolls his eyes and digs into his bowl of Cheerios.

One day, Sebastian is going to let them go all Thunderdome on each other and congratulate the winner. Of course, he'll be short one best friend, but that's bound to happen eventually.

"I hate you two," Mason grumbles to the lip of his cup. "You're like an awful bromance."

"Hey!" Willie protests. "You wanted to marry me yesterday."

"I was mistaken."

"Whatever."

Leaning back, Sebastian bites his lip. Mason is territorial when it comes to friendships, but he'll get over it. The thing about this team is, there's always been a lovefest between the players. All the testosterone and machismo exists on the field and in the locker room, where they can grab their crotches and have pissing contests. But this team has a thing for waxing poetic about their undying love too.

Mason pushes hair off his forehead. "Get a room already."

"You're disgusting." Sebastian shakes his head at him.

"And you're just a boring virgin."

Sebastian's mouth tightens as he whispers, "I'm not a virgin, dickhead."

"Oh, that's right. Just with guys, correct?" Mason's far too smug, as if he's shut Sebastian down.

Sebastian sighs through his nose. This is an excellent time for him to reevaluate his reasons for being Mason Riley's best friend.

The dining hall stinks of sweaty soccer players, but it's the smell of all the foods Sebastian used to love that he's struggling with: burnt bacon, fried eggs, stacks of rubbery pancakes. He frowns at his stomach. If it wasn't for those chants in the back of his head, the echoing voices of his bullies, he'd be stuffing his face the way Charlie is.

Get a grip, come on. He cautiously glances around the room.

Grey smiles at him from the coaches' table. It's empty, though, like her eyes. She wants to belong among them, but no one is welcoming her.

"Are you going to bother speaking to her?" Willie asks Mason.

"Maybe." Mason pauses dramatically. "I haven't decided."

"Wait, what? Dude, you're such a dick to girls."

"Shut up, Will," Mason bites back.

Today, Sebastian's not in the mood to play Dad and break them up. He waves to Grey—damn Mason—and she brightens up like the neon lights of Times Square.

"You're full of shit, Riley," Willie says, pointing his spoon at Mason.

"Because I don't suck up to Coach's daughter to get a better playing position?"

"I'm not friends with her because of that."

"No?" Mason asks. "Oh, I forgot. You have to be friends with *everyone*."

It's true. A world where Mason Riley is actually right is just ridiculous, but Willie has the heart of a damn puppy. Some people are assholes. They don't deserve Willie.

"So that's it?" Willie asks, incredulous at Mason's careless shrug.

"I haven't decided."

"Asshole."

Mason arrogantly says, "And proud," just to rile Willie more.

They'll be at it for hours. Sebastian turns to converse with his teammates. Between the repetitive "That's what she said" jokes and boasting about a championship win, Sebastian manages to fit in. Guys argue over the best players in the league, the endless war of Seattle or Dallas. They laugh with Sebastian instead of staring at him when he talks.

Popularity isn't his thing but, with these rowdy boys, it's good to know he matters. It also scares him that life has become just two things for the past four years: graduating and soccer. Shouldn't there be something else?

Emir walks into the dining hall, dragging his feet. He balances a tray in one hand and a can of Red Bull in the other. His appearance is sleepwalker-lite: hair spiked up, the sleeves of his shirt pulled over his knuckles, his scowl halfhearted. He's almost soft and inviting.

That's a big *almost.*

Sebastian wants to kick himself. He shouldn't be staring at Emir. And he sure as hell isn't going to admit to himself the reasons why.

Emir's lost. His eyes scan the room for somewhere to sit. Just as with Grey, no one makes the effort to help.

In the world's biggest mistake, Sebastian says, "Hey," circling his fingers around one of Emir's thin wrists.

Emir freezes, glaring at Sebastian's hand, then his eyes. An eerie hush falls around them.

Sebastian attempts to lock onto his bravery. He almost succeeds, but then Emir hisses "What?" in a hostile voice, and Sebastian falters.

He struggles against the boulder in his throat. "Um," he tries with the entire team's eyes on them.

He gets it. Willie, Mason, and he are pretty much the Three Amigos around here. It's not an exclusive club. Zach and Sebastian have known each other all their lives. And Charlie and Mason have been terrors together since preschool. But there's always room for more. Sebastian knows Emir. Well, he *did*, so Emir can fit in too, right?

Sebastian sheepishly offers, "You can sit with us if you want," when Emir's face softens just a little. Foolishly, Sebastian takes that as the universe giving him a thumbs-up.

Emir, exploding Sebastian's theory, whispers, "Not happening, dude." He twists his arm free and stomps away.

"Burn," someone hisses nearby.

Sebastian wipes the wounded expression off his face. But his heart hammers like a fifty-piece drum section at a parade as Emir sits at his table in the corner. Sebastian turns away and glares at his untouched food.

"What's with him?"

"Does he *love* soccer, like the rest of us?" Jack says to Gio.

Mason says, "I told you, bro. He doesn't like us."

Sebastian wants Mason to shut the hell up, but he forks at his food for something to do. It doesn't hold his attention long. Since he's an epic idiot, his eyes find Emir looking back at him. Tears sting his eyes from their staring contest, but Sebastian holds the stare until something calm replaces the anger in Emir's face. It's a start.

Emir looks down first. His spoon draws lazy circles in his cereal. He's so tense and small. All their lives, Emir has been smaller but faster than Sebastian. He could outrun Sebastian any day of the week.

It's as if they're still running from something.

"Hurry up, slackers! Scrimmage on the field in fifteen!" Coach Patrick barks from the doorway. The collective groan only intensifies the glee in his eyes.

Mason clears his throat. He says, "I don't think Shah is going to last long."

Sebastian's a total jerk for not saying anything back. He hopes this time Mason is wrong.

THE RUSH OF A SWEATY, sunbaked scrimmage is just what Sebastian needs. His teammates show off their new skills, which are terrible imitations of footwork they've seen in the latest FIFA video game. It's classic. Most of them fall on their faces.

The workouts afterward are worse. Once again, they are a disorganized pack of rabid cubs, and the coaching staff makes them suffer. This form of torture has to be illegal.

Coach O'Brien shouts at the defensive line: "Knees up! Eyes forward! How do you expect to beat those Spartans if you can't keep up with the ball?"

"Vamos, hombre! Is that the best you've got?" Coach Rivera yells. "Want another thirty minutes of cardio added to tomorrow's practice?" His dark eyes narrow at Smith, who is struggling to keep up. "Smith! Where's your form?" he asks after a sip of his cinnamon coffee.

"At your wife's house," Smith mutters.

"I heard that! My *husband* would appreciate it if you picked your crap up one of these days." Grins are rare for Rivera, but his lips twitch when Smith trips over his own feet. His nascent smile fades just as quickly as it came when he starts yapping at Jack and Robbie for falling behind.

Coach Patrick paces the field end to end. "You all play like you've never seen a soccer ball! This isn't tryouts." His feet leave tracks in the grass. "Less than two months," he shouts. Without his hat, his scowl is visible and demands one thing of every player: gratitude. He expects nothing less than discipline on the field. "That's all you've got 'til we meet the Spartans at home. If we're going to win any games, you better survive working as a unit. I don't see any heroes around here."

"Riley would disagree, sir," Zach says, hacking. He's still breathless from the suicide drills.

Mason counters with, "Just repeating what your girlfriend tells me." He's just as winded as Zach. They flip each other off, earning another lap from Coach.

Yep, they're doomed. Might as well forfeit the trophy now.

The team scrambles through basic drills and ball control techniques. A zigzag of orange cones is set up for passing exercises. Upperclassmen practice block tackling midfield. On the sidelines, the freshmen compete for who can puke colorful streams of Gatorade the farthest. Sebastian doesn't hoot at them as the other upperclassmen do. He was the same as a frosh and he made varsity. They can too!

His afternoon is spent in his home, the penalty box, fending off shots from the offensive line.

"Too much force!" He smacks away another ball from Kyle. He's a transfer from Bloomington West with way too much confidence in his kicks. Every shot is predictable, and Sebastian barely puts forth effort.

Kyle replies, "Screw you," but Sebastian shrugs it off. In time, Kyle will find his bearings.

It doesn't help that Willie's crowing from the sidelines. He shouts, "Bombs away!" when another guy misses.

Sebastian ignores his friend's manic sense of humor to observe the obvious: Willie's bad knee, bandaged and iced, is propped on a bleacher below him. It's a sure sign he's already overdone it.

Sebastian tries to sound admonishing when he says, "Willster," but it doesn't work.

"You can't beat Hughes! He's like the Eyrie castle on *Game of Thrones*!" Willie yells. He's an invaluable asset, as much the team's cheerleader as their best defenseman.

"William!" Coach Rivera barks from midfield. "Hughes doesn't need an ego, quit it!"

Willie shrinks from Rivera. The roguish glint in his eyes indicates this silence is temporary.

Grey, next to him with her clipboard in her lap, chews the top of her pen mercilessly. She takes notes on every player as if she expects there will be a quiz. Sebastian likes that she's got a good head on her shoulders. He could encourage her to pursue the coaching thing if she can get her mind off Mason, the reason behind her lip-biting and her stone-cold posture.

Mason sinks ball after ball into the goal Jack's protecting on the other side of the field. "Ding-dong!" he howls, grinning wolfishly at Jack's pathetic defense.

Grey pumps a fist in the air, screeching, "Yes!" She cringes, red as a ripe strawberry, as the other guys hoot at her.

Mason groans, "Christ," and gives her a dirty look. Zach is blowing him kisses from the sidelines, so Mason mouths, "Eat shit," but Coach Patrick catches him. He slinks back into position to prepare for his next kick.

Sebastian has no interest in getting involved in that love boat. He stumbles off the field to flop next to Willie in the bleachers, where Willie brandishes a Gatorade. "Anything good happen?" Sebastian asks once he's cracked the Gatorade and had a sip.

Willie points toward Jack's side of the field. "Emir has potential." Sebastian shrugs slightly and stays quiet. Willie continues, "He'd make a good wingback."

Sebastian studies the pitch; his eyebrows furrow at how scattered Emir is. He seems determined, but nothing else.

"We need one," Grey chimes in. "To replace Kendrick." She is nothing but positive about the team's prospects.

Sebastian shrugs again. Kendrick was decent, but completely replaceable, last season. Emir is faster and has the potential to be better. "Sweeper," he suggests, tapping a finger on his chin. Willie gapes at him. "With practice, I mean. Reminds me of Cameron."

"Geoff Cameron?" Grey asks.

"Wait, *the Geoff Cameron*," says Willie, way too skeptically.

Sebastian nods. "Potential, right?"

Willie goes paler, as if he can't tell if Sebastian's finally taken one too many soccer balls to the head, but Emir *is* fast. He steals the ball without sweating. It's the lack of coordination afterward that does him in.

Willie rants, damning Sebastian's very existence. That's no surprise. Geoff Cameron is a legend to Willie, and Sebastian said it mostly to piss him off.

He ignores Willie to observe Emir scooping the ball away to win another one-versus-one battle against Smith. He's fascinating. His prideful stance is maintained the entire time Coach O'Brien barks at him for sloppy footwork or while Carl points and laughs.

Tipping his Gatorade for another sip, Sebastian whispers, "Awesome." He almost chokes while swallowing, though. Emir is eyeing him. Busted! Wait—did Emir just smile? Nope. Sebastian must have a concussion. Emir's turned away, so he'll never know.

"Watch out!" Grey yells. Kyle is coming upfield too fast. *Wham!* Emir's folded up on the grass. Shit, that'll leave a mark. Being laid out protecting the goal far too often has taught Sebastian that.

"Eyes ahead of you, Shah!" Coach O'Brien snaps, while Hunter runs to help Emir up.

"I'm fine," Emir mumbles, getting to his feet without Hunter's assistance.

Hunter's affronted expression lasts a bit too long before he shakes his head.

"C'mon kid," Coach Patrick, stern but fatherly, says. "Shake it off, Shah. Don't let it beat you."

Kyle babbles apologies, but Emir doesn't make eye contact. He grabs his ribs and flinches before limping back into position. He doesn't say a word, but glares at a ball.

"Wow, dude, that's uncool," Zach says, stretched out a few bleachers below them. "He totally blew Hunter off, the dick."

Sebastian rubs his sweaty palm over his mouth, so he doesn't say the wrong thing. Emir isn't being an asshole on purpose. Putting his finger on why will take time.

"Dunno, Bastian," Willie says, their shoulders touching. "He doesn't look much like Cameron to me, bro."

Sebastian ignores a hardcore desire to roll his eyes. Willie is cool, but sometimes he reminds Sebastian of Mason. Sebastian doesn't want to be told he's wrong yet again.

Coach Patrick has an arm around Emir's shoulders. He's giving Emir an earful, one of Coach's notorious fatherly talks, but Emir doesn't seem all that interested. He's glowering; his chest is heaving.

"Maybe he doesn't want to be here?" Grey suggests.

"Huh, maybe." Sebastian slumps; his throat holds in the words "He needs a friend" because he's a major tool.

"You'll get it, Emir," Grey shouts, clapping. She receives a hopeful nod from Emir, and suddenly Sebastian wants that for himself. There's only one way to get it.

 6

"WHAT THE HELL ARE YOU doing here?"

Well, it's definitely not the reaction Sebastian anticipated, but he didn't know *what* to expect when he found Emir.

An early end to practice meant dinner was dull and noisy. Afterward, Sebastian dodged Willie and Hunter, who pleaded with him to hit the rec hall for root beer floats, Sebastian's favorite, and some team bonding. He wasn't in the mood for belching, corny jokes, and guys acting like kindergarteners. Sebastian doesn't need the root beer float, anyway. But he regrets not hanging with Willie and Hunter, who remind him of the dudes from *Wedding Crashers*. It sure as hell would beat standing beside a cabin under Emir's death glare.

"Um, hello?" Sebastian tries.

Emir narrows his eyes. He has this whole "being a prick" thing down to a science. "What are you doing here?" he repeats.

"Okay." Sebastian drags every letter out. "So, we're not past that part yet?"

A half-burnt cigarette hangs from Emir's lips. His nose releases a plume of blue-gray smoke. "No," he grunts, leaning his head back, eyes closed.

Shadows bank the confined space between cabins here, an obvious spot for Emir to sneak a smoke. Sebastian lucked out catching him. Okay, he pulled a real stalker move, standing on his cabin's porch to see if Emir would sneak off to the pitch to practice again.

"Are you not going away, mate?" asks Emir, his index finger tapping ash off the end of his cigarette. Gray snowflakes catch on the breeze.

"Not likely," Sebastian says around a tight throat.

He's bold enough to move closer; fallen leaves crunch under his shoes. Carly smokes, so he's accustomed to the stench, but it doesn't stop his nose from wrinkling. "Gross," he says.

"Whatever." Emir is unfazed.

Sebastian's satisfied that he received a response. The sky is pre-thunderstorm charcoal. It hides a full moon, which freaking *bites*, because it eliminates Sebastian's one excuse for acting weird about this Emir situation.

"So." Sebastian stops when his voice cracks. *Hello, puberty!* He quickly pulls himself together. "Are you okay?"

Emir snorts; smoke trails escape the corner of his mouth. "Sure. Now will you go away?"

"Apparently not," Sebastian teases, too hopeful Emir will crack a smile. He doesn't, but his scowl softens, encouraging Sebastian. Emir is wearing a cutoff T-shirt that exposes his arms and the gnarly purple bruise from the hit he took during practice. "That looks painful."

"It's nothing."

Sebastian wants to call Emir on his bullshit. His thumb presses against the mark to prove his point. It's the dumbest thing he could do. What kind of idiot provokes an already pissed-off bull?

"Bloody hell, mate!" Emir hisses, jerking back. "Are you brain-dead?"

Sebastian shrugs and leans lazily against the siding of the cabin. He likes Emir's British accent. As a kid, annoyed with the teasing he received, Emir tried to hide it.

"That's pretty bad."

"Are you a bloody doctor now?"

"You don't have to play tough."

Emir takes another drag before he says, "It's nothing, okay?" His voice is pleading, as if he already has enough of the world on his shoulders and Sebastian isn't helping.

"Okay," Sebastian says.

He turns and is greeted by the boy from his childhood, the one who hated losing to Sebastian at video games but could never stay angry. "Let's play again and I'll show you," he'd demand until they were going at it again for hours. Sebastian hasn't had a memory that amusing since he and Emir stopped being friends. It's a punch to the throat.

"Shit happens." Emir stubs his cigarette in the pine needles under their feet. He sniffs, crossing his arms. "What's it to you?"

"It's my job," Sebastian feels compelled to say. Before he can explain, Emir snorts.

"That's right. Captain, yeah?" He's mocking Sebastian. He's reverted to whatever screwed-up version of Sebastian's ex-best friend he's become.

"*Teammates*. And we take care of our own around here."

"I'm not anyone's teammate."

Sebastian turns on the charm, smiling. "You *could* be."

Emir glares, taking them right back to zero. "Do you honestly believe they want me around? We're not friends."

"I believe…" Sebastian takes his time because he's walking a thin line. "You need to get to know them, and vice versa."

Emir says, "That's hard to do when I'm too busy sucking on the pitch to pay attention to any of them." He pushes his beanie back. Soft hair falls over his brow. "I'm rubbish."

"You're not," Sebastian says too quickly, caught staring at Emir's pink, very kissable lips—

Whoa. Hell no. Absolutely not in a million freaking years.

"Mate?" Emir seems puzzled.

Sebastian, blushing feverishly, turns away. Searching for words, he coughs into his hand. "We used to be friends," comes out, because his timing is atrocious.

"What?"

Sebastian wants to veto any other form of speech. "Sorry, I meant," he says and then heaves in a deep breath. "Do you want to leave?" Sebastian stares at his shoes. The old, discolored laces are a temporary distraction.

Thick, sticky silence forces Sebastian to lift his chin. Around them, crickets sing an ode to his stupidity.

Emir, chewing his lip, replies, "No."

Sebastian sags happily against the cabin. He blurts, "I can help," like a teen excited over meeting Shawn Mendes. What the hell is he doing? "I mean, I'm not the best—"

Emir guffaws. "Bullshit."

"I'd like to help you."

"What for?"

Sebastian isn't offended, especially since Emir's eyes seem candid rather than agitated. "I dunno," Sebastian replies. It's obvious this isn't like old times and Emir doesn't want to rekindle their friendship. He's doing this for the team.

"I'm not a charity case, mate." Emir starts to walk away.

Sebastian *should* let him go. Common sense isn't his strong suit, though, and he grabs Emir's wrist before he can get too far. "I'm sorry," falls out of his mouth. He's thankful Emir doesn't yank away. All he wants is thirty whole seconds of Emir's trust instead of the glaring. Sebastian says, "I want to help, okay?"

Emir's throat makes a noise when he swallows. His eyes shine in the dark; his breaths are slow.

Sebastian waits.

"What if they don't want me here?" Emir's tone is hesitant; his eyes flit to the trees rather than Sebastian's face.

Sebastian could easily throw together a TV-dad speech about being a family, togetherness, and the beauty of team unity, but this is Emir. Sebastian unwraps his fingers from Emir's wrist. He's embarrassed by how long it takes Emir's skin to return to its normal color.

"You've gotta try," he says, willing confidence into his voice. "I'm not giving you an option."

"Is that a threat?" One corner of Emir's mouth lifts. "It won't work."

Sebastian waves him off, chuckling. "See you in the morning!" He likes that, temporarily, Emir isn't scowling or seemingly ready to punch him in the back of the head. He strides away exceptionally fast. *Get out before you screw this up.*

"You'll regret it!"

"I doubt it!" Sebastian waits a whole five seconds before he twists his head around. A slight smile has graced Emir's lips. Maybe this is the start of something amazing.

 7

"TRAITOR!"

Sebastian isn't shocked that his cell's only response to this accusation is to continue its shrieked alarm. He smacks it silent and is rewarded when the screen goes dark.

Willie, immune to unwanted noises, continues to snore and mumble about Mason's treacherous Mario Kart gameplay. "Kiss my ass, you cheater" is muffled by a pillow.

Sebastian rolls out of bed. He stretches until his neck cracks. He goes through the motions of getting ready for another day: pulling on loose, comfy clothes, then his sneakers; dragging a hand through his gold-brown hair until it's artfully messy; stealing Willie's iPod.

Yawning, he steps into a still-cool summer morning. The low sun creates a campfire effect across the sky: orange and yellow lick the indigo out of sight. "Good morning, Oakville," he croaks, lips twitching as the birds chirp a response.

The dirt path between him and Emir's cabin looks like a trap. Despite last night's talk, Sebastian is apprehensive. This could be an elaborate prank by Emir, his dark revenge for whatever happened between them that left their friendship toast—well, not toast, but ambiguous.

"Man up," he mumbles, lifting his chin. He can do this. But when he knocks at Emir's door, no one answers. "Perfect."

Sebastian taps an impatient foot on the wooden porch. A brilliant idea that could also be horribly idiotic hits him. Jogging to the side of the cabin, Sebastian finds the window. He nudges and—*crack!* "Awesome," he whispers. Window locks, like everything at camp, are old and worthless. The window slides up with a shudder.

He's no future Olympian, but Sebastian has strong calves from soccer. Leg day finally pays off as he vaults inside.

"Oh, shit."

Sebastian collapses in a heap on the wood floor. It's unnatural for his body to pretzel like this. He doesn't break any limbs, so it's a victory.

From Sebastian's current angle, it looks as though Emir has a room to himself. "Huh," he whispers. Surveying all the extra space in the room, he stands and dusts himself off.

The air is heady with incense and cigarettes. Emir has created one giant bed by pushing the twin beds together. Sebastian forgot how *neat* Emir is. Everything is in its place, clean and organized, except a small crimson rug trimmed in gold that Sebastian trips on.

"*Crap.*"

Emir remains peacefully asleep under a messy tangle of sheets.

Sebastian almost considers leaving Emir to his dreams. Then he remembers Emir's scowling and frowning, and his guilt dissolves. He shuffles to the bed and repeats, "Hey," until Emir stirs.

Emir, gloriously stubborn, turns and cuddles a pillow.

"You're kidding, right?" Sebastian complains, but Emir simply curls into a fetal position. His breaths are still even. "Are you related to Will?"

Emir's response is a soft, easy exhalation.

"Dude," groans Sebastian, flopping onto the edge of the bed. He considers Emir. Against a white pillowcase, dark hair lies like spilled ink. Sunbeams bronze his brown skin. Prickly morning stubble sprouts from his chin.

Sebastian decides to go with Plan B. When they were younger, sneaking into each other's room while the other slept was the norm. Spare feathers from old pillows were used to tickle each other awake, or sometimes a finger, like the one Sebastian uses now to graze Emir's cheek and the soft skin under his jaw.

Emir's nose twitches.

"Cute." Sebastian chuckles, skimming Emir's chin. "You're not so bad asleep." He's on the verge of brushing Emir's lower lip when a pair of silver eyes pop open and lock on him. Sebastian recoils at the glare-of-certain-death. His arm jerks his hand out of harm's way.

"What the actual hell?" The sun gleams in to highlight Emir's frown. "This is a nightmare."

Sebastian says, "Time to practice," as if this is so normal.

"You prick," Emir says, voice cracked with sleep. He turns away and tries to bury his head under a pillow, but Sebastian snatches it away.

He's already taunting the tiger; he might as well see how far he can get.

"Go away!"

A witty response is on the tip of Sebastian's tongue, until he notices Emir is shirtless. A sick hawk with spread wings and sharp talons is inked inches below his nape, between his shoulder blades. Sebastian's brain short-circuits, distracted by the beautiful detail.

He sputters, "What the—" but stops short, horrified about staring at Emir *like that*. "Dude," he gasps, losing a battle with his stupid mouth. He's thrilled when Emir turns over and glares. "Um, Emi…"

Emir's eyes are immense.

Sebastian hasn't used that nickname since before they were teens. Now, he's blurted it as if they're still killing goblins and ogres on his couch back home.

"Did you—"

Frantic, Sebastian interrupts Emir. "I'm here to help, remember!" It's supposed to be a question, but Sebastian's voice goes screechy at the end, making it a shouted declaration. He should've quit while he was ahead.

Emir raises a thick eyebrow. "Help or torture me?"

"Both?" It's not his best response, but he's stuck on the tattoo and how the pillow crease on Emir's cheek makes him adorable.

"You're disturbing."

"Does that mean we can get started?"

Emir glares at the ceiling. His brooding gray eyes shine. His jaw is tight, as if he is coming up with creative ways to kill Sebastian.

Sebastian finds the overacting more amusing than intimidating. "I'm not leaving, man," he tells Emir.

Emir puffs out a breath. "Noted, mate."

Sebastian scoots off the bed and ruffles his hair. He stands to the side and waits for Emir to follow. If he must, Sebastian will drag Emir's ass to the pitch. His mind is set, and Sebastian's no quitter. "Emir," he says, voice edging on frustration.

"Bloody prick." Emir finally rips the sheets away and crawls off the bed. He's small in nothing but red boxer-briefs. "I've barely gotten any sleep."

"Why?"

"I just…" Emir pauses, pink tongue brushing his lips. "This place freaks me out, okay? I've never been away from my family—"

"But we used to have sleepovers at my house."

"That was *different*," Emir snaps, eyebrows furrowed. His tensed muscles strain under his skin.

"How?"

Emir frowns before shaking his head. "You don't get it," he mumbles. "That's when we were friends" is implied. Sebastian deems himself an asshole for broaching the topic when Emir says, "Just let it go."

Sebastian does. He's not here to put bandages over wounds that still haven't healed. "Okay," he whispers, running a hand through his hair again. "Are you up for practicing, then?"

Emir sighs. "Whatever," he says through his teeth. "Could you like, um, stop *staring*?"

Sebastian's skin prickles. Emir is standing there, all skinny limbs and compact muscles, hairy legs, and a flat belly. Sebastian is confident in his bisexuality; how's he supposed to look away from a half naked guy? But this is *Emir*, who has a very strong dislike for Sebastian.

"Sorry," he stammers, spinning on his heels so his back is to Emir. "Really, *really* didn't mean to do that."

Emir chuckles. "'S cool. I'm used to people staring at me." His voice is hoarse. "They say some pretty harsh things."

"What do they say?"

Emir laughs acrimoniously. "You don't want to know. They don't compliment my eyes or the smoothness of my skin."

Sebastian can imagine the cruel words from kids who don't understand someone who sticks to himself. They don't share any classes; Emir's book-smart, unlike Sebastian, who'd rather read comics than learn trig. But Sebastian knows Emir's refusal to socialize *invites* the talking. Surviving high school is about having two things: confidence and friends.

Emir lacks both.

"For what it's worth, I think you're okay," Sebastian says while Emir locates clothes, hopping behind Sebastian's back in a search for shoes.

"You don't know me."

A wrinkle forms between Sebastian's eyebrows; his shoulders stiffen. He needs a subject change before Emir tells him to go to hell. "What's the rug for?" He rubs his index finger over an eyebrow.

"None of your business."

Bad idea, confirmed.

"Can we just get this over with?" Emir's breath ghosts the side of Sebastian's neck before he walks around to face him. His clothes are similar to Sebastian's, but looser around his slight frame.

Sebastian forces a tight smile. "If we hurry, we can grab a late breakfast."

"Whatever, Bastian." Emir is already halfway out the door.

❀

"You don't have to go so hard," Sebastian says as Emir stumbles to keep up with him.

Gasping, Emir flips him off. Roadkill sounds more alive than Emir. Sebastian's jogging at half his usual pace, but he'll give Emir credit for trying. He's not a total asshole; he's just not a morning person. The sun washes over them in neon waves of orange and yellow. Sebastian's clothes are sticky with sweat. Adrenaline works through his blood like electricity, and he thrives on it.

It's a good morning.

"You're a masochist," Emir says.

"Break?" Sebastian offers, then snorts when Emir nods furiously. He wheezes when they slow down.

Emir's soaked shirt clings to his chest and stomach. Across his face, sweat glitters like stars in the sunlight. "I hate you right now."

"I can take it." Sebastian shoves Emir's shoulder. Emir counters with a fake punch that reminds Sebastian of being kids.

"What does running have to do with my lack of soccer skills?" Emir asks.

"Stamina."

"I haven't had any complaints about that before."

Is Emir implying...? Sebastian hastily explains, "You're no good on the pitch if you're laid out, short of breath."

"I hate this." Emir grunts, lifting the hem of his shirt to wipe sweat off his face. The shirt is lowered, revealing a pout.

Sebastian is amused, but also horrified at the stupid *He's adorable* chant smacking in his head like a racquet ball against Plexiglas. Maybe he has heatstroke? It's a feasible explanation and much cooler than the truth: hormones.

"Drinks," Sebastian suggests. The desire to get the hell away from Emir is strong. He ducks off into a nearby gas station to purchase two Gatorades with a few dollars stuffed in his shoe.

Cherry-red liquid dribbles down Emir's chin as he guzzles. After a breath, he says, "Thanks."

It's a warm morning; wafts of breeze circle their awkwardly silent walk to camp. During their run, Emir looked almost ready to start a conversation, but they had only huffs and grunts with little eye contact.

The dirt road crunches under their sneakers. They sip their Gatorade as if it's the most fascinating thing ever. Sebastian's forfeited the idea of doing anything other than bicker until Emir asks, "Why soccer?"

"What?"

The skin around Emir's eyes tightens. "Why soccer, mate?"

"Oh." Sebastian pushes hair off his forehead. "It's a good story."

Emir raises his eyebrows.

"Because of Coach Patrick," Sebastian says. "He's a hard-ass, right? Real piece of work. But he made being on the team about finding yourself first. Winning and being the best guy on the pitch came second." He grins crookedly at the sky, where puffy clouds drift by.

"Yeah?"

"You know Willie is gay, right?" Sebastian checks for a nod from Emir. "And Mason is—"

"A whore?" teases Emir.

"We like to use the term 'experimenting,' dude."

Emir's eyes roll dramatically.

"Anyway," Sebastian continues with a chuckle hanging in his throat. "Coach doesn't care about that stuff. A fourth of our team is gay or bi or curious, but we still get respect from the other guys. For once, sexual orientation in sports isn't a negative."

Emir scratches at his stubble. "Pretty cool."

"It *is*!"

Sebastian's never had to put any of this into words but, now that they're discussing it, he wants to grab a megaphone and shout to anyone he passes how epically awesome Coach Patrick is for giving him this gift.

Ahead, the road grows narrow, signaling their close proximity to camp. Shadows from thick canopies of emerald cool them. Sebastian's mellow from the quiet buzz of bugs all around.

"And you are...?" Emir leaves space for Sebastian to fill in.

It's heating up, and Sebastian uses that as a perfectly lame excuse to himself for his flushed skin. He says, "I'm bi. I'm into dudes and girls."

"I know what bi means."

Sebastian, flustered, quickly says, "Cool. Yep, I'm bi." Emir's unfazed nod relieves him. Despite the team's rules, Sebastian isn't rocking rainbow flags and announcing his sexuality at school. It's always tricky coming out to a new guy. Emir's no exception. "That okay?"

"Yeah," Emir replies with sheepish eyes. "Gay. Me. That's what... I'm gay."

"Sweet."

Nostalgia, along with Emir walking closer, is making Sebastian's skin tingle. He takes a gamble. "So, why soccer, for you?"

"It's not my thing, right?"

"No" rolls off Sebastian's tongue, but his brain yells *Yes*.

"It just happened," Emir says, his expression pained. "Kinda." He rubs a hand over his face, and Sebastian is prepared for Emir to tell him he's doing this for all the wrong reasons. "It's my abbu."

"Your dad, right?"

Emir says, exasperated, "Sorry. Never mind."

"Wait. I didn't mean to be rude." It's been so long since Sebastian's heard Emir speak in Urdu. The Shahs are British Pakistani. Sebastian's forgotten most of the words he heard so often around Emir's house. He says, "Abbu. That's *father* in Urdu."

"Yeah," Emir says, fondly impressed. "I can't turn it off sometimes."

Sebastian admires Emir's jaw and cheekbones. He resembles his mom, whom Sebastian remembers being lovely and smelling like summer. Emir's nose and his quiet disposition come from his dad. Mr. Shah always said nice things to Sebastian.

"It sucks when it comes out at school. The stuff people say. They talk about my accent, my parents, my skin…" Emir's voice trails off; his narrowed eyes stare at the ground. "Just because I speak funny or don't look like them."

"Yeah," whispers Sebastian.

Emir twists the cap of his Gatorade back and forth. "Anyway, my dad is a huge soccer fan. Since forever, he's spent Saturdays crashed on the couch with games on the telly. Premier League, the MLS, whatever he can find."

Sebastian snorts. Oliver is the same. And Sebastian is always right next to him; they're two couch potatoes arguing over their favorite players while Lily brings snacks and root beers. "Boys will be boys," she'll say before warning them to use coasters.

"I'm here because he loves the sport as much as he loves his family and," Emir pauses for a deep breath, as though he's about to reveal the secrets of his soul, "I want to impress him."

Sebastian likes the range of pinks in Emir's cheeks. Very irrational thoughts about how *cute* Emir can be make his stomach queasy. Sebastian shouldn't go there when Emir is being vulnerable.

"Is that stupid?" Emir asks, chewing his lip.

"No."

"It's my last year before college, and Abbu has done so much for my family that I feel like I owe him this."

Emir walks as though the whole world is pushing on his shoulders. Sebastian gets that. The burden to make your parents proud while still feeling clueless about what you're doing with your own life is a struggle.

"You're not doing this for you?"

"No," Emir hisses. "I'm here to make Abbu proud. I can do that without any pity, okay?"

Sebastian stops mid-step, stunned.

"Thanks for the run," Emir spits. He tosses his Gatorade bottle and turns away. Over his shoulder he says, "How about we not do this anymore."

"'This' what?"

It's as if the sound of Sebastian's voice makes Emir glower all the more. "You pretending to give a damn if I make it or not."

Sebastian blinks hard, wanting to shout, "What the hell?" or punch Emir or walk away.

Emir leaves first.

And Sebastian has to question his own rationality, because he still wants to help Emir—if not for the team, for whatever he must have done to screw up what he and Emir had.

 8

LATE IN THE AFTERNOON, COACH O'BRIEN'S whistle blows a final time.

Thank God, because Sebastian is exhausted and cardio sucks, especially in the dead heat of summer on an endless green field with no shade. Sebastian could definitely live without this. He jogs off the field, dodges other players to get to a paper cup of ice cold water, and then finds Willie.

"I was thinking," Willie starts, and Sebastian's lips quirk at the gleam in his eyes. Last year, when he shared a science class with Willie and Mason, all of their worst ideas started with, "So I was thinking," or, "I promise it won't get us arrested this time," which was a clear indication that, yes, they would get arrested or at least serve detention. And yet Sebastian always went along with whatever ridiculous idea they suggested.

Willie says, "Jacobs's School of Music."

"For college?" asks Sebastian after a gulp of water.

Willie nods, adjusting the bag of ice on his knee. Sebastian drags a hand over his mouth. Willie's blue eyes are spacey, like a child fantasizing about Christmas morning.

"Why?"

"It's not far from Bloomington. Pops can visit, and music's the perfect major for me." Willie's a music junkie; his weekends are spent playing bass in a punk cover band. Sebastian's been to a few of their shows. Willie's got skills. "Or I could just go to college in the city."

Sebastian makes a face. They've agreed against one thing: State University. It's either a specialty school or getting the hell out of Bloomington, starting fresh.

"What about New York?"

Willie, in a perfectly spot-on Brooklyn accent, repeats, "New Yawk?"

"They've got the Red Bulls professional team. And the schools are good. Sweet living, you know?"

"It could be, but what about being closer? Somewhere we both could go?"

Sebastian tosses an arm around Willie's shoulder, pulling him in. "But imagine it: a crappy apartment in the city, cab rides every morning, making the team—"

Willie clears his throat. "Sorry to disappoint you, Bastian but..." He points at his knee. "I don't envision taking this all the way like we planned."

Willie is through after this season. He has two options: surgery or lifelong rehab. An operation before college is a death sentence for an athlete. Recruiters aren't scouting injury cases.

"Yeah," Sebastian mumbles. "Guess so."

Willie smiles just enough to hide the mourning in his eyes.

"Bloomington's cool," Sebastian says with a shrug. "Mom wouldn't complain." But Sebastian's daydreams about sharing a shithole dorm at Bloomington University with Willie and hitting the bars for weekend college games on a widescreen TV aren't enticing enough. He wants out. Life after high school is a mystery, but Sebastian won't solve it in Bloomington.

Hunter plops down next to Willie. He announces, "Pasta and salad for lunch today," with all the dread of a prisoner about to be executed. "Have we not suffered enough?"

Willie chuckles. "Nope."

"Well, then." Hunter leans on Willie. "At least you have to die with me."

Hunter and Willie slip into a private conversation. Sebastian doesn't mind. He's spaced out, anyway. On the pitch, Coach Patrick and O'Brien discuss strategy. The defensive line is coming together nicely, except for Emir.

He can't pass accurately and has zero coordination. It's as if his foot's allergic to the ball. But he outruns all attackers, beating them to their next move. If he can just harness that, maybe Sebastian can work around the rest.

"Keep it up, Shah!" Coach Patrick yells, glancing at his clipboard.

When Emir stumbles again, Coach O'Brien tosses his hat on the green. His hair is thinning; sunlight glares off his skull. "Why do you have two left feet? Is that possible? Jesus, Mary, and have mercy, kid, where is your head?"

Carl shouts, "Up his ass!" while chasing a ball.

"Hey!" Gio yells, pointing at Carl. "Don't screw up his concentration."

But it's too late. The ball's rolled too far in front of Emir, allowing Kyle to sidestep him and make a play.

O'Brien fusses, "Carl, you wanna do some more laps? We can skip lunch if you'd like?"

"No, thank you!"

"Then give the lad a break," O'Brien snaps. His scowl exaggerates his wrinkles. "Try again, Shah."

Sebastian's bony elbows rest on his knees. He's drained his cup, but keeps it close to his mouth, hiding how intensely he's studying Emir.

Emir's expression reads as if he'll march off the field and quit. Then, something flashes in his eyes, a reminder, before he marks another player to steal possession of the ball.

Yes!

Sebastian doesn't scream but he might do a small fist pump out of view. He's a dork, okay, but Emir did it. Of course, he doesn't keep control of the ball. Robbie swoops in like a hired assassin to take it back, but it's enough for Coach Patrick to nod his approval when Emir passes.

"What about fullback?"

Sebastian startles. Hunter and Willie have stopped their random geeky ranting to turn their attention back on him. Willie's expectant face means the question was obviously for Sebastian.

"Emir?"

Willie rolls his eyes. "Well, not for them." He points to the gaggle of freshmen doing passing drills—badly. They are no doubt headed for the reserve team at the end of camp. Or, as Mason appropriately calls it, soccer limbo.

Hunter says, "I don't know if he has it in him. But defense is definitely his strong point."

"Yeah," Willie concedes. "Definitely defense."

Sebastian can teach Emir to be a great defender. *I'm the team goalie; defense is in my blood.* And he trusts Willie and Hunter's judgment, even if they're now arguing about who'd be the better soccer player, Mario or Luigi. At least they're interested in Emir's success. Now, if Sebastian can convince Emir that he isn't helping because Emir's a charity case.

On the sidelines, Coach Patrick is talking to Emir; his thick hand squeezes Emir's bony shoulder. Judging by his stance, Coach's giving one of his famous pick-me-up speeches, something he doesn't often do publicly. When a player is struggling, Coach pulls him into the office, shuts the door, and recites every *Rocky* quote possible. It's repetitive, but Coach never lets anyone feel like a failure.

When Coach walks away, Emir kicks at the grass and mumbles. Most of the guys steer clear of him. His tightly-wound shoulders don't invite company; nor does his otherworldly frown.

Sebastian bounds down the squeaky bleachers. His heart hammers triple-time; a black hole gapes in his stomach. Willie calls after him, but Sebastian's feet keep pounding on wood that's sure to snap. The other guys might crack on him later, but he doesn't stop.

"Wait up."

Emir spins around with an annoyed sigh. "Please, don't do this."

"But—"

"Don't."

Sebastian shakes off the chill spreading through his body. He rubs Emir's shoulder; the sweat makes Emir's shirt stick to his skin. Oddly, it's not gross.

Emir lowers his eyes. "You don't have to—"

Sebastian cuts him off with, "Meet me here after dinner," as if Emir wasn't speaking.

"What for?"

Sebastian raises his brow. "Do me a favor and meet me here, okay?"

Emir nods, whispering, "Okay" with little fight in his voice. It's progress.

The sun, warm and bright, beats relentlessly. Emir's a siren drawing Sebastian in with his face rather than his voice. Sebastian, realizing he's doomed, snatches his hand away to shake off whatever that was.

Emir's mouth goes soft. Sebastian is hit with the thought of kissing Emir, which is just horrible. It's difficult to resent someone while wanting something more.

"Hughes, lunch! I'm starved, bro!"

Sebastian's appreciation for Mason's whiny voice is immeasurable. He steps back, still breathless, needing to get away from Emir and unsure he's cool with that. "Okay," he says, too low, then jogs toward his friends. They've lagged just enough that Sebastian doesn't have to run.

"Pasta time," Hunter says, piggybacking Willie with Mason to his left. Sebastian flanks Mason's other side, keeping his head lowered. He doesn't say anything.

At least in the dining hall, Sebastian can escape Emir. Too bad there's nowhere in his head to retreat from the thought of sliding his mouth over Emir's.

A true tragedy.

 9

FROM THE EDGE OF THE pitch, the sun skids across the sky like a red cannonball rolling toward nothing. It leaves only purple and orange bruises from a war between light and dark. In the evening glow, Emir is soft, approachable. Without a beanie, his hair is fluffy. A thrift-store T-shirt and loose sweatpants compliment his cozy appearance. Granted, Sebastian's view of Emir lately has been nothing but rough, so maybe he's simply appreciating the moment.

Emir, humming to himself, juggles a ball between his feet. It escapes, but he chases it down, finally moving freely. When no one's watching, pressure doesn't exist; it's like dancing in the dark. But Emir can't control the ball for long.

Cicadas hum their nightly hymns, but underneath them Emir sings Michael Jackson. Music was always like magic for Emir. Eight years ago, it was all Emir needed to be himself around Sebastian.

"Shit."

The ball wobbles from between Emir's feet. In the middle of the pitch, Sebastian effortlessly stops it with one foot. He says, "That was good," with too much glee in his voice.

Emir flinches at being caught. "It was *okay*."

"Give yourself some credit," Sebastian says, using the toe of his foot to scoop the ball into the air and then bouncing it off a knee. "Just keep going."

"What if I quit first?"

"Is that the plan?"

Emir's shrug is about as convincing as a puppy's growl. "I haven't decided," he says when Sebastian passes the ball back to him. He fakes left, goes right, but Sebastian's right in his face, grinning.

"Waiting for me to convince you?"

Emir says, "Waiting for you to fail," but his lips twitch upward.

"That won't happen."

Emir rolls his eyes, trying to work around Sebastian. He sweeps the ball past Sebastian, making a run for it. Sebastian catches him, but barely.

"Not bad," he says, spinning around Emir.

"I'm barely trying," Emir says, breathless.

Sebastian relaxes. Well, he tries to relax, but his pulse pounds in his ears. They're face to face, waiting for the next move. And Sebastian, having another idiot moment of epic proportions, brushes sweaty hair off Emir's forehead with his fingers.

Emir, who is an inch or two shorter than Sebastian, peers through his eyelashes. He doesn't say anything, but he looks ready to speak.

"Um, yeah." Sebastian overheats.

Emir says, "Sure," and leaves it at that.

They pass the ball back and forth; the sun sinks behind the trees. At five minutes to eight, the halogen floodlights that surround the pitch click on, illuminating the greens in lustered silver.

"What're we here for?" Emir asks.

"To make you better." Sebastian is trying to remain focused on the benefits to *the team*, not on his hormones.

Emir mumbles, "Horrible plan, mate."

"Just give me a chance," Sebastian insists.

Emir chews his lip. He reaches to brush the hair off his forehead, but Sebastian's already done that. Emir's hand dangles mid-air; a blush overtakes his face. "So," he starts and then pauses, as if the world anchors him to the ground when he wants to fly. "Let's do this, then?"

Under the hazy, firestorm sky, they practice. Sebastian teaches Emir passing first. "That's better." He applauds Emir's ability to control possession of the ball for more than ten feet. Of course, Emir still keeps his head low, glaring at the ball as if he's willing it to follow his commands. But Sebastian is content with his growing coordination.

Eventually, he'll advance their training to marking an attacker, slide tackles, and complicated tricks, like hitting a header so the ball flies to your teammate.

The sky spits out stars as time slips between them.

Sebastian pushes hair off his brow and says, "Do you think you can get it back here to me?"

Emir groans softly, spinning in the grass. "Demanding asshole." He clumsily works the ball back upfield.

"I heard that!"

"Good!" Emir gripes, but his laughter betrays him.

Sebastian rubs sweaty hands over his shorts. He usually wears gloves when he's protecting the goal. He's anticipating a shot attempt from Emir, but it never happens because Emir loses control of the ball.

"Bugger." Emir makes a face. "See what you've gone and made me do."

Sebastian snorts, flipping Emir the finger. "You just need more help."

With total lack of common sense, Sebastian runs up to Emir, then comes around his backside to align his chest with Emir's spine. He fits his arms around Emir's lean frame; his hands smooth Emir's waist. "Personal space" has vacated his vocabulary.

"This okay?" Sebastian asks.

Emir flinches, then nods.

In his head, Sebastian has ruled this a "teaching method," though no one's ever given him *this* brand of attention. "Follow me." Emir's muscles are coiled, but when Sebastian whispers, "I can help," he leans into Sebastian's chest.

Sebastian hooks his chin over Emir's shoulder. "Less focus on what you *want* the ball to do," he says, moving them in tandem toward the ball. "More on the way the ball wants *you* to move."

Emir turns his head just a millimeter, and asks, "How do I do that?"

Sebastian clears his throat, his flow slightly disrupted by the brush of Emir's soft but still stubbly cheek. "Stop forcing yourself."

"It's not that easy."

Sebastian tightens his fingers on Emir's hips. "Relax," he says, his lips skimming Emir's ear. Their feet guide the ball closer to the penalty box.

"I can't relax with your," Emir says, sounding smug, and with a deliberate arch in his spine, "*junk* against my bum, mate."

Sebastian gasps and pulls away from Emir to chase down the ball that's strayed from between them. His gnarly, cool-as-shit impersonation fails miserably. What did he expect? He wasn't *purposefully* trying to do that.

"Shut up," he says dejectedly.

"It's cool, Bastian."

No, it very well is *not*, since Sebastian has to turn away and adjust everything under his shorts.

Sebastian is disarmed by Emir's easy grin when they're face to face again. Emir wiggles his eyebrows and says, "I don't mind a guy's..." He waves a hand at Sebastian's waist. "On my bum, but I usually don't mix stupid sports and sex. It's a rule."

"It's not stupid," Sebastian says, piqued. "*Sports*, I mean, okay? Don't put down soccer, because it's all I've got these days."

Emir's mouth droops. "I didn't mean to..." He shoves a twitchy hand through his hair.

Sebastian shrugs. It's not as though Emir knows or understands how big soccer has been for him, how it's given him something to be proud of. It's been a purpose. Which is hard to explain to anyone who acts as if high school is just a stepping stone. To what? Once soccer is over, Sebastian's sure as hell his future is DOA.

"Maybe we should call it a night?" he suggests.

"Wait, can't we, um..." Emir's voice is broken and small when he says, "This is important to me, Bastian."

Sebastian hates realizing he's Emir's last chance. "C'mon," he says, waving Emir over. He's in front of the posts and instinctively ducking into position. "Take a shot."

"Yeah?" Emir doesn't wait for Sebastian's response; he lines up for a kick.

Sebastian swats the ball away. "Again."

Emir's next shot is easier to block; the one after is too. Sebastian tosses the ball right back at Emir. He's pissed at the world, not Emir, and takes it out on the ball.

"Better."

"I can't tell." Emir takes another rip at the ball.

Concentrating on Emir's improved approach, Sebastian loses track of time. Emir's stuttering shuffle toward the ball turns into a stiff glide. That encourages Sebastian to fight harder guarding the posts.

He hasn't had this much fun since he was a rookie.

"Why goalie?" Emir asks.

Sebastian chest-bumps the ball away. He's impressed when Emir uses the inside of his foot to catch it. "You don't want to know," he tells Emir.

"I do," Emir argues.

"I tried every position my freshman year. The glory is in being an attacker," Sebastian explains, leaning over to catch his breath. "It's why everyone loves Mason."

Emir's mouth twists, but he keeps quiet.

"I'm not as good as him," Sebastian says.

This time, Emir snorts his disapproval.

Sebastian pinches his sweat-soaked shirt to pull it away from his skin. "I wasn't quite the defender, like Willie," he continues. He jumps to stop the ball, then tuck-and-rolls with it wrapped in his arms. "I was a certified benchwarmer."

"A water boy?"

Sebastian tosses the ball back, amused. "I wasn't cool enough for that."

He is mesmerized by Emir's new ability to maintain focus and dribble the ball. Emir's face is shining with sweat, his eyebrows are lowered, and his mouth is pinched. But he's into this.

"I was bad." Sebastian laughs, self-deprecating.

"Ha! Couldn't be worse than me."

"Anyways," Sebastian says, rubbing his finger over an eyebrow sticky with perspiration. "At the end of the first season, our goalie graduated. I went out for goalkeeper because, well, why not? Jack was a whiny brat. I figured I could be as good as him."

The ball soars high, and Sebastian meets it midair with both hands. Emir grumbles, "Thanks, asshole," when Sebastian tosses it back.

Sebastian falls back into place. "I did all I could to get better. Extra time at home or camp, wherever."

"And?"

Sebastian waves his arms around in a "here we are" gesture. "My first game was against the Spartans," says Sebastian, looking into the distance.

It took an overtime period before they dragged those pretentious assholes to the ground. The score was two to zero, and the crowd went bananas when Mason scored the winning goal. But Coach Patrick dug his fingers into the collar of Sebastian's jersey and hauled him to the front of the team so he could soak in the fact that he shut out their rivals. That feeling still hits him with shuddering waves of warmth.

Emir stares at him as if Sebastian's just had a war flashback. Sebastian doesn't care. Memories like that are hard to come by. Most of the time, it's school or relationships or trying not to screw up and get grounded before the next party—and the endless awkwardness.

Sebastian is determined to hold on to those memories.

Emir says, "I'll never be like you."

Sebastian blindly catches the ball Emir pelts at him. "Hey, are you trying to quit again, Shah? Save it, I'm not interested."

Emir laughs, then licks his dry lips.

Sebastian gets stuck on how he'd really like to suck Emir's lower lip, winces, and leans over to conceal his excitement.

"Thanks, Captain."

Sebastian is so completely thrown by Emir's words that he doesn't pay any attention until—the ball zooms right past the side of Sebastian's head.

"Goooal!" Emir howls like a Telemundo announcer. He runs around maniacally, cheering and high-fiving imaginary teammates. If he doesn't quiet down, he'll wake a coach, but Sebastian lets him have this moment. Maybe he'll reflect fondly on this in a few years.

Sebastian's happiness, for Emir, for the night, for the small victories, is unexpected. He waits until Emir slows down, breathless, before tossing another ball at him. "Again?" he says.

Emir says gleefully, "Yeah, again."

They go for another hour. Emir is unable to sink another goal, but it doesn't matter. He's high off the last one. It's enough to keep a warped smile on Sebastian's mouth.

"I killed the giant," Emir keeps saying. Sebastian rolls his eyes every single time.

He teaches Emir how to do keepie-uppies. They laugh and shove each other until they're too sleepy to keep going.

❀

WEEKENDS AREN'T A FREE-FOR-ALL, BUT a coach can only shove so many practices and *Hoosiers* references down teenagers' throats before they rebel. The coaches give them mercy, with limitations. First, a curfew, a respectable one, too, because what teenager is ever in bed before midnight on a Saturday? Second, a bed check in the morning to make sure no one's gone missing or run off to marry a townie in the night. That's all.

After Saturday afternoon's required lunch, the madhouse cracks open.

Half of the team piles into the first available car or walks into town. The seniors usually sneak in cheap beer or rum, which doesn't always end well. Sebastian and a few others keep everyone in check, mostly.

"Do they need chaperones?" Coach Rivera asks.

"Let them go." Coach Patrick smiles. They're standing near the picnic area, observing. "It's not like we have bail money, anyway." Coach's anticipating his own weekend routine: beer, pizza, and a *Rocky* movie marathon. All his best speeches come from Sylvester Stallone quotes.

A convertible, top down, speeds off with Jack straddling a headrest. "Que Dios nos ayude," Rivera says. "God help us." He's a devout Catholic and often calls on his religion in moments like this.

Mason is perched on the hood of his car. Guys shout for him to hurry up. Tires spin, creating a fog of dirt. But Mason doesn't move. His hair is slicked back; he's wearing a loose tank top and green skinny jeans. Sunglasses slip from his brow to his nose. He winks at Sebastian. "Ready to destroy this place?"

"Um, no," Sebastian says with a laugh. "I don't want to know what the inside of juvie looks like, bro."

"Boring." Mason cocks his head back. A night in juvenile detention would be a dream come true for Mason. "Will has my back."

Willie climbs into the back seat. With his pale skin and over-gelled hair, he would look ridiculous in an orange jumpsuit.

Charlie's old Civic sputters past them. Icona Pop's "I Love It" shakes the interior. Last year, the seniors made that song their anthem, singing it endlessly in the showers. Those guys were ridiculously comfortable with their sexuality, so no one gave them shit about it.

"Fifty bucks says Zach gets harassed by a cop first," Hunter says.

Mason whistles his approval. "I'll take that bet." He's king of the jungle on his car-throne; all his loyal subjects salute him on their way to Oakville. He says to Sebastian, "That is, if Bastian doesn't save their asses first."

"Hey," Sebastian protests. "Wasn't it I who made sure you didn't get locked up two years ago for possession of greenery?"

"Touché." Mason nods, looking grateful for the reminder.

"Dude, you should have a cape," Hunter says. Sebastian beams—he's been thinking the same thing. "And spandex," he adds, and then Sebastian loses faith in Hunter's sanity.

He glances up the road. His purpose for tagging along with the guys is simple: to protect them. The coaches don't insist on caging the team in the campground because of Sebastian; the unsaid expectation is that Sebastian will make sure everyone does the right thing.

Sebastian wants to ask them, "What seventeen-year-old knows what *that* is?"

He tries not to let it bother him too much, though. He has fun with the guys, so it's a fair trade. Well, mostly it is. Plus, he needs a break from training and dining hall food.

"Should we invite him?" Willie points to a cabin, where Emir is sitting outside.

Mason hastily replies, "No."

"Seriously?" Hunter asks.

"Dead serious, dude. He doesn't like us. If he did, he'd sit with us during meals. Or, you know, *talk*."

Sebastian doesn't understand why Mason loathes Emir, but he's got his own issues to deal with. He's kept their training sessions a secret, and Emir never says a word to him in public.

Also, there's that minor wanting-to-kiss-Emir thing.

Emir's on the steps with an open book in his lap and an unlit cigarette behind his left ear. He appears uninterested in his surroundings. But his eyes are guarded, not letting anyone in.

"Whaddya say, Bastian?" Willie asks.

Sebastian eyes his feet and shrugs.

"Let's just *go*," Mason insists, climbing off the hood to hop in the driver's seat. "We're missing the fun."

"I'd call it mayhem," Hunter jokes.

Emir's eyes meet Sebastian's, and Sebastian's about to say something, go against Mason's bratty attitude and invite him along, but Emir shakes his head. He and Emir can resemble friends away from everyone else, so why not around Sebastian's friends?

"Yo, Bastian," Mason shouts.

Sebastian falters. Screw Mason and Emir. He wants to tell Emir to get off his ass and come along, but Grey skips up and plops down next to Emir.

"Aren't you going?" she asks.

Emir glances at Sebastian before lowering his eyes. "No, that's not my crowd."

In the background, Mason tuts.

"Well," Grey says, pushing curls off her face, "They never let me tag along."

"Because you're twelve!"

"Willie wants me to come along," she says to Mason.

Willie ducks when Mason twists around. He cuts a finger across his throat as if Willie is dead to him, at least for the next hour or so. "No effin' way, Patrick," Mason tells Grey. "The kids stay at home."

"I'm the one who saves your ass when you come back, drunk and out of your mind." Grey's fierce stare pins Mason down. "I never rat you out. Doesn't that count for something?"

Mason mumbles, "Thanks, but no," with a scowl.

Grey's usual neon vibrancy begins to dull.

Is that what it's like having a crush on someone who doesn't want you back? It steals your light?

"Whatever, Mace." Grey rolls her eyes, but hurt tilts her lips downward. She turns back to Emir. "I'm not twelve, and I'm fun." She sits taller, as if it'll make her older than sixteen and cooler too.

Emir bites on his lopsided grin. "You think so?"

"Oh, I *know* it," Grey assures in a way that could be misinterpreted, but then she giggles so hard she goes red all over, ruining the effect.

"I'm not," Emir says, lifting his book. "But you can chill if you want. I've got sisters back home, so I'm sure I can handle you." He points a finger in her face, warning, "But no trying to braid my hair."

Grey lifts her hand to pinky swear. The easy bonding between Emir and Grey intimidates Sebastian. They barely know each other. Doesn't he deserve that? Why does Sebastian get Emir the Asshole, with bitchy accessories?

"Whatever," Sebastian whispers. And he most certainly doesn't pout or stomp away like a kid, but he does climb into the passenger seat with a little less of a glow.

Willie tries to give him a fist bump. Sebastian returns it, half-assed. He kicks his feet up on the dash while Mason cranks up the car.

"I'm not gonna say it"—Mason totally does—"but he doesn't like us."

Sebastian ignores him. Emir just did Mason a solid by taking Grey off his hands, and he's blind to it. He closes his eyes as Mason drives them away.

 10

"So, what're you having to drink, sweet cheeks?" Liza, with her blue-tinted hair, kind face, and soft wrinkles around her eyes and mouth, asks. She snaps her gum, waiting patiently.

Sebastian doesn't know why he bothers running his eyes over the plastic menu. He's been to the diner enough over the last three summers. Nothing about it has changed, not the stench of grease-dripping burgers or the collection of framed vintage photos featuring Marilyn Monroe, James Dean, and Audrey Hepburn from *Breakfast at Tiffany's* lining the pastel blue walls. The neon vinyl stools complete the nod to '50s nostalgia.

Sebastian sits alone. He smiles at Liza. "Can I have a—?"

"Root beer, right?"

"Valerie Jones," Sebastian says, his mouth curving slyly. Val is another girl who's big on nicknames and never forgetting a face. It's ironic, because Sebastian can't forget her doe-brown eyes, sculpted rosy cheeks, and snarky smile.

She teases Sebastian with a raised eyebrow before hugging him. He reciprocates with one arm, breathing in her coconut suntan lotion.

"It's still root beer, right?" Val asks.

Sebastian nods a confirmation for her, then Liza.

Liza rolls her eyes. He's ordered the same thing forever, including the free slice of pie Liza slides him after every meal. "I'll let you two catch up," she says, snapping her gum. "Just call me when you're ready to order the usual." She saunters off with the limp of a grandma who's been on her feet too long.

Val peeks around him, tilting her head. "Alone?"

Sebastian doesn't mind being by himself. It's easier to keep track of the team, who bookend the booths inside the diner. They're lean but big, taking up as much space as possible. And they're loud, rowdy guys, knocking back milkshakes and clearing their plates as if they're starved. The slop here beats anything the dining hall produces.

Sebastian's head has been stuck on Emir. That doesn't make for good conversation with this wild bunch. It's not that he *can't* talk about his attraction to dudes, it's just that—well, the team hasn't made their minds up about Emir yet.

Neither has Sebastian.

"Just chilling," he says with his best laid-back shrug.

"Still the babysitter?"

"I prefer the term 'Big Brother.'"

"Bastian," Val says, skeptically, "you're half the size of some of those beasts." Her nose wrinkles at him in an intensely loveable way.

"Enjoy," Liza says, sliding him his drink. An extra scoop of ice cream sends root beer burbling over the rim and a cherry sits on top. "Hey! You make a mess, you're licking it up!" She scurries to a table stuffed with defensive players.

Val's chin is on her knuckles. She fills their silence with eyebrow wiggles and grins. They've always been good at replacing useless words with goofy facial expressions.

"Are you alone?" he asks.

Val jerks a thumb toward a corner booth where three gorgeous girls share a plate of fries drenched in ketchup. Their fine cheekbones and shiny hair scream "Private School Life." "Friends from school," Val explains.

Sebastian makes a horrified face.

Val rolls her eyes. "They're visiting for the weekend. Brunch with my parents tomorrow 'cause my life is so glamorous." She twirls a finger around her head. Val doesn't take anything too seriously, except for Mason Riley. Well, she *did* take him seriously, but a lifetime happens between summers.

"They look like fun," teases Sebastian.

"Oh, yeah," Val says, playing along. "About as much as future sorority-row, trophy-wives-in-training can be."

Sebastian lets Val steal a sip of his drink. She crinkles her nose, gags, and passes it back. "Awful." Then, seriously, she asks, "Are you still with Sam?"

Somewhere between the breakup and realizing he didn't love Sam, Sebastian developed a certain face at the mention of her. Mason told him the expression makes him look like a zombie, which is fair, since he was pretty dead during the last half of their relationship.

"Ouch," Val says, holding back a laugh. "That bad?"

"Kinda."

Behind Sebastian, Mason is holed up at a table with Willie, Hunter, and Charlie. Judging by all the hand gestures and *Macbeth*-like reenactments, it's obvious Mason is talking about the family trip to California three years ago.

Val gives him an equally undead look when Sebastian turns back to her, so he avoids broaching the subject. She sighs. "It's like us." She lowers her chin.

"Yeah?"

"It's for the best. It's my last year of high school." Val's lips twist into a smirk. "Carpe diem and all that shit they teach us."

Sebastian chuckles and swigs from his soda.

"I'm going to design school in Paris."

Sebastian's eyes widen. Val's voice sounds certain as she explains her plans; her next four years are mapped out. He's blown away, mainly because Sebastian has no idea what he's going to do with his next *four months* besides play soccer. He's jealous of people who are certain of their future before it happens. How can anyone know what they'll do with their whole lives, when he can't figure out where or even *if* he's going to college? But here's Val, not having a single panic attack about life after high school.

"It's great," Val continues, as though he hasn't been lost in space. She tucks a lock of hazelnut-colored hair behind her ear. "I'm in control of what my life looks like after graduation. I can decide whenever."

It all sounds so easy. Once she's away from high school and not worried about silly romances, she'll have it all together. Sebastian doesn't believe it's that simple, but he likes the dream she's selling.

Also, Mason is a total douche-canoe for letting her go. Sebastian doesn't tell her, because it's clear she's already had that epiphany.

"So that's it?"

"Life goes on after high school, Bastian." Her hand covers his on the counter. "We all move on."

Sebastian wants to tell her life is impossible to figure out. How does he silence all the huge, monstrous fears biting at his mind?

"Well, well," Mason interrupts, sliding between them before Sebastian can get a word out. His back and elbows rest against the counter as he eyes Val wolfishly. "Looking good, Jones."

"Good to know," she says.

Mason's face goes blank, then confused.

"Well," Val says, hopping off her stool. She leans over Mason to kiss Sebastian's cheek. "Always good to see you, Bastian." She saunters back to her table.

Mason's jaw tightens; his fingers curl and uncurl at his sides.

"Mace, do you—"

"Let's get out of here, bro," Mason says with a snarl, breathing heavily. He glares at the empty stool as if Val will magically reappear, and then jerks his head toward the door. "I heard Zach found some townie to buy beer."

Mason and Willie are opposites when it comes to discussing the F-word: feelings. That's not Mason's thing. When Sam broke up with Sebastian, Mason punched him in the shoulder and passed him a Heineken. "Drink it away" is Mason's motto, his coping mechanism. Sebastian blames Mason's dad ditching him and his five younger sisters. Mason's claim to fame is being a soccer god in Bloomington and a badass. Alcohol camouflages the scars from his youth, but strength isn't measured by a guy's ability to drain a six-pack and not cry.

Mason looks ready to rip a hole in someone's chest when he snaps, "Let's *go*, man."

Sebastian sighs. Mason gathers the other players while Sebastian checks with Liza to make sure all the tabs are taken care of.

He doesn't even get his free slice of pie.

❂

THREE HOURS AND FOUR MICHELOBS later, Sebastian wonders if the entire night was a spectacularly awful idea.

He's still very sober, so he doesn't understand why walking a straight line should be so difficult, unless it's because he has a nearly two-hundred-pound *slug* named Zach hanging on him. They've been struggling to make it to Zach's cabin for ten minutes. Bearing most of Zach's weight, Sebastian anticipates their eventual collapse into the dirt.

"Bro, the ground is…" Zach pauses to hiccup, then laugh, and says, "*moving.*"

Decision made: This night is the *worst.*

Most of the team made it back before curfew, though some were toppling over like building blocks. The sober ones, cranky freshmen, try to help where they can. "No brother left behind" is the golden rule among the Lions, a rule Sebastian's dying to break because Zach's exhaling rank, basement-ass beer breath in his face.

"Do you see it? We're, like, hovering."

"We're not," Sebastian tries, but Zach's already on another tangent.

Sebastian's friends are no help. Mason's taking a leak on a bush. Hunter is sprawled in the back seat of Mason's car with his head in Willie's lap as Willie destroys a John Mayer song with his off-key singing. *No, Willie, your body is* not *a wonderland.* Sebastian's on his own, doing a mental headcount as he lugs Zach over dirt and pebbles.

"I can fly!"

"Shut up." Sebastian has one arm around the small of Zach's back. Zach is freakishly tall, something Sebastian isn't jealous of. But it makes this whole tandem-walking thing weird. "You're gonna wake the coaches," he warns, as if that might work.

"Then they'll see I can fly!" Zach's eyes are shadowed by his disheveled hair, but the moon shines off their hazel color.

"Perfect."

At this rate, weight training in the fall won't be necessary.

"I love you, man," Zach slurs, head lolling to one side. "Like, you're my bro and my captain and—"

"Okay, got it." Sebastian carefully prevents Zach from teetering over. If he can get Zach to focus a little, they'll make it to the door before he turns twenty-one.

Sebastian lets Zach talk, because Zach can concentrate on his limbs when he's yapping about whatever's on his mind. Zach badgers him about always being sober, something Sebastian does for *his* benefit. And, for the record, beer tastes like sour mouthwash and bile. No one is convincing Sebastian otherwise, not even the guys.

"I'm not wasted," declares Zach.

"Not at all," Sebastian lies. Zach stumbles, and Sebastian's legendary reflexes kick in. He stops Zach from face-planting into a bush.

Zach mumbles gratitude before launching into a story about that time Sebastian *did* get loose with the guys. At Carl's last party. Sebastian was just so done with Sam's shit, he had a healthy hit off Mason's joint, coughing violently before mellowing out with vodka. He was a champ for not passing out, or flirting with a wall, as Jack did.

"Dude!" Zach gasps as if he's been kicked in the face. "I totally did something stupid, didn't I?"

"Well." Sebastian considers listing all the things Zach did. He can't hold in "You nearly puked all over Val's friend."

Zach turns pale. "Was she pretty?"

"They were *all* pretty."

And they were, not that Sebastian flirted with any of them. One girl, with eyes like a Disney woodland creature and an uneven smile, was cute. He usually would've at least made an attempt to flirt, with his corny jokes, but tonight he couldn't get past how her eyes were green instead of gray thunderclouds. Massive downer.

"So," Zach says, tipping forward, "I didn't get her number?"

"Nope."

Zach and that girl would've had a lovely story to tell their grandchildren about how they met: "Yep, I nearly blew chunks in her hair and then asked her to the movies!" More romantic comedies should start that way.

"She wasn't interested anyway." Zach vainly attempts to stand erect. "She had goals, and a high school loser like me wasn't good enough."

"Hey," Sebastian says. "You're not a loser, Zach." Obnoxious when he's drunk? Sure. But not a loser.

Zach grins lopsidedly, as if he almost believes Sebastian. Guys like him—Zach lives in a rundown home with a chain-smoking father who would rather yell at the TV than come to any of Zach's games—don't always win the cheerleader types. Zach isn't what Sebastian would call fragile, but anyone's entire universe can be shattered when it involves approval from family or someone you're attracted to.

"Maybe she heard you were a virgin," Sebastian says with a labored chuckle. Humor is always good medicine for unhealthy thoughts.

Zach, shitfaced and wobbly, scoffs. "I am not. I get plenty of tail."

"That's not what the girls in Bloomington say."

"Liar!" Zach smacks a hand over his eyes, sputtering. "You're a dick, Hughes."

Sebastian pauses so Zach can regain his breath. He leans over as if he might finally hurl. Sebastian hopes not. These are his favorite low top Chuck Taylors; the fabric is worn and faded.

"Cool?"

It takes a second before Zach nods, pulling a grin out of thin air. "You should've scored with someone tonight. Get over the whole Sam thing, you know?"

That's all Sebastian is, right? Soccer, graduation, and Sam. These days, Sebastian wants his life to be made up of soccer, soccer, and more soccer. But he's over it, the Sam part. Some exes are just a sentence in the story of life, not the defining chapter with all the drama and awesome climax.

"Maybe next time?" Sebastian offers.

"Yes! Next time, I'm so gonna get you laid," Zach says. "That's life goals, bro."

Great. This is all Mason's fault, like so many things in Sebastian's life, and he'll make Mason suffer for not helping him drag Zach around.

Zach yawns. Sebastian grimaces because, *really?* Zach has the nerve to be tired when it's Sebastian who has Mount freakin' Olympus hanging off his shoulders?

"Are we there yet?"

"Dude, are you shitting me, like—"

"Hey."

Sebastian barely recognizes the groggy, soft voice before another arm loops around Zach's back. He inclines forward, a difficult task considering how bulky Zach is. Emir's sleep-mussed hair and weary gray eyes heighten his moody expression.

"What are you—?"

Emir grunts at Sebastian. "You looked like you were about to die."

I am. Sebastian smiles.

Emir yawns, then makes a disgusted face. "He stinks."

Sebastian, no longer carrying the weight of Godzilla on his own, laughs until the knot of frustration unravels in his belly. He doesn't care if Zach balks because, for once, he's not trying to save one of his teammates' asses on his own. When he strains to gaze around Zach, Emir's amused expression greets him.

"So," Emir says as they lurch closer to Zach's cabin, "do you do this often?"

Sebastian says, "No, but… I'm the only one who watches over them," to his feet. He's not embarrassed but sometimes saying the truth out loud makes it sound worse than it is.

"Huh."

"And I could've done it by myself," Sebastian says hastily, but that's not being defensive. He just doesn't want anyone calling him a victim.

"You think so?"

"Maybe?" Sebastian's not sure. "I was almost there."

Emir *pffts*, and it forces Sebastian to accept that, nope, he wasn't all that close.

Behind Zach's back, their hands brush occasionally, fingers almost linking as they try to realign him. Goosebumps spread from Sebastian's neck to his chest. The touch of Emir's soft hand has him dizzy, a problem he's never had with other guys. It's scary, because that puts Emir in the small category of Guys Sebastian's Been Attracted To.

"Did we wake you?" The stranglehold his throat has around his words mortifies him.

He can't tell if Emir is nodding or shaking his head until Emir says, "Still can't sleep proper around here."

Sebastian hums. The whole night, including this moment, is a train wreck.

And to add to it, Zach says, "Well, if it isn't the great Emir Shah," as if he's just noticed Emir is under the wing of his arm. "So, what's your story?"

"My what?" Emir cranes back.

By tugging Zach in his direction, Sebastian desperately tries to make sure they all don't eat dirt.

"Your story, man," Zach says, exasperated. "No one *knows* you."

"I like it that way."

Sebastian's brow furrows. It's not the answer he expected. Then again, *nothing* about Emir has been predictable.

"Oh, come on, man," Zach says. "Everyone needs a story." He stops, causing Sebastian to groan, before he considers Emir. "What are you? Brainiac? Band geek? Art geek? Goth? You're definitely not part of the jock crowd."

"I'm not a stereotype." Emir glares as if he might just drop Zach, but he doesn't, and Sebastian is relieved.

"Okay, but you're very," Zach says, then takes a deep breath, "quiet. It's scary. How are you going to make friends with us?"

"I'm not here to make friends."

Things are seconds from going nuclear. Sebastian tries to walk a little faster, but it's difficult since neither Zach nor Emir is cooperating. He's tired and confused by Emir's constant hot-and-cold vibe. All he wants is his bed and for everyone to shut up.

"Are you playing the weird-kid angle?" asks Zach, hacking a laugh at Emir's scowl.

"I'm not playing anything—"

"When we were kids," Zach barrels on, "you didn't say a *word* unless Bastian was around."

"Zach," warns Sebastian, because he doesn't need this right now.

"No, no," Zach says. "What's wrong with the rest of us? I don't get it. I don't get *you*, Shah."

Sebastian almost drops Zach trying to read Emir's face. He's red all over and breathing hard; his eyes are glassy. His jaw works as though a mouthful of profanity is going to fly out, but he doesn't say anything. He glares straight ahead. It's a girl-from-*The-Exorcist* vibe.

Zach swings his arms off both of them. He stumbles, then regains his balance. Puffing boozy breath, he smirks over his shoulder at Emir. "Here's a tip, Shah: We're a family on this team—"

"Zach, man, *please*," Sebastian begs.

But Zach continues, "If you want in, you better learn there are more guys than your superhero Bastian."

Zach sways side to side, then stumbles up the porch. He thuds his shoulder into the door a few times before it pops open. Then, it smacks shut.

Sebastian turns, whispering, "Emir," but it's useless.

Highlighting his shaking shoulders and red face, moonlight haloes Emir. Tears haven't drowned his eyelashes, but they're threatening. "I need to get to bed," he says in a broken voice.

"Wait, just let me—"

"Here's a fun fact: Everyone in high school is a dick," Emir snaps. He waves a hand around. "Your friends aren't excluded." He wipes a finger across his left cheek, giving Sebastian just enough time to pull something poignant out of his ass.

The words never come. At least, not until Emir stomps off, head hanging and fists shaking.

"Thank you."

11

CAMP HAVEN IS A GHOST town the next morning. Most of the team sleeps through breakfast. Their buzzes give way to headaches, exhaustion, and fits of nausea. Guys creep zombie-like into the rec room for a monster FIFA tournament on the Xbox. A handful hide behind sunglasses from any threat of light.

Sebastian skips his morning run. He hardly slept last night. He declines Kyle and Gio's invitation for a round of ping pong. He's no good to anyone when his mind is drifting, lost at sea without a buoy. He's drowning in Val and Mason, Zach's attitude, the team, and Emir Shah.

Why is it so hard to get the one person who *dreads* seeing you off your brain? It should be a piece of cake.

Sebastian's brain is so stuffed full of shit that Emir just circles around the surface like flotsam in a clogged drain.

The lake is a good place to free his thoughts. Sunlight glints off the water, gold against azure. Robins and sparrows chirp their sweet anthems. He presses his phone to his ear, flops on the wooden dock that stretches a few feet into the lake, and dips his toes in the cold water.

"Bumble Bee!"

Sebastian winces. One day Lily will realize the nickname is childish and tragic and finally stop calling him that.

They go through their usual catch-up; Lily carries most of the conversation. He hasn't got much to say. Her voice is enough until she says, "Something's on your mind, Bastian," and he considers belly flopping into the lake and drowning so he'll never have to admit to her how screwed up he is.

"It's nothing."

"Sebastian William—"

Oh, shit. Lily only uses his middle name when he's on the verge of pissing her off beyond repair.

"It's no biggie, Mom. It's just—our first game against the Spartans is so soon."

She hums. "Your mortal enemies."

Sebastian does a pretty great job at holding in his sigh. "I'm nervous; it's a big deal. We need to beat them." His feet kick up a splash; sunlit, golden droplets ripple the lake's surface.

"Well, sweetheart," Lily says, "win or lose, what's the most important part?"

"Kicking ass and winning the championship."

Lily has always been blasé about his swearing, thanks to Carly, who has pulled enough outrageous stunts and brought home enough questionable boyfriends for Sebastian to get a pass. "It's about *you*," she says, her tone serious. Sebastian quickly sobers. "This has been your dream, right? Making the team. Having this journey."

"Yeah."

"And now you're the best goalie in the conference—"

"I'm not the best."

"Whatever," Lily says with an almost audible smile. "The nerves are normal."

But what about the pressure of keeping everyone in line? Figuring out his life's aspirations? Also, these weird prickly feelings about his ex-best friend? Of course, he doesn't mention any of that to her, but they're recurring nightmares.

Maybe someone should create new hashtag: "Life's complicated, but so is math."

Lily talks randomly about his dad, the family dog, Thor, and her garden. She brings up school, and he sneakily avoids the topic because, *no way*, he doesn't have the strength for a discussion about college. Sebastian isn't ready for the reality of being an adult: earning a degree, starting a family, and living the dreams his parents have for him.

Lily says, "It'll all work out."

He can't help but reply, "That's what you're supposed to say."

"Well, it's true!"

"You can't prove that."

"I don't need to, Sebastian William, I'm your mother."

Sebastian lets the subject die. He's already pushed her far enough and he doesn't want to ruin the moment.

"Maybe if you find a nice girl, who's not Sam, you might stop being such a pest," Lily says, half laughing, half hopeful.

He should tell her. Hands down, being bisexual is the one part of his life Sebastian hasn't had to *think* about. It's also the one thing he hasn't had to be great at, not the way he's had to try to be a good friend, to be a perfectionist on the pitch, to make an impact.

It's scary, coming out to his parents. When it comes to being anything other than straight, it seems there's a fine-print clause: a penalty for full disclosure when you belong to the LGBTQ community. Sebastian doesn't get it. It shouldn't matter if he falls for a girl or boy. Love is supposed to be a happy, comforting emotion, but it always comes with conflict. And being anything but straight means making these huge declarations to the people closest to you.

Why is coming out to loved ones like giving a speech in your campaign for President?

"Bastian?"

He chokes. His parents won't hate him for who he is, but he's not certain they'll understand him either. "Yeah, Mom," Sebastian stutters. "Maybe I will find someone." And the rest, he keeps to himself.

Sebastian stares at the screen after they hang up. He stands, feeling lighter than before. He jogs back to his cabin.

MIRRORS AREN'T THE FRIENDLIEST OF objects. Sebastian decided that years ago, but it's inescapably clear now that he's standing shirtless, inspecting his body.

In his head, on repeat, he hears it: "Bastian the Trashcan, Bastian the Trashcan…"

Behind him, Willie and Hunter are bundled under an afghan on Willie's bed, snoring and dead to the world. Willie's face is mashed in Hunter's neck. Hunter's fingers are twisted in Willie's hair; their lower halves are tangled. A pair of cuddling bros.

Sebastian figured they'd be like that for another hour, which was all the encouragement he needed to change clothes for a late run. Then he caught a sideways glimpse of himself. Now, he can't move his feet.

He's repositioning his body to appear *normal*. Yes, he likes some things about himself: his skin has a natural, creamy tan and he has a broad chest and narrow hips. But the flaws stick out. He's lost definition in his arms. His metabolism finally caught up with his growth spurts, so his belly is softer. He pulls at the extra tissue above his hip and hisses, "What the hell," when it stretches painfully.

Sebastian's tried changing his diet, more time in the weight room, counting calories, anything to make a difference, to end those taunts in his brain. But in the reflection, an older version of that bullied kid glares at him.

"Shit."

The knot in his chest expands. Emir would never go for him. Not that Emir *wants* him, but why would he? Sebastian's not in Emir's league, at least, not physically.

"And these are the days of our lives…" Willie mumbles in his sleep; one leg hangs off the bed. Hunter is squeezing an arm around him so they both don't roll off. It would be a viral hit if Sebastian recorded it on his phone, but he decides not to.

Bro code.

Sebastian eyes his reflection one last time. "Screw you, evil mirror" is implied when he flips himself the bird. He tugs on a tank top, steals Willie's iPod, and heads for the door.

He can still squeeze in a run before lunch if he hurries.

12

"Beckham is a legend."

Jack is pointing an accusing plastic fork at Gio. He's got a pale, freckled rat-face that's slowly turning red as Gio scoffs. His eyes are bloodshot, adding to his deranged look.

Gio says, "He's got nothing on Ryan Giggs, amigo."

Groaning, Jack drops his fork and throws his hands up.

It's late afternoon, and the team has finally spun into the dining hall like a category five tornado. This argument, and a few others, is prominent between soccer players at Bloomington High. Sebastian skipped the lunch line after his jog and plops down at their table with a protein shake for a front-row seat.

He's betting on Kyle's usual Ronaldo favoritism or—

"What about Rooney?"

Bingo! Sebastian chuckles to himself. He turns back to Mason, who seems to have a kickass hangover and is poring over a cup of coffee.

"That looks gross," Mason says, eyes barely open. Sebastian takes a huge slug of his shake. Mason's still wearing pajama bottoms and his hair is floppy, as if it took an army just to get him out of bed.

Sebastian wipes his mouth with his hand. "So does your face," he says, and is rewarded with a middle finger salute. He slouches in his chair. It's plastic and uncomfortable, but he makes do by propping his feet on an empty seat next to Willie.

Willie and Hunter are leaning into each other. They whisper as if they're plotting a bank robbery. That wouldn't end prettily.

"What's in there?" Mason waves a hand at Sebastian's drink.

"Whey, green stuff, bananas, more green stuff."

Mason shudders. "I'm gonna puke in your mouth, man."

Sebastian shies away from Mason. Projectile vomit wasn't on today's lunch menu.

"Here."

Sebastian isn't always the most observant person. He is, however, frozen in shock at the sight of Grey sitting across from them at their table. She waves dainty fingers; her curls are tied in a ponytail. Sebastian curves up an eyebrow.

"Take two," she tells Mason, pushing a pill bottle at him. "They're for motion sickness but should do the trick. And they're herbal."

"Who and what is happening?" Mason asks. "Willie, dude, did you do this?"

Willie is bright red, laughing at something Hunter says, and unaware of Mason's existence.

"Don't be a jerk," Grey mumbles.

Mason snatches the bottle; pills rattle inside. He pops the top and downs two, grimacing. Over his coffee cup, he glares weakly at her.

"These will kill me, won't they? Is that your plot?"

"You think I want to kill you?" Grey asks.

"I think you want to do a lot of things to me." Mason leaves his statement open for interpretation.

"Listen." Grey sighs, rubbing her temples. "I caught Charlie ralphing his guts up in the bushes and covered for you guys when Rivera came asking about it. I deserve a 'Thanks, Grey' at least."

Mason gives her a thumbs-up before returning to his coffee.

Lifting an eyebrow, Sebastian turns to Grey. "Really? *This?*" he asks, pointing at Mason, who has found a conversation with Charlie to keep him distracted from Grey.

Willie peeks at them. Sebastian *knows* he invited Grey to their table. Willie's that guy who's friends with everyone. The entire senior class back in Bloomington gets a high-five or a "Hey, beautiful" for the girls. Popularity's easy for Willie. Sebastian's wagering on Willie for Homecoming King.

Around Sebastian, guys talk about SAT scores, AP classes, and prom. Willie raises an eyebrow dramatically when Hunter mentions attending UCLA. Mason's still undecided. Sebastian slouches, waiting for a subject change, and Coach Patrick provides it.

"Guys, guys!" he yells from the front of the room. "Rest up today. Tomorrow, we start practicing for the Spartans. I've got some footage of their spring practices. Are we ready?"

Grunts break out around the room, steady as the rhythm of a drumline.

"You're gonna take them down this year, right?"

Now tables rattle; a few guys slam their trays.

"We're Lions, correct?"

Growls and roars echo against the walls. Jack tries to maul Smith. Coach is great at riling the guys up. Sebastian chews his thumbnail. Coach Patrick will always be his favorite.

"He's stressed about the first game," Grey confesses when the room starts to clear out. She fiddles with a curl. "Our offense is good, but the defense needs work."

Sebastian nods; he has his elbows on the table with his chin in his hands.

To his left, Mason says, "Then I guess Willie better get back on the field."

Eyeing the table, Willie tugs a hand through his hair. His mouth is drawn into a thin white line. Hunter pulls on Willie's ear until he lifts his chin. They get lost in a conversation about video games.

Sebastian hasn't figured out how to get Willie out of his funk, but at least Hunter's around.

"Go, Bloomington!" someone shouts on the way out the door.

"Go, Lions," Sebastian whispers.

The bank of windows on the side of the room lets in blasts of sun and heat that make Sebastian want to go for a swim. At the table under the windows, Emir is folded awkwardly with a comic book balanced on his knees. A mostly untouched bowl of fruit sits by his elbow. Trails of dark fringe fall over his brow, helping to hide his eyes. But his mouth is hanging open; he must be captivated by whatever he's reading. Sebastian stares at his lips, slick with spit from a pink tongue, and—

"Bastian, bro."

Mason snaps fingers at him. Sebastian nearly falls out of his seat but catches his balance by smacking his hands on the table. It almost tips over. Four sets of wide eyes stare at him, and his cheeks burn. Breathless, he tries to speak but only gets out, "Um, yeah, swimming sounds like a great idea!" He's pretty sure no one was talking about swimming.

"Okay," Mason drawls with a raised eyebrow. "I need a nap, but yes. Go. Swim away."

Sebastian wants to bang his head on the table.

"Cool," Willie says, because he is a godsend. "I could use a dip."

"Me too." Nodding, Hunter slings an arm around Willie's neck.

Sebastian sags in his chair; his chin nearly hits the table. He peers at Emir's table, praying his moronic display has gone unnoticed, but Emir hasn't moved an inch. Obviously, Sebastian isn't worth noticing.

⚽

SEBASTIAN WAKES UP ON MONDAY with orange sunlight beating against his eyelids. His cell, still hell-bent on betraying his rest, squawks. Sebastian almost tosses it across the room but remembers his mom won't buy him another one, so he rolls his eyes at it instead.

He makes it through his morning routine of clothes, sneakers, and stealing Willie's iPod: a major accomplishment Sebastian completes with one eye open. He records a video of Willie making out with his pillow. He'll use it for blackmail if Willie ever tells anyone Sebastian ate a cricket on a dare.

Camp Haven is quiet, the morning hues of tangerine and ocean blue painted across the cabins and trees. Sebastian squints against a glaring sun. He's in that hazy space where he's not asleep but still dreaming, and that's his only reason for stumbling to Emir's cabin after he brushes his teeth.

The window is already propped open. Sebastian's sense of comfort quickly fades. This might be a trap. Maybe thumbtacks are waiting on the other side of the window.

"Nah." He laughs to himself, pressing his arms on the ledge of the window to vault inside.

Sunlight draws crisp edges in the cabin. Emir is tucked into a small ball, buried under mounds of blankets. His head is sticking out. He's sucking his lower lip like an infant.

Looks are definitely deceiving.

Emir rolls away from the sunlight, exposing his shirtless back when the blankets slip lower. Staring at the hawk tattoo between Emir's shoulder blades, Sebastian bites hard on his own lip. He's always wanted a tattoo of his own, but this sweet piece of artwork drives the thought home. His mind starts to drift in a wicked daydream of tracing all the ink under his fingertips while Emir gasps and—his whole brain derails.

"Okay," he whispers. "That's not healthy, at all."

Floorboards creak on his way to the bed. Sebastian pauses. Emir's shoulders rise and fall; the side of his face reveals a mask of peace. His hand curls into a fist on the pillow.

The urge just to let Emir be *almost* beats out Sebastian's plans to wake him.

Sebastian's hand is cold against Emir's sleep-warm back. Goosebumps raise across Emir's skin. Sebastian's fingers outline every knob on his spine. "Emir," he whispers. Emir is icy and petulant, so words like cute and adorable should not be crossing Sebastian's mind. "C'mon, man. Get up, Emir."

Emir shakes awake like a puppy, nose twitching and body convulsing. His eyes pop open, then glare. "What the hell, Bastian?"

Sebastian wants to point out that Emir was expecting him, since the window was open, but he says, "I—"

"Nope. No way, mate. Go away." Emir turns to snuffle into his pillow. "Not happening."

"Emir—"

Emir, completely destroying all of those "innocent" thoughts that crossed Sebastian's mind, starts to hum. He curls inward as if he can disappear.

Sebastian knee-walks his way onto the bed. He jabs a hand under the blankets and tickles Emir's ribs until he jerks and yelps. It's a small victory. "You know you want to—"

"Kick your ass?"

Sebastian can't figure out how Emir can be so devilishly handsome while peeking through his eyelashes. "Funny," he says.

Emir squeezes his eyes shut. He tries to squirm away, mumbling, "Go screw yourself," but his expression is soft, like a feisty kitten coming down from a catnip high.

Poser. "Time for a run. All of the experts, and Oprah, say exercise is good for you."

"They lied, all of them. Horrible, disrespectful lies," says Emir. "Now leave."

Sebastian squawks pathetically before flicking Emir's spine. "Don't be a dick," he says, then pulls on Emir's resistant shoulder. Sebastian's stronger than Emir, which pleases his ego. "We're doing this. You're going to get better."

Emir growls like a sleeping lion. It doesn't help that whatever is going on below Sebastian's belly likes that noise. Horrified, he turns away to take a deep breath and calm down. He's disappointed in his body, because getting aroused while trying to wake a teammate is so inappropriate.

He imagines crying babies, Mr. Drake's boring history class, *anything* to stop images of Emir, neck kisses, and their bodies tangled. He's seriously frying brain cells. Emir isn't helping one bit by complaining, "You aren't going away, are you?" in a husky voice.

"I mean..." Sebastian's sweating. His fingers are curled in Emir's sheets. "It's not as if you *asked* for my help, so, whatever. I can ditch, if you want." He didn't mean it as a desperate question, but it comes out that way. His embarrassment is at nuclear levels.

Emir sighs. "No, it's okay." He rolls over behind Sebastian and pushes up on his elbows. Sluggishly, Emir crawls from under the blankets. He plops down next to Sebastian. The frustrated line between his eyebrows is replaced by a sleepy smile, and he shoves Sebastian's shoulder when he stands. "I really hate you."

"Well, thank baby Jesus, the feeling's mutual!" Sebastian teases. Then, seriously, he says, "Do you?"

"Nope," Emir says around a yawn, standing on his tiptoes with his hands stretched toward the ceiling. "But you're annoying in the morning."

Sebastian can take that. But his brain only accepts Emir's attitude because his eyes are busy darting over Emir's body. In just a pair of briefs and socks, Emir's sepia skin pales to gold under the sunlight. He's on the skinny side, but small muscles are defined everywhere. It doesn't help that his hair sticks up in a tall fluff. And then there are his narrow hips, angles hiding behind the waistband of his underwear, the material stretched—

"Um."

Sebastian snaps his head up.

Emir's headshake is followed by laughter. He says, "Hey, it's cool. Don't you ever get morning wood?"

If there was a blurb in the biography of Sebastian's life, those last two words would be bolded and italicized. He clears his throat, then shrugs, playing it smooth. He focuses on the nearby wall, studying its matte-finished, golden wood—

Christ, his mind is seriously screwed up, and the wall is no longer a good distraction.

"Dude." Emir punches Sebastian's arm. "It's a guy thing, I get it. You're just sizing up the competition, right?" At the mahogany dresser in the corner, he pulls out clothes. In a mildly deprecating voice, he says, "I'm not that impressive."

In what alternate universe? All the gold hexagons the sun creates over Emir's skin accentuate his amazing features. His messy hair is an inky spiral. And just when Sebastian can get past Emir's appeal because he's been an uncalled-for asshole, Emir turns his head, and his blinking, pale gray eyes attack Sebastian.

It's an unfair use of good genes.

"Bastian?"

Sebastian raises his hand like at roll call during homeroom.

"What time is it?"

Sebastian pulls out his phone. "A little after seven."

"What the bloody hell," Emir whines while pulling on a hoodie.

Obviously, Sebastian's ears burn with love at Emir's British accent coiled around his name. It's all downhill from here. By the time he stops spacing out and drooling, Emir is at the door, fully dressed, scowl included.

"You coming?"

Sebastian scolds his brain for thinking *not yet.*

Emir taps his foot. He's gone from sleepy morning nymph to raging demon in five minutes flat. "Let's get this over with."

Sebastian couldn't agree more. Then he can run to his cabin, put a sock on the door, and pray Willie has an extra-long breakfast.

13

Sebastian is ready to take on giants.

Their run through Oakville was uneventful. Sebastian spent most of it shuffling through playlists. Emir kept pace while panting like an asthmatic dog. Sebastian was running at half-speed, but he'll credit Emir for his efforts. It was an equally brutal and amusing sight.

And now a very determined monster is staring him down from halfway up the field, complaining, "This is pointless!" like a disgruntled Godzilla.

"Emir," Sebastian says while Emir stares resolutely at the ball in front of him, "I'm not letting you give up, okay?"

"No," Emir says, as peevish as ever. "It's stupid."

"It's not. You've got this, dude." Waiting for Emir's attack, Sebastian sways into position.

Emir dribbles the ball. He's improved. He's not starting player material, but he shows promise. And his confidence when he doesn't lose control of the ball as often gives him presence. He's a cub growing into a wolf.

"Shouldn't I be practicing to be a midfielder?" he says, gaining range as he dribbles closer.

Sebastian vacates his box to scoop the ball away from Emir. "You'll make a better sweeper." Sebastian spins around Emir only to be caught mid-motion. He grins. "You remind me of Piqué."

"Who?"

Sebastian zigzags, but Emir's on his heels. The sky is a splash of Caribbean blue today; sparse clouds make room for the heavy gold sun. The scents of summer grass fill Sebastian's nose, but, with Emir this close, musk and sweat and something spicy underlie everything.

"He's a professional—you know what, never mind." He backtracks, but Emir isn't fooled and gets a foot inside to steal the ball. "We need a sweeper," Sebastian says.

"Isn't that what Will is?"

Sebastian pauses, resting his hands on his hips. "He's out, bad knee." They'll be lucky if Willie has a handful of games in him. Nearly every doctor in the entire state has warned Willie that he risks blowing out his kneecap if he plays. Their eyes meet, and Sebastian says, "We need an alternate."

Emir stops, resting his foot on the ball. "So, I'm a Plan B." Out loud, it's harsh, but Sebastian can't argue with him.

"You'd be the most important player on the field."

"That's *you*," Emir says with a corner of his mouth raised. It's a clever diversion, giving Emir just enough time to maneuver the ball around Sebastian. The goal is a few feet away. But Emir gives himself away by leaning too far to his left.

Sebastian fakes with him before slipping a foot in to pop the ball away.

"Sucker."

Emir has a frustrated hand in his hair. "I don't know if I could do it."

Sebastian does keepie-uppies midfield. His tongue hangs out of the side of his mouth. "Try," he says, half to Emir but also to himself, because he wants to believe he can make Emir into the player he's shown potential to be.

Emir exhales shakily, proving he's not sold on the idea.

"Think about it. You could make a big difference and show your dad how incredible you are."

Emir teeters from foot to foot. His tiny, pleased smile shocks Sebastian's gut.

"Yeah?" Emir's eyebrows and mouth inch higher. "Okay."

"Okay, then let's do this, dickhead."

Sebastian waits until Emir is in a defensive crouch, leading the ball up the grass until they meet near the goal. Emir shoves. Sebastian pulls. Their feet fight over the ball. Soccer is a contact sport, so it's not as though Sebastian is out of line for grabbing Emir's shirt. Emir is so fast, he needs a way to counter.

"Mine!"

"Not so fast."

The ball is knocking around like a pinball. Their contacts have become more aggressive. Emir cheats, grabbing the waistband of Sebastian's shorts. Sebastian's hand jerks Emir's hip. They're nearly nose to nose, struggling not to lose their balance.

"Loser," Emir says, getting the ball away from Sebastian. He dribbles it upfield. Sweaty and gasping, he turns to wave a hand at Sebastian like Neo in *The Matrix*. "C'mon," he taunts.

Sebastian is enjoying Emir's burst of ego. He won't mind deflating it in a few seconds.

Emir fakes right. Sebastian charges forward to wrestle the ball away, but Emir is shoved bodily against Sebastian. He's a torch against Sebastian's exposed skin.

Sebastian trips on the ball, ready to eat grass on his way down. Emir catches his elbow. Sebastian cups a hand around Emir's neck, pulling until they collide.

They burst into laughter. And then Sebastian kisses him.

It's so quick, their mouths just smack.

Sebastian should write it off as a mistake; this isn't a real kiss, where you're lightheaded afterward or shoving your tongue down a hot guy's mouth to taste the flavor of his gum.

This is nothing at all.

Sebastian barely keeps himself from falling on his ass. "Shit." He meant to keep that in his mouth, the same mouth that's currently buzzing with electricity.

Emir is pale, blinking. *Perfect. I accidentally, I repeat, accidentally, just kissed him and he's ready to puke.* He didn't *want it,* not the way Sebastian did, according to his lower half.

"Okay." Emir pushes hair off his forehead and looks around.

"Okay," Sebastian repeats in a wobbly voice.

If this is where Emir rejects him, Sebastian is completely cool with it. It was a mistake: no foul, no harm. He can live this down. He hopes.

"So," Emir whispers. He locates the ball and kicks it to Sebastian. "Good practice."

"Yeah," Sebastian says, absently catching the ball with his foot.

"But the whole sweeper thing," Emir is waving a hand around; his face is scrunched, "I don't know about that. Just— let's focus on other stuff." He shakes his head, then jogs away before Sebastian can swallow the massive lump clogging his throat.

Should he apologize for kissing Emir? Ask him to keep practicing? Sebastian doesn't know. He doesn't know *anything*, and that's not the worst part. He grits his teeth and stares at the sun. He's hoping for clarity, but the light just makes him see spots. Eventually, he dribbles the ball back to the Hot Box. He leans against it, face pinched. It's hot, but Sebastian's brain sticks on how much hotter it was with his fingers holding the back of Emir's neck when they kissed.

BY DINNER, SEBASTIAN IS RESTLESS and not very hungry. He shows up in the dining hall, though. If he doesn't, Willie or one of the guys will hound him until he does. Over the years, he's become the "glue" for the team and, usually, that's an amazing feeling. This evening, he can't get out of his own head enough to savor his coolness.

"Prom, yay or nay?" Jack, who has beady dirt-brown eyes, asks Gio while pointing a plastic knife at him. Dinner is dry chicken, again, and all Sebastian's managed to do is hack it to shreds as if he's Leatherface.

Gio shrugs, munching on carrots. "If I can find the right girl—"

"None of them want you." Jack wheezes at his own joke.

Gio flips him off, then says, "I could take *your mom*. She's pretty hot."

"Christ, dude," Kyle chokes, milk spluttering from his mouth. "The disrespect, man."

Gio chugs his Coke. Sebastian's always surprised at how Gio owns his smugness without being an asshole. He reminds Sebastian of a super-young Benicio del Toro.

Sebastian leans back in his chair, fascinated by how his teammates carry their own senses of self-awareness, as if life is so easy despite their setbacks. They've all had shit shoveled on their dreams. Some of them won't have enough money to attend community college when they graduate. But none of it weighs them down. They carry on, cracking jokes and living each day as if they're high in the clouds. Sebastian has no clue how to earn, let alone keep such impenetrable confidence in his future. Instead, a giant pile of choices waits at his feet.

"Okay," Mason says, stealing the cup of Jello from Sebastian's tray and Willie's too. He shoves a spoonful in his mouth. "Who wants to explain to me how junior made it to our table again?"

Grey's shoulders drop at Mason's callous reference. "I invited myself."

"You've got balls," Mason says, making a face. "Okay, maybe you don't, but you know what I mean."

"Audacity," Grey clarifies. "And yes, I do. Why, are you attracted to bold women?" She bats her eyelashes.

"One," Mason holds up a finger, "you're a girl, not a woman. And two," a second finger pops up, "I don't understand you enough to be attracted to you."

"So, there's hope?"

Willie chokes on a laugh and thumps his chest repeatedly. This is all his fault.

Mason glowers at him and then cocks his head at Grey. His glare is intense, as if he's attempting to shoot lasers and evaporate her. "You think you're cute, don't you?"

Grey's mouth does this little quirk that's more shy than confident. "Sometimes," she says, barely lifting her shoulders.

Mason ignores her to spoon Jello into his mouth before starting in on Willie about what he's wearing: a neon-green Barbie tank top with a rainbow on it that says "California Dream," simultaneously owning his sexuality and his awesomeness.

Sebastian slouches, examining Grey. Soft, half-moon dimples form around her mouth. Her curls fall around her bright eyes, brown against green. It's as if—

"Are you wearing eyeliner?" He inspects her. She kicks his shin under the table and Sebastian jolts, almost knocking everything over.

"Dude!" Mason scowls and protects his Jello. "You need to get *whatever* under control."

Sebastian frowns, rubbing his shin. Grey stares, slit eyes warning *I will make sure you never have children* as she pouts. Sebastian rolls his eyes. It was an observation, not an attempt to ruin her whole scheme to woo Mason. She wasn't making much progress, but he doesn't want to burst her bubble.

"Okay," Hunter says, plopping down next to Willie. He runs a hand through his hair. During the school year, he wears it close to his scalp in a fade, but he has naturally dark, springy curls for the summer. It looks good with his soft features. "Someone has to go sit with him." Hunter is referring to the table in the corner.

Sebastian doesn't make eye contact with anyone, including Emir.

Grey sits taller for a better view. "He might not want to be bothered."

"He never wants to be bothered," Mason complains. He licks his spoon clean while maintaining a frown.

"That's the point!" Hunter says. "He needs a way in."

Sebastian tucks his chin. He can't tell them that *he* is Emir's way in, if Emir would quit acting as though he doesn't exist when the team's around. Also, if Sebastian ever gets over what happened earlier, which is impossible since he hasn't stopped replaying it in his head.

"I don't think he likes me." Willie pouts.

"*Everyone* likes you, Willster," Sebastian says.

Hunter nods, shifting his hand from his own hair to Willie's fluffy blond mop. Willie leans against Hunter like a pleased puppy.

"Yeah," Mason sighs, elbows on the table. "Somehow, I've got a weird boy-crush on you too."

Grey giggles. Willie flushes, sticking his tongue out at Mason. Something cold flicks over Hunter's eyes but he hides it with a lazy laugh. *That's* definitely new.

"So." Grey crouches, like she's planning a big secret mission to help Emir. "Who's gonna do it?"

"Not me," Mason insists.

Willie shrugs. "I'm out."

Hunter's frustrated groan prevents attention from falling on Sebastian. He's grateful. He's on the verge of a heart attack, sweating as though he's just finished a lap around the pitch.

"You all *suck*," Hunter announces. His chair screeches as he grabs his plate of food.

Sebastian's still learning things about Hunter. His parents are intensely religious. He's an AP student and sits with the geek squad during lunch. But he's been friends with Willie since sophomore year. Also, he's in good standing with Zach and his cronies. In fact, Hunter's well-liked by a lot of students; he once got his name on the ballot for class president.

Hunter is bold, too, a fact proven when he crosses the room and parks himself in an empty chair at Emir's table.

"Oh, shit," whispers Mason. "He's gonna die."

"I *truly* liked him." Grey sighs, as if she's imagined a black ensemble to wear to Hunter's funeral. She rests her cheek on her knuckles.

Sebastian sits very quietly. He's trying to maintain a blank face. This could go perfectly or end in blood. He doesn't know. But he doesn't want anyone connecting him and Emir.

Emir startles, then frowns at Hunter's presence. Hunter, with his winning smile and electric eyes, talks as if they've known each other for years. Maybe they share AP classes, since Emir's a brainiac too. Maybe they just haven't been project partners or discussed *Big Bang Theory*-genius stuff.

"There it is," Mason hisses.

Emir squints at Hunter, then returns his attention to the book he was reading. Hunter's face falls. Another person Emir's shut out.

"Okay, boys, wrap it up! Bright and early tomorrow!" Coach Patrick booms from the entryway and claps his hands.

Grumbling, the team powers through their meals.

At Emir's table, Hunter sits alone, frowning. Sebastian can barely react when Mason whispers, "Total waste of time," in a voice oddly similar to the one in Sebastian's head.

 14

SEBASTIAN IS IN AN EPICALLY sweet mood the next morning, despite aching like a tackle dummy after a college football practice. Last night, he raided the Hot Box for a spare ball, sandbags, and a few cones to spend hours running drills until his legs gave out on him. He needed the distraction, and now his body is paying for it.

"You're dead to me," he mumbles to his cell as the alarm chirps. It's mocking him, so he stuffs it under his pillow, hoping it suffocates. He considers sleeping in. The vicious orange sun is bursting through the window, and Sebastian just can't do it.

"Stupid sun and routines and *life*," he says, hopping out of bed. He shivers—the floor is subzero this early—and dances around the room to find socks. He finds them on Willie's side of the cabin.

Then it hits him: No one is snoring or making out with a pillow or sleep-talking.

Willie's untouched bed indicates he crashed at Hunter's. And then, another epiphany smacks Sebastian: Hunter is crushing on Willie. That would explain his I-will-destroy-you death stare when Mason implied liking Willie in a sexual way, as well as why he's so clingy.

Mason and Willie would make a horrible couple.

Hunter hasn't shown any interest in anyone. He's always been single, and never talked about a girl or a guy he might have a thing for. Sebastian figured it was because Hunter's parents were hardcore religious and constantly on him about his studies. But maybe it's because he's not quite comfortable in his sexuality?

Sebastian taps his chin. He shouldn't be so worried about his friends' love lives when his own is screwed up. "Whatever," he says with a sigh, dragging a hand through his hair. Hunter's a cool guy and Willie's earned "little brother" status in Sebastian's book. He can only hope for the best.

But for right now, Sebastian has an entire cabin to himself. *What to do?*

He's a teenager, so his options are always sleep, food, or sex. Sebastian's leaning toward the last option, but he has one mission on his mind: *Emir Shah.*

The moment doesn't totally go to waste, though. He's wearing nothing but his boxers, socks pulled up to his shins, and a pair of Willie's cheap sunglasses. Sebastian skids across the hardwood floor to "Old Time Rock and Roll" blaring off his cell, à la *Risky Business*, like a big kid.

Later, after he finds his sneakers under his bed and a pair of running shorts, he stands in the doorway of his cabin. The leaves are bright green; streams of sunshine break through the gaps. Morning breeze shakes the tree limbs. Sebastian has a clear view of Emir's cabin at the end of a row. He's stalling. Sebastian wants yesterday to be a blur, a bad dream, but it's not. It's vivid, in color, and it haunts him like a bad trip.

I kissed Emir.

He can't forget the little things about Emir: his wide, clouded eyes, his stunned breathing, his tongue brushing his lips. Sebastian's head is filled with happy Taylor Swift pop love songs instead of kickass rock anthems, songs that do not evoke magically falling in love.

It's not a big deal. He rubs his temples. Emir's just a guy.

He is so *not* just a guy. He's Emir Shah, one-time best friend of Sebastian Hughes. Angry, gray-eyed, wickedly handsome when he scowls—

Sebastian groans. "Oh, what the…" He's doomed.

Marching to Emir's cabin with his hands stuffed in his pockets, Sebastian decides that if he doesn't bring up the kiss, then it never happened. What he can't decide is if he *wants* to forget it ever happened. But before he can work out how he'll get over that part, he spots a Post-It stuck to Emir's window: *"Sleeping! Don't wake me! —Em."*

Sebastian glares. He rips it off, crumples it, and tosses it to the ground. Fine, whatever. He doesn't have a single cell in his body that gives a shit if Emir improves or not. Emir's frustrating. And he's making Sebastian miserable.

"Asshole." Sebastian jogs toward the hiking trails. He doesn't need Emir to have a good run. He'll just slow Sebastian down, anyway.

Sebastian stops a few feet from the trail. In a cloud of blue smoke, Emir paces a lazy circle. He's wearing shorts, his BHS sweatshirt, and a beanie pulled close to his eyes. His long, thin fingers idly hold a cigarette with a mound of ash at the end as if he's forgotten about it.

A knot of confusion spreads from Sebastian's chest to his limbs, like an infection. He clears his throat. Emir stops cold when Sebastian says, "What are you…?" but the rest of the question never makes it out of his mouth.

"Morning," Emir says, voice rough with fatigue and smoke.

Sebastian crosses his arms over his chest. He's trying hard not to lose his mind over how soft and pink Emir's mouth is when it curls around the end of his cigarette.

Jesus, I need professional help.

"I couldn't sleep." Emir drops his cigarette and grinds it out. "I blame *you* for that."

"Happy to help."

"I've been waiting on you."

"Why?"

"Because," Emir says.

"That's not an answer, Emi," Sebastian says, faltering, because, *shit*, he didn't want that silly, childhood nickname to slip out. He flinches when Emir's eyes widen, only momentarily.

"After I did my Fajr prayer—"

"I'm sorry, what?"

A wrinkle appears between Emir's eyebrows. He says, exasperated, "The *Fajr*, the dawn prayer we say as Muslims. You don't remember?" He waits.

Sebastian nods slowly because he does, vaguely. He's only seen Emir's parents praying on those mornings when he sneaked over to wake Emir. But they were so young, and Sebastian was clueless about the religious terms used by the Shahs.

"I'm used to having to explain my religion to everyone," Emir continues. "People talk about my skin color, my accent, my faith." His cold and fragile tone shakes.

Sebastian steps forward. He knocks their shoulders and raises his eyebrows. It's a weak attempt to communicate that he remembers. He still likes Emir for who he is, every part.

Emir sags. "Faith is a big thing for Abbu, so I try not to disappoint him."

"That's cool," Sebastian says, because he hasn't thought of something better.

His slight height advantage means Emir raises his chin to smile at him. It cracks open Sebastian's brain; old memories flood out: playing video games, eating lunch side by side on the playground, backyard races, Sebastian's constant attempts to impress because Emir was so *epic*.

"We should, um," Sebastian stutters, rubbing the heel of his hand over an eye.

"Time for a run?"

"Yes!"

Sebastian could point out that a run after smoking isn't wise, but he's not here to highlight Emir's bad habits. Plus, he can totally use it later, when Emir is being a jerk because Sebastian wants to add an extra mile to their run.

"Also," Sebastian grabs Emir's wrist, his thumb pressed to the pulse point on the inside. "Hunter's a good guy."

"What's that mean?" Emir asks, brow furrowed.

Don't be a dick to him, Sebastian wants to say. Instead he says, "I saw what happened yesterday. He's a good guy, Emir."

Emir considers him through slit eyes. Then, after taking a deep breath, Emir nods. "Time to run," he whispers, freeing his wrist from Sebastian's grip.

Sebastian doesn't argue. He gives Emir a head start and catches up when the sting in his chest subsides. It's a relief when neither of them mentions the stupid kiss or not being friends anymore.

⚽

THE DINING HALL IS EMPTY after practice. It reminds Sebastian of a post-zombie apocalypse. Coach O'Brien confiscated half of the team, including Willie and Mason, to go replay footage of the St. Catherine's boys in the rec room. Everyone acts as if the tension buzzing from the coaching staff about the Spartans game is normal.

Sebastian fears that, this time, they'll be in over their heads. He plays it cool, though, parking his exhausted body at their table by himself. Summer is at its height; a mild heat wave is only tolerable because they're so close to the lake. He kicks a foot up on a chair, studying today's lunch: yogurt, a granola bar, and an especially green protein shake.

Is this what college is going to be like? Unless he's willing to die a boring death by staying in Bloomington, he'll be solo while Mason heads to Michigan, where his uncle is in good with a few of the coaches, and Willie does the local thing.

Sebastian frowns at his yogurt.

"You look funny when you're thinking."

When Emir plops down on the tabletop, Sebastian's eyes open wide.

Emir says, "It's disturbing." He makes a face that Sebastian supposes is the one he was making a minute ago. It resembles a dog's when the vacuum cleaner comes on.

Sebastian, his body betraying him, shivers. He replies, "I do not," without the conviction he wants.

"Yes, you do!" Emir's feet rest on a chair, Willie's chair, as he bends to steal the granola bar from Sebastian's tray. It won't be missed. "Actually," Emir continues as he points a finger at Sebastian, crunching on granola, "you used to make that same face when Mrs. Callaway made us read *My Side of the Mountain*."

Mrs. Callaway was a tyrant, always making them read books that put Sebastian to sleep. *The Hobbit* was an awesome exception. "Literature was boring," Sebastian mumbles.

"If you were struggling, I would've helped you." Emir's mouth slants and his brow creases when he adds, "Back then."

Sebastian's skin prickles from his chest on up. He chews his thumbnail; confusion and conflict fester in his system.

Emir sits, inscrutable, as if they're not walking on this very thin sheet of ice.

Tension and his warped sense of timing make Sebastian ask, "What happened?" before he realizes what's coming out of his mouth.

Emir chews granola slowly. "Remember when I went to England for a summer?"

Sebastian nods. After fifth grade, Emir's family left, and he didn't hear from Emir at all. It was their first Fourth of July without viewing the fireworks from a tree in Sebastian's backyard while fireflies hovered around their ankles. No one explained to him what happened. Life simply ripped Sebastian's left arm off and told him he didn't need it. And, sure, Sebastian could've tried to find Emir, but he was *ten*. He knew how to operate his Xbox, not set up a Facebook account.

"My grandmother, my nani, was sick for a long time. Then, she died," Emir says, face pinched as if the memory's still fresh. "We stayed in London because my mom was too shook up to function."

Sebastian chews his lip, wanting to say something but unsure what.

"And then I came back."

He came back in the middle of the school year, when Sebastian had filled the emptiness left by Emir with Willie, Mason, and Zach, and was living in an alternate universe where his new best friends were Mason and Willie. Then, out of a wormhole, Emir returned with a different view of Sebastian, as if Sebastian was an alien and not the kid who'd sat alone on a couch, missing a goofy-grinning, skinny kid no longer there to help him bomb zombies.

Sebastian kept his distance. Emir did too. Their lost friendship became a passing thought.

"I get nervous around people," Emir says, staring at his knees. "People call me weird all the time, but I'm just extremely shy. It's easier for me to stick to myself." He hunches forward, growing smaller.

Sebastian absently puts a hand on Emir's knee.

The tops of Emir's cheeks blush rose. "So, no, I didn't mean to be an asshole to Hunter. I'm just not good with people. The only person I never had to *try* with is you. We got on well, and then you were gone."

Sebastian sinks in his seat. It's not a sucker punch catching him off guard, but it aches. He would gladly have made room for Emir in his crowd if they actually talked once Emir came back. That's mainly Sebastian's fault too. Why the hell isn't working through feelings a class offered to middle school kids? As soon as puberty hits, all of a sudden people find reasons not to like you: weight, height, acne, sexuality, race, parents' income, whatever. Confidence is earned by how many flaws you can find in someone else.

"Once high school started…" Emir trails off for a moment. "It's bloody easy not to want to make friends with people when they stare at you." Emir sighs. "The crippling shyness is just a bonus."

"I went through it, too."

Sebastian is overwhelmed by the reality that what ruined his friendship with Emir was a misunderstanding. They're not mortal enemies, but each have some major self-esteem issues to work through.

"I never noticed what people said about me when you were around." Emir smiles at his knees. "That's the thing. I spent so much time caring about you, I didn't know anyone else existed."

Sebastian slumps, but he's not willing to admit that Emir's confession knocks him back.

The dining hall is slowly starting to fill. Players walk in laughing; loud conversations are punctuated by trays dropped on tables. Emir tenses under the hand Sebastian has on his knee.

"Sorry," Sebastian says, nervously, pulling away.

"I should go." Emir pushes off the table with one hand. His cagey eyes look around. The noise is getting louder. His mouth pops open and his eyes scan Sebastian as if he's about to say something else. Instead, he nudges through the congestion at the entryway to leave.

"Bro," Mason says, smacking his tray on the table. Willie follows; Hunter and Grey squeeze into the other side. "What was *that* about?"

Sebastian frowns. "Nothing." But it's a pretty big something that he hasn't got a clue how to explain.

"But that was Shah, at our table," Mason says, annoyed.

"Just drop it." Sebastian's face is hot, his shoulders are way too tense, and he hasn't had time to process the last ten minutes. Explaining any of that to Mason is an unnecessary task.

"But he hates us."

"You," Hunter corrects, biting into his ham sandwich. "He hates *you*, Riley."

"Whatever." Mason rolls his eyes.

Sebastian's hands shake, and a crackling fire licks at his chest. He's not a violent person, but hell, he wants to punch something or someone. Also, he wants to ask Mason if he'd ever let Emir *sit* with them? If, outside of camp, Mason would have a civilized conversation with Emir the same way he talks to all those assholes at their school who pretend to be his friend? But he can't, because Mason has been a good friend. Along with Willie, he filled that gap in Sebastian's life where Emir used to be. For that, Sebastian's grateful.

"So, you guys aren't friends?" Willie inquires, confused.

"No," Sebastian says, but the lie sticks to his throat. "I don't know. Let's just talk about something else." His hairline is sweaty; his stomach gnaws its way into his chest.

After a silent conversation with their eyes, Willie and Mason shrug. Mason goes on about Coach's plans for their first game. Willie complains about the heat. Sebastian can deal with his nauseated stomach as long as he doesn't have to talk about Emir.

He steals glances at Emir's empty corner.

The topic turns to the pro leagues. Grey says, "I think—"

But Mason clears his throat, "Show of hands for who doesn't care what The Brat thinks?"

Of course, Mason is the only one with a hand up, but it's enough to awaken a little hurt in Grey's eyes. She lowers her chin.

Sebastian slips an arm around her shoulders. "Don't worry about it," he whispers. He wants to tell her that Mason's an asshole with a good heart, that his only example for treating someone he might care for was his father, the deadbeat bastard who ditched his mom while she was pregnant with Mason's youngest sister, but that's not his baggage to unpack.

Pride overruns Sebastian when Grey smiles with her eyes. Maybe he's not so bad at this friendship thing.

 15

RAIN PLINKS STEADILY ON THE cabin's roof while thunder rumbles in the distance. Fat, heavy, gray clouds sit in the sky like a fleet of battleships making port. A storm is approaching. This early, the rain's as cold as it is annoying.

Sebastian shakes out his hair; his Bloomington hoodie does little to keep the rain off his head. *Why didn't I just sleep in?* This is lazy, beneath-the-covers weather. Now he's ruined his own day by fighting for ten minutes to drag Emir from under his blankets.

"You're bloody insane!"

"Are you gonna get up now?"

Sebastian's smart enough to know that if anyone saw them right now, with Sebastian straddling Emir's hips, Emir's wrists pinned to the bed by one of Sebastian's hands, and Emir's legs kicking wildly as he tries to squirm away, it would appear pretty suspicious. But the moment "You look like a wet, pathetic dog," popped out of Emir's mouth, it was on.

"I hate you!" Emir says through laughter, freeing an arm.

Sebastian's quick reflexes keep Emir from punching him in the chin. Emir is freakishly strong for someone so skinny. "I've heard that before," he tells Emir, locking his wrists above his head.

"Bastard!"

Sebastian coos at Emir almost adorably. He will never be adorable, though. Not ever. He is ruthless and cunning and a Bloomington Lion!

A very clumsy, preoccupied lion who notices three seconds too late that Emir has wretched an arm free and is tickling Sebastian's ribs. It's all over in a yelp as limbs smack against the ground. Sebastian gets an upside-down view of Emir's smug grin as he peeks over the edge of his bed. He's going to kill Emir, or at least mangle his stupid face, once he figures out if it's medically appropriate for his ear to be kissing his knee.

"Jerk," Sebastian grumbles, twisting until he's certain he hasn't broken something. He stands and dusts himself off. Emir shrugs with a bashful smile, as if he didn't mean to nearly paralyze Sebastian.

Sebastian accepts the half-assed apology.

"It's raining," Emir complains when Sebastian insists they practice. It's hard to take Emir seriously with his hair standing up at absurd heights.

"Rain or shine, the team plays."

Emir falls back on the bed; his face is covered by a pillow. Sebastian can't make out everything he's saying, but he's heard quite a few of the words used in Judd Apatow movies. He waits, impressed by how long Emir shouts into his pillow. The wet cold makes Sebastian desperately crave his bed.

Finally, Emir climbs out of bed. That's good, because Sebastian is tempted to drag him, half naked, kicking and screaming, into the rain. Emir stomps around like one of Mason's little sisters when she's pissed he won't play Barbies.

"You will suffer," whispers Emir, too close for comfort. Warm breath skims against the side of Sebastian's face before Emir continues shouting about how soccer sucks.

Sebastian, deft as a ninja, pulls his hood over his head to hide his mortified expression.

"You look like your dad," Emir says while destroying his cabin in search of clothes.

"Do I?"

"Oh, my god, you're a bloody Manchester fan like him, aren't you?"

"Of course!"

Emir chucks a shirt across the room; a pout puckers his lips. "Yeah, whatever. Have you taken Ms. Haverly's history class yet? It's proper dreadful, mate."

"Really?"

"The worst."

They fall into an easy conversation about more teachers they hate. It's weird, at first, but Sebastian doesn't want to give Emir a reason to shut down again. Then he changes the topic to last season and the guys. In the middle of Sebastian's ranting, Emir says, "Zach's pretty good." His head is stuck in the collar of his shirt, so it's muffled.

Sebastian steps forward and tugs down the shirt. "He's come a long way," he tells Emir, trying not to laugh at Emir's tousled hair. But then his eyes drop. Emir is pants-less in tight boxer-briefs. Sebastian tenses.

"Too bad he's such a dick," Emir says through a yawn.

"It was a rough night for him, that's all."

"If you say so."

"Get to know him."

Emir hums, running fingers through his hair. "Maybe I will, if I'm on the team long enough."

"You'll be fine, man."

"Quit being nice," Emir says with a huff negated by his tiny grin.

"It's my job," Sebastian says, gently punching Emir's shoulder.

The heavy clouds hood Emir's cabin in dramatic shadows. His eyes shine silver and moss in the dark. The cabin is eerily quiet with just the echo of thunder and the constant *plink-plunk* of rain on the roof.

Finally, Emir says, "I'm not going out in *that*," with a frown. Now Emir's eyes remind Sebastian of a cold, gray sky in November. All of this is unhealthy for his overcrowded brain.

"What's a little rain?" he asks, pretending he didn't just choke on the words.

"That's a *lot* of rain, idiot."

Sebastian doesn't even flinch. Emir's insults bite with less venom now. He retaliates by punching Emir's arm; Emir slugs back with a high-pitched laugh. Sebastian has an urge to toss Emir on the bed for a wrestling match. But that could lead to— no, it *would* lead to—something involving a lot less clothing.

And there it is, like a kick in the head. Would Emir kiss him back? Does Sebastian *want* Emir to kiss him back?

"Let's get this over with." Emir sighs.

Sebastian follows Emir to the door. In the back of his mind, he's stuck on how their brief kiss seemed like a wild summer in the heart of an ice storm.

"LET ME WIN!"

"For what?"

"Because I said so!"

Raindrops drip from the end of Sebastian's nose over his top lip to his unruly smile. His clothes are soaked from the storm.

"I don't do charity, Emir," he yells over the rolling thunder. "Beat me!"

The howling wind carries away Emir's shouted "Arsehole!"

Sebastian's laugh echoes in his ears. He licks the metallic flavor of rain from his lips. Emir slicks the limp fringe off his forehead and focuses on the ball. They've bypassed drills today and started their morning with an epic scrimmage that has gone scoreless.

"Let's go, rookie."

"Rookie?" Emir's voice squeaks.

"Yeah, you heard me." It's a diversion; Sebastian goes for the ball. Emir one-ups him, spinning while the inside of his foot keeps the ball close. His speed is a nice counterattack, but the grass is slick. It's impossible for him to get far without stumbling.

Emir goes down hard in a patch of mud, screaming, "Kiss my ass!"

Sebastian doubles over, hands on his knees, hacking a laugh into the cold. His hair's gotten longer over the summer; it drips into his eyes as Emir gives him a middle finger salute from the ground.

Okay, so it's not exactly Godzilla versus King Kong, but Sebastian's sure Hughes versus Shah is still pretty legendary.

Emir grumbles, "I had you," as Sebastian helps him up. He's got an ugly brown smear from his armpit to his thigh. His hair sits drab and flat on his forehead.

Sebastian tries, and fails, not to snicker, gripping Emir's hand until he's on steady feet. Then his hand lingers in Emir's. His fingers weave between Emir's as if they belong there.

"You're getting slow."

"Bite me, Emi."

"Or I could kiss you."

"Wait, what?" slips out of Sebastian's mouth, but he's too late to recognize the distraction. Emir sweeps his foot between them. He snags the ball, and Sebastian is left in awe as a rookie smeared in mud takes the ball all the way up the field for a goal.

Emir meets him midfield, smiling wryly. Sebastian stands, hands on his hips, scowling, but he's impressed.

"Ready?"

Emir drops the ball between them. "Are *you* ready, Hughes?" he asks, wiggling his eyebrows.

"I guess you're about to find out, dude."

Emir's mouth opens to retort. Sebastian uses the advantage to swoop in and steal the ball. Emir is shouting after him when he's already down the field knocking in a goal. It's a total douche move, but he fist-pumps the air when Emir finally reaches him.

"Again," demands Emir.

They trade goals, back and forth. Their cleats are caked in mud; brown and green are the new colors of their clothes. Thunder booms off to the left. Rain turns to mist. Their battle continues without a break. Breathless and red-faced, they keep going.

"You're cheating!" Emir whines.

"You kicked my *shin* last play, Emi," Sebastian argues. His feet try to keep up with Emir's and come up short. Emir weaves around him, but Sebastian manages to hook a few fingers in Emir's hoodie to drag him back.

"Cheater!" yells Emir. His thin fingers coil around Sebastian's hips, tugging. The ball pops out and rolls away, but they still wrestle for control.

Emir has Sebastian's nape in a cold hand. Sebastian is sneaking a hand under the hem of Emir's hoodie when Emir says, "You lost," with a trembling laugh.

"Did not."

"You let me win?"

"Maybe."

They're so close, their foreheads are a sliver away from touching. Raindrops are translucent pearls on the ends of Emir's eyelashes. Sebastian's faint breaths are rough. His chest squeezes tight at the curl of Emir's smirk. *Abandon ship!* blares in his mind, but he can't.

Their hips press together. Emir flushes; the world around them blurs. Sebastian has no idea why he's leaning back until the light pressure of Emir's thumb registers. It traces lazy circles on the nape of his neck. Sebastian bites his lip, unsure.

And then, Emir's breath hitches and that's all it takes.

It just happens.

This kiss is nothing like the first one. It's mutual. It's deliberate. Emir pushes as much as Sebastian pulls. It's needy. Wet mouths move as if there's not a second to lose. They'll never be able to dance around this kiss. Sebastian likes that; he's also half panicked over it.

Emir makes a choked noise. He presses farther in, as if he's never been kissed this perfectly, and Sebastian's brain goes offline.

Well, no, he has one very clear thought: *Emir Shah, Emir Shah,* more *Emir Shah.*

With his thumb at Emir's jaw, Sebastian takes his time. He's never kissed a boy. *Holy shit,* Sebastian is kissing his first boy, and it's Emir Shah.

Emir's mouth is something Sebastian needs more of. Sam was a lazy kisser; her mouth was flavored by pink bubblegum. They shared nice, but emotionless, kisses. Emir's different. He tastes bitter and cold from the rain.

A slip of tongue catches Sebastian off guard, but he goes with it. His palm is heated by Emir's cheek.

Emir jerks back, mumbling, "What are you doing, Bastian?"

Rain sticks Sebastian's eyelashes together when he blinks. He shrugs, hand still on Emir's cheek. He says, softly, "What *I* want."

It's difficult to read Emir's expression with their foreheads pressed together. Sebastian sees more shock than anger, but he's prepared for Emir to push him away or punch him. His ego will be bruised, but Sebastian can take it.

Hell, what are the chances I'm Emir's type?

"I…" Black pupils expand, shrinking gray irises. Emir surges forward, kissing Sebastian again.

"*Okayyeah,*" Sebastian mumbles against Emir's mouth. He succumbs to the hunger in his belly. He grabs Emir's hoodie and drags him closer. His thigh fits between them, and Emir uses it like a cat rubbing against a post to scratch an itch. Sebastian is okay with that.

Rain pounds over them. It mutes the weird noises Sebastian makes, sparing him embarrassment. He'll revisit how whiny he is while kissing at a later date. *Much later.* Right now, Emir's tongue explores his teeth, while his own hands examine the lean-meets-muscle of Emir's body. Nothing will ever make him pull away.

Of course, he's *so* wrong.

At first, it's just a whoop. Then they hear a howl, voices getting louder and closer.

Emir jerks away, pushing Sebastian back with a newfound force.

"What the—" Sebastian stumbles; his eyes are moon-sized.

Emir scrubs the back of his hand over his mouth.

The team comes into focus. The rain turns to a light mist, but Sebastian's certain no one saw them kissing. He swallows whatever lump is caught at the back of his throat when he spots Mason leading the charge.

Emir shifts farther away.

"Who doesn't love a good practice in the rain?" Mason, with wolfish eyes, rubs his hands together.

Jack elbows him. "Let's see what these freshmen are made of."

"They're all better than you," Hunter says. The gray, overcast sky washes out his usually ochre skin. Behind him, the players crow.

The team's arrival kicks Sebastian in the teeth. If he wants to be captain, he can't go around making out with teammates.

"Boys, scrimmage!" Coach Patrick blows his whistle. "Hughes, Drews, pick your squads!"

Sebastian does a quick headcount. Willie's missing. He's sitting in the bleachers next to Grey.

"He's resting his knee," Hunter whispers.

Sebastian doesn't tell Hunter he wasn't looking for Willie. His eyes find Emir, who is glaring at the mud on his shoes rather than Sebastian.

"I want Riley," Jack says, startling Sebastian.

"Shit," Sebastian mouths. Picking Mason should've been automatic.

Mason stomps over to Jack's side.

"Fine," Sebastian says, glancing at the leftovers. And then he says, proudly, "I'll take Emir."

The gasps are audible. Emir stands wide-eyed, hands jammed in his pockets, eyebrows raised. He skulks over, shoulders tight.

Carl whispers, "This is going to be good," too loudly.

"Shut up," Sebastian says. "Face it, Mason's our strongest attacker. If he's on the other team, I want a good defender, like Emir. It's called *strategy*." He doesn't flinch when Jack sucks air through his teeth as though Sebastian's digging his own grave. Jack is an intolerable jerk, and his opinion doesn't matter.

Coach clears his throat. "Enough," he warns, when a few guys snicker. He doesn't tolerate bullshit; he always preaches about every member of the team being invaluable. They all have a role to play. Sebastian's not sure if that's from *Remember the Titans* or *Any Given Sunday*, but he agrees. Emir is as important as Mason.

"Right on, Bastian," Hunter says.

"Jesus freak," Carl replies, chuckling.

Hunter peers at Carl. "Let's hope God blesses me not to humiliate your sorry ass all over the field today." He bows his head. "Amen."

To the left of Sebastian, Coach smiles, as if he's impressed with Sebastian's speech or his decision-making skills, or maybe he's just trying not to laugh at Sebastian for picking a very green Emir.

This could all go horribly wrong in about five minutes. But first, they finish divvying up the remaining players. Sebastian steals Hunter and Smith, because Jack is too egotistical about picking Mason to remember he needs to build an offense around him. Jack gets Gio and Zach too. Sebastian settles for two freshmen over a shivering Kyle.

"C'mon," Coach barks. "If any of you catch the flu because picking sides took so long, Drews and Hughes will be cleaning up your puke."

The field is a slick surface made for disaster. Jack has stacked his team offensively, but Sebastian's squad is balanced with players interchangeable by position. It's a small advantage. He won't stop Mason, but he can slow him down.

"Hey," he calls to a sulking Emir. "We're gonna win."

Emir tilts his head to the heavens. "We'll lose," he says weakly.

Sebastian says, "And if you're wrong, we run an extra mile tomorrow," before swatting Emir's ass; he puts a hand over his own mouth to hold back a laugh.

Emir narrows his eyes as if unconvinced. At the last second, he smiles. Sebastian relaxes, content in his tiny victory.

Mason's eyes are rimmed by hurt or anger. "Good luck," he scoffs, and trudges to his end of the field.

Sebastian shrugs. His mind is on one thing: crushing Jack's team.

They lose, one-zip, but to Sebastian's holy grail of delight, it's not because of Emir, who holds his own against Jack's team. He defends Sebastian's box the way a knight defends his castle. Midway into the game, Emir goes toe to toe with Mason, putting on an epic show of fast feet. His nerves are visible: stiff shoulders, shaky legs, a wan expression every time Mason isn't looking.

Sebastian's proud he survived.

Their downfall is their lack of offense. Smith's way too cocky for a sophomore. Kyle is all over the place. And Mikey, a freshman who's more bones than muscle, bombs a penalty kick in the first five minutes.

Coach, disgusted, shouts, "Who taught you how to play, son?" while tugging the brim of his beat-up BHS Lions snapback low enough to hide his scowl.

Gio steals the ball when something goes wrong on an easy passing play between Smith and Kyle and cracks the ball right into Mason's path.

Sebastian isn't embarrassed to admit he and Willie spent an entire winter break repeatedly viewing the original *Star Wars* trilogy. The team's defense racing behind Mason is like a fleet of TIE fighters trying to chase down the Millennium Falcon; it's not possible.

Mason yells, "All the way, Hughes!"

Then Emir steps into his path.

Mason has a lot of tricks in his arsenal. He's got sweet feet, but Emir's high-speed. Mason spins. Emir counters. Mud and grass fly as they fight for the ball.

Kyle screams, "Get the damn ball, Shah!"

"Not happening." Mason jerks left. Panting, Emir lurches with him. Sebastian bends into position. He's prepared for anything. But Mason takes a fall to draw a foul against Emir. It's a stunt he's seen Neymar pull when stuck with a tough defense.

"Shit! Come on, Shah. Keep your hands and feet to yourself!" groans Mikey, knocking Emir's shoulder when he passes.

Rivera stands over Mason. "Okay, Riley?"

Mason clutches his shin. He puts on a cheesy performance: groaning, rolling in the mud. His overdramatic stunt wins him sympathy points.

"I didn't," Emir says, then pauses, a hip cocked out, hands trembling as they rub across his face. He exhales. "It's bullshit," he says, glaring at Mason as if he might punch him.

Sebastian seconds that idea. He also wants to smooth a hand over Emir's hair and tell him it's nothing serious. He doesn't.

"Boys, you know the drill." Coach eases players away to help Mason up. "Penalty kick for Riley."

"It's cool, Shah," Hunter says, softly, patting Emir's ramrod-stiff shoulder.

Emir doesn't jerk away. He nods with defeated eyes and his hands balled into fists.

Frustration contorts Sebastian's face. His focus has gone haywire. He glares at Mason as Mason lines up with the ball. Mason raises his eyebrows. His mouth curves up smugly.

They lose because of Sebastian. One penalty kick, he missed one stupid penalty kick.

After the scrimmage, from the center of the bleachers, Willie yells, "Great plays, Hughes!"

Sebastian puts on a fake grin. He salutes Willie and Grey while stalking off. He's soaked, mud squishes in uncomfortable places, and he was ridiculously sloppy. They'll never beat the Spartans, or anyone in the conference, playing like that.

Zach reels an arm around his slumped shoulders. "You did good, Captain." He's smiling; his messy hair hangs in his eyes.

The rest of the guys shout their agreement, something Sebastian appreciates, but he's not mentally ready to say anything back. He does, however, spy Mason limping off the field. A smug grin dominates his face; he doesn't care how he got the win.

Sebastian's had enough.

"What the hell, Mace?"

Mason turns, eyebrows lifted. "What's up?"

"What's up?" Sebastian repeats, flustered. He pokes Mason's chest with a dirty finger. "You pulled that shit on purpose."

Mason sniffs, glaring at Sebastian's finger. "It happens all the time, Bastian."

Sebastian wants to punch him. He wants to punch his best friend. Because of Emir. "It doesn't make it right."

"And it doesn't make it right that you're all pro-Shah, either."

Sebastian's upper lip curls. "Are you serious?"

Mason replies, "Deadly, dude."

"So that's it? You're jealous of *Emir*?" Sebastian's voice rises. He's incredulous. His head throbs. "He's scary-good, bro, how could I *not* pick him?" He doesn't care about Mason's skeptical expression, because he's wet and cold and so over this whole picking-Emir thing.

Mason's dripping brown hair hangs in his eyes when he rolls them. "You're being a douche, Bastian."

"You made Emir look bad back there."

"So what?" Mason throws his arms up. "All of a sudden you care about Shah? People think he's a joke."

Sebastian says, "You're the joke here, dude," with more frustration than he's ever directed at Mason. Their squabbles are brutally short, ending over pizza and laughs. After Mason's dad left, Sebastian unconsciously adopted Mason into his life, and a reason to eject him has never existed.

"Don't be a tool," Mason says through his teeth. He blinks so much, Sebastian's not sure if it's rain or tears wetting his cheeks.

"You didn't have to do that, Mace. He didn't deserve that."

"It is what it is. Get over it." Mason's neck is stretched; his repressed swallow is visible. Cold blue-green eyes match the stubborn jut of his chin. "I don't get you, bro. Ever since he came around, you've been picking sides and... I just don't get you."

Me neither. If the roles had been reversed, Emir would've stood up for him if someone was being an ass. At least, the younger Emir would have.

"Not cool, Bastian." Mason knocks his shoulder against Sebastian's as he stomps away.

Sebastian doesn't say a word to stop him.

When he turns, Sebastian catches Emir shivering and smiling sheepishly at Hunter's reenactment of a big play Emir made during the game. "Dude, it was like, epic!" Hunter shouts, jumping up and down.

Emir lifts his chin higher. He bites his lip, turning it red and swollen, soft-looking.

Hunger that has absolutely nothing to do with food erupts in Sebastian's stomach. It spreads to his chest. His heart slams into his ribs like a gorilla trying to break free of a cage. Emir looks just as hungry. "Holy shit," Sebastian says under his breath.

Emir walks across the field toward his cabin quickly, as if he's trying not to be caught.

And Sebastian, confused but excited, uses the returning storm as camouflage. He pulls up his hood and hugs himself against the pulsing downpour. He ducks between the trees like a special ops soldier. Nothing can get in the way of what he wants more than anything: *Emir*.

 16

EMIR IS PERCHED ON THE edge of the bed in the dark when Sebastian walks through the door. For once, it was slightly ajar, as if Emir was waiting for Sebastian. He's not expecting candles and a killer Ed Sheeran love anthem when he closes the door. Things like that happen in Anne Hathaway movies. But he doesn't know what to do because the shadows hide Emir's expression.

"You're thinking too hard."

Maybe its Sebastian's voice breaking the silence or being soaked to the bone in the aftermath of the scrimmage, but Emir says, "Now you know what I'm thinking?" with an accusatory tone.

"Possibly." Sebastian flails his arms. "If you'd give me a chance to, I dunno, get to *know* you more."

"You knew me once."

Sebastian grinds his teeth. He gets it. He messed up a long time ago, but Emir did, too. This isn't all on him. Sebastian was—Sebastian *is* a good friend, but Emir won't give him a bloody chance…

Now the damn voices in his head have replicated Emir's accent!

"I was just coming to tell you," Sebastian sighs and runs a twitchy hand through his damp hair, "that you did great, Em."

"Is that all?"

No. Sebastian doesn't say it. He just doesn't understand when simply talking to a friend, or whatever Emir is, became an exercise in ripping open his stitched-up heart to let his emotions bleed all over the place.

"I'm not the enemy," he says, stepping forward. "I'm not."

"No." Emir's mouth gradually twitches downward. "You're just the guy who won't leave me alone."

Sebastian winces. Fury bubbles in his throat. Emir's being an absolute asshole. So, no, Sebastian isn't going to leave until he figures out what the hell's going on inside him that draws him to someone who seems to hate his guts.

"So that's it?" He's shouting, but whatever. "You want me to back off?" Sebastian stalks over to Emir. "Just say something!"

Emir doesn't, but he stands and closes the distance between them.

Sebastian's ready for whatever Emir's got. He is so exhausted, trying to fix busted-up relationships while other friendships circle the drain. He's tired of trying to be this amazing version of a guy that everyone else sees but Sebastian can't find when he stares in the mirror. If Emir punches him, he'll knock Sebastian off this damn pedestal he never asked to be on in the first place.

"Just do it." Emir grabs the front of Sebastian's drenched hoodie and pulls at the fabric. "Do something," he growls. Gray eyes dance in the dark, but Emir's cheeks are red and his nose is scrunched.

"What?"

"Stop…" Emir's voice dies off. Sebastian gazes at the wet corners of his eyes. Emir's breath catches before he says, exasperated, "Stop, and do *something* to me."

Sebastian's reflexes work faster than his brain. He wants something, wants *this*. So he nuzzles Emir's throat. He drops kisses under Emir's jaw. Sebastian waits. Emir chokes back a gasp, and then Sebastian's fingers dig roughly into Emir's hips, lifting him up in one quick motion. He pushes Emir against the closest wall. His lips are near Emir's, but never close the gap.

"Bloody pain in the arse."

Emir shoves his mouth over Sebastian's. He trembles. His legs curl around Sebastian's hips.

Sebastian's strong enough to support him. "Is this good?" he asks, a little too happy, but also nervous.

Emir nods, still kissing.

A hand in Sebastian's hair pulls sharply. Sebastian follows; tension seeps from his muscles. His fingers dig into Emir's thighs. This will undoubtedly end in fire and desperation and—well, he's not sure what else, or if he's prepared for it.

Then again, Sebastian's never prepared for Emir Shah.

A gasp turns into a chuckle. Emir nips at his jaw, then lower, toward sensitive skin along his neck. No one has ever done *that*. Sebastian's high, breathing as if he's run five miles.

"Holy shit."

Nothing more creative comes out of Sebastian's mouth. That's mainly because his mind is on how he was certain Emir wanted to murder him five minutes ago. Maybe he will—after they're through kissing, of course.

Their foreheads knock. Emir's tongue meets the seam of Sebastian's lips. "Shut up."

"I can't help it."

The kisses, their hands scrambling for new areas to touch, Sebastian pinning Emir to a wall—it's all *ridiculous*.

"Shut your bloody mouth, Bastian."

Sebastian can't take him seriously, not with the crinkled nose and the corners of his mouth quirked. He says, breath slowing, "Do you have something to shut me up with, Emi?"

Emir trembles; his pupils are blown into silver-lined black holes.

Sebastian wants to touch Emir's swollen, red lower lip. He also wants to smooth that wrinkle between Emir's eyebrows. "Stop thinking."

"I'm not."

"You're a bad liar."

Sebastian's hips meet Emir's. He worries Emir might not want that, but the soft hitch in Emir's voice counters those concerns.

"This is a bad idea." Emir's fingers curl in Sebastian's hair. His thumb rubs the skin behind Sebastian's earlobe. "Whatever we're about to do."

"*Are* we about to do anything?"

They crack up together. It's so obvious. Every taut muscle in Sebastian's shoulders relaxes. The skin around Emir's eyes is crinkly-soft. It's awfully hard not to appreciate all the friction going on below their navels.

"So?"

Sebastian asks, "Am I supposed to make a decision on where this is going?"

Emir's fingers are at his jaw, rubbing at a smudge of dirt from a dive he made during the scrimmage. "Where is it going?" he whispers.

Sebastian has no clue. What will life be like thirty seconds from now? In twenty minutes? A week? Where's his life going and how long does he have to decide?

Arousal beats out analytical thinking. Sebastian just wants to kiss Emir again.

Being a wicked mind reader, Emir angles his head up, then leans forward. The kiss is imperfect, noses bumping, teeth clicking, but it works.

"Let's just," Sebastian pauses to kiss words away from Emir's lips, "see what happens."

SEBASTIAN'S WEIGHTLESS; HIS HEAD IS in the clouds. He doesn't know if that's how fooling around with another guy is supposed to be, but it's a good start.

He's staring at the ceiling from Emir's bed. They're breathless and rank. The fuzziness in his head keeps him squinting at shadow puppets created by the darkening sky. Should he leave? This was a one-time thing, right?

Emir drapes an arm around Sebastian's naked torso, pulling him closer. Sebastian doesn't resist. He'll admit it: He's desperate for the attention.

"Hey."

He turns, raising an eyebrow at Emir. Sebastian's waiting for this sappy moment to end, because he's two seconds from burying his face into the side of Emir's neck. Emir's crinkly eyes are all Sebastian needs.

This is a scene out of a horribly clichéd romance movie, starring a guy who's hotter than Sebastian. He tells Emir as much, then shivers when Emir cracks up. "It's not *that* funny," Sebastian says, but it actually is.

Outside, rain falls in a steady *drip-drop-plop* on the roof. It makes their silence eerie. Their breathing is still heavy. Sebastian should say something. "Should I go?" he asks while Emir's finger drags figure-eights along the nape of his neck. It's not his brightest moment. His brain is still frozen on what just happened, so he flounders.

Emir's silence is an indication of his own confusion.

Sebastian pulls the sheets away and starts to move until Emir says, "Wait." Emir's mouth is open with nothing coming out, but his eyes say every little word he's too stubborn to utter.

"Okay."

Emir's chest makes for a pretty flat pillow, but Sebastian rests his head on it. He's enjoying the murmur of Emir's heartbeat. It's mellow, like that bit in "Bohemian Rhapsody" when everything goes from awesome guitar solo to melancholy Freddie Mercury ending. Emir's fingers moving over his scalp help, too. Sebastian's head is clear of all the gunk clogging it up.

"Maybe we should—"

"Shut up."

Emir's tone is betrayed by a stray smile. It confirms one thing for Sebastian: If Emir isn't going to kick him out, Sebastian doesn't plan to say a damn thing about it.

The rest, well, he doesn't care right now.

 17

"It's late."

Sebastian startles; his heart nearly high-fives his tonsils when he spins around. Willie is parked on his bed, staring at him through groggy eyes.

"Um."

Willie yawns. He's sitting with one foot under him. His pale fingers pick at invisible lint on his sweatpants. His lips are tugged into a thin line. "You missed dinner," he says, absently combing his shaggy hair.

The gurgle from Sebastian's stomach confirms his hunger. "Yeah." Sebastian's rubbing the back of his neck, unsure of what he's supposed to say. Should he explain himself? Will it matter that he was with Emir? "I was—"

"Shah, right?" Willie's dark eyebrows push wrinkles into his forehead.

Sebastian sags in the entryway. The storm has let up, leaving behind a cloudless black sky and a heady breeze. Everything smells like pine. Sebastian was already experiencing sensory overload from the scents of Emir's cabin; earthy from mud, sour from sweat, honeyed from Emir's boyish musk.

"Sorry."

Willie slants his head.

"What? I mean," Sebastian pauses, staring at his dirty cleats. "Should I be?"

"Are you being smart about this?"

Sebastian knows what the "this" is, but he wants Willie to say it out loud. Is Sebastian being smart about Emir? About his place on the team? About what he wants to do after high school? Maybe he can accept that he has no idea what to do with the things that are in his control. For now, he is stuck in a loop of indecision.

Part of him just wants to go back to Emir's cabin, back to where they spoke softly about the most random things, like the anime Emir is into. "It's *cool*," Emir insisted. Sebastian, making faces at the images Emir swiped through on his phone, thought otherwise. But lying in a bed with Emir half-twisted around him made up for that.

The moon lights the sky through the window behind Willie's shoulder. Camp is dark and lifeless. It was perfect for sneaking back here while praying none of the coaches would catch him. Being benched would've been totally worth it for the things he did with Emir.

Now, the sky is frightening, just like having to "'fess up" to Willie.

"Bastian?"

"I don't know," Sebastian says, shrugging.

Coming out to Willie was one of the easiest things he had ever done. "Hey, you know how you're into guys and stuff? Yeah, well, me too. Dudes and girls, I guess. No, I *know*. I like girls and guys," he rambled, while Willie nodded with a lazy smile. Then Willie hugged him, patted his head, and whispered, "Okay, pepperoni or veggie pizza tonight?"

Sebastian has no clue why telling Willie he's starting to like-*like*—which sounds silly and juvenile in his head—Emir is such a big deal.

"So is he like…" Willie makes weird, convulsive hand gestures Sebastian can't interpret, but he gets the gist: *Is he your boyfriend?*

"Nothing," Sebastian says, hanging his head. "It's nothing."

He kicks the door shut, then walks to his bed. He sits gently, though his whole body is exhausted. His fingers curl over his knees. The lie stirs nausea in his stomach. He can't talk to Mason about this, not without judgmental eye rolls and sour comebacks. And Grey well, they've never had the version of a heart-to-heart that includes discussing *Sebastian's* romantic problems.

Willie should be his rock. He's all about emotions and making fun of serious situations.

Sebastian is aware that he's awful at sorting through his feelings enough to *talk* about them. He sits silent. Willie gives him a long, unreadable look. It makes the back of Sebastian's neck cold.

"I like him," Willie finally says with a yawn. He fluffs a pillow and lies back. "Emir, I mean." He closes his eyes; slowly, his breaths even out.

Sebastian doesn't *want* to care about anyone's opinion. It's his friendship, not theirs. But being a teenager is one good day of being a superhero, followed by a hundred days of being self-conscious about every little damn thing. It's one big, selfish moment when you don't give a shit about other people's opinions, but you still want your friends to love who you are and what you do.

Sebastian falls back on his bed. The hum of cicadas and Willie's snoring fills the cabin. His stomach turns. Why isn't life like being ten years old again, when graduating to junior high and catching Pokémon was such a big deal?

❖

By tradition, bonfire nights only happen a handful of times. Sebastian needs more of them. It's a Saturday night in mid-August, and Oakville is muggy. His teammates dump piles of wood in the center of a pit Charlie and Gio dug an hour ago. Sunset-pink skies frame the trees.

Zach grins, arms stuffed with cheap beer. "Brews and tunes, dudes."

Hunter hauls supplies from a pantry raid: graham crackers, chocolate, marshmallows, and sodas.

"Sweet," says Mikey, grabby hands already extended.

"What, wait." Zach sighs. "Who invited the frosh? We said no freshmen, dudes."

The rules of bonfire night are pretty simple: drink, bond, and no freshmen. The last part is for the safety of the frosh. They're still lightweights, and it's difficult enough to keep the upperclassmen from streaking when they've got a good buzz, let alone some fourteen-year-old newbie.

Their chosen spot is where the woods nudge up against the shoreline of the lake. It's around a point from the campground, hidden from the coaches. It's perfect for reflection while summer dances around them on its last legs.

"I'm cool, man," Mikey tells Zach: code for *I'm not a narc.* Since the scrimmage, Sebastian hasn't minded Mikey's attempts to fit in.

"Whatever." Zach cracks a beer and passes it to Mikey while pretending he doesn't exist.

Sebastian leans lazily against a red maple. The team fills out the circle around the fire. Everyone is wearing a BHS Lions sweatshirt or hoodie. Firelight edges the trees in burnt orange.

It's been a week of constant drills and Coach shouting "I'm gonna whip you all into shape so we can crush those Spartans" any chance he got. In the dining hall, one frosh collapsed face-first into his pasta. But not one player quit.

Smith says, "You're crap at handling wood, Keating." He passes around burgers from the diner. His hair is a cotton candy explosion of pink, blue, and blond. It's either awesome or an experiment from his older sister's cosmetology class gone wrong.

"Yeah? That's not what your mom says."

A roar of laughter erupts. Corners of his mouth pulled up, Smith salutes Zach with his beer. It's clear the team needed a good laugh to squeeze out all their nervous energy.

Mikey, already high off too much sugar and booze, asks, "Do you honestly think we'll beat the Spartans this year?"

Zach, clearing his throat, narrows his eyes at Mikey. "Damn right." He takes a gulp of beer. "Do you know why, kid?"

Mikey shakes his head, far from affronted.

Zach points at the faded mascot on Mikey's obviously secondhand hoodie. "Because we're a pack. We've got pride."

"Pride," chuckles Gio, jostling Willie with his elbow.

Willie rolls his eyes.

"We're a family," Zach says, serious as a heart attack. "You bunch of assholes are *my family*, so I'll make sure we tear them apart." He lifts his beer can. The fire spits and crackles a rhythm over the silence.

Charlie whispers, "Hell, yeah." He clinks his can with Zach's. That's all the others need before they growl and chuckle, letting Zach's moment of vulnerability pass without jeers. Some days, Zach is a better leader than Sebastian will ever be.

Zach turns his head and drags his knuckles over his eyes.

Leaders can be vulnerable, too. Sebastian isn't alone in his uncertainty about the future. And he isn't alone in leaning against a tree, either.

"Hey."

The sun coasts out of view. Next to Sebastian, Mason chugs a beer. Eyebrows raised, he cocks his head.

Sebastian has no idea what to say, since this is the first real word Mason's said to him since their blowout on the field. Cottonmouth sets in. Sebastian's tongue is heavy behind his teeth. He wants the awkwardness to go so he can have his friend back.

Mason considers him. He says, "Okay," as if all is forgiven.

That's it, huh? Sebastian's shoulder to shoulder with Mason. The air between them isn't completely clear, but Sebastian settles for Mason's off-center smile and the scent of smoke wafting toward them. This is their brand of normal. It's not messy, filled with hug-it-out confessions.

"You're being a loner." Mason flicks his eyes toward the team. "I'm not."

"Totally are, bro. What's up?"

Sebastian rubs a hand over his eyes. He wants to tell Mason about Emir, about how nice things are, or how he's freaking out about their newly re-formed friendship and how he's waiting for it all to fall apart.

He says, "I'm cool, dude," because he's not ready to go there.

Mason is. "So." Mason lowers his beer. "Where's Shah? You didn't invite him?"

"He wouldn't come."

It's another thing Sebastian can't wrap his head around: how different Emir can be when it's just the two of them. No longer rude or abrasive, he's still painfully shy with the guys, but he can laugh in Sebastian's ear every morning after their jog.

"He needs to be more involved with the team."

"Why, so you can be an ass to him?"

"You're really raw about what happened, huh?" Mason seems exasperated, but Sebastian doesn't care.

Frustration has been building, because Willie, who's an unbelievable mind reader about these things, gets it, but Mason just doesn't. Today, Sebastian is a superhero. He says, "Yes, I am, Mace. Emir is a pretty awesome guy and, once upon a time, he was my friend. You're my friend, too, but you've been an ass for weeks about him." He exhales, jaw tensing. "I'm over it."

The crinkles in Mason's brow are his tell. He's processing.

Sebastian beats him to a response.

"You're amazing, man; like, I don't know any other guy like you, on or off the field," he says. "When I told you I was bi, I thought you'd ditch me, but you didn't." Now his cheeks feel flushed, but Sebastian has to get it out. "You're so cool about everything, so I need you to lay off Emir because I like him. I want you both around, just not like this."

"So," Mason says, smirking, "I'm amazing?"

Of course Mason only hears *that* part. "Shut up," Sebastian says, punching Mason's arm.

"It's hard." Mason scuffs the toe of his shoe. "Outside of my mom and sisters, all I have is you and Will." He presses his elbow against Sebastian's. "I never hated Shah, but he's so closed off that I'm suspicious he's got evil intentions. It comes out the wrong way."

Sebastian snorts. "Definitely."

"Shut up, I'm trying."

"This is you *trying?*"

"This is me trying."

"I hate to break it to you, but you suck at it."

Mason laughs. Sebastian does too. And maybe it's not the best "I'm sorry" or "I think you're amazing, too" Mason can offer, but either way, it's pretty cool.

By the fire, Willie studies them. Guilt plunks into Sebastian's stomach like a boulder. He should talk to Willie. They're not estranged, because they stay awake for movie marathons on Willie's laptop or to talk. What they don't talk about is Emir, who has become this big, ugly secret wedged between them. And Sebastian's the jerk, because Willie hasn't ratted him out to the team. Sebastian can't figure out how to approach Willie about whatever he is and isn't doing with Emir.

"Poor Hunter." Mason cracks another beer; foam bubbles off the top. He slurps it up, then says, "Dude has totally been sweet on Will's ass for months now."

The fire casts orange light on the side of Hunter's face, on his white teeth and scrunched eyes. He winds an arm around Willie's shoulders. He isn't standoffish, but Hunter's not affectionate with a lot of people, not like this.

Willie tunes up someone's beat-up acoustic guitar. He launches into Radiohead's "Creep" the way all good dudes do.

Before Sebastian can ask, Mason swigs more beer, then says, "Last weekend, after I noticed he looked ready to crack when Willie was being flirty with Kyle, he told me."

Sebastian is pretty sure there's nothing to worry about. Kyle's been dating the same girl, Lisa Kowalski, since sixth grade.

"Shame he doesn't have the balls to say anything to Will." Mason's mournful, as if he's hoping for some magical, fairy-godmother, happy ending. It'd be wicked.

Sebastian hugs himself against the cool draft from the lake. The breeze carries a smoky scent, like dragons' breath, from the bonfire. From this vantage point, Willie's cheeks are pink. He flubs lyrics while giggling at Hunter. His body is curled over the body of the guitar. Sebastian gets a clear look at the familiar, longing gleam in Hunter's eyes.

"Now that Will's done crushing on you, maybe he'll give Hunter a chance."

Sebastian nods, then—*Wait, what?* His head snaps in Mason's direction. He mouths "Oh, hell" at the same time Mason cringes, whispering "Shit."

"What do you mean—?"

Mason cuts him off. "Nothing, dude, nothing at all. I'm wasted; like, *Jesus*, how many beers have I had?"

"Two."

"Only two?"

"Yes, Mace, only *two*."

"Two too many then." Mason gives Sebastian a "You really didn't know?" look that makes Sebastian's stomach drop. He's sweating, ready to hurl. No way in hell would Willie ever crush on *him*.

Mason's holding up a hand, the universal sign for *Calm the hell down*. He sighs, as if he's in epic trouble. "Fine," he grumbles, jutting his chin in Willie's vicinity. "Yeah, Willie's been impossibly sweet on you for about a year and a half. Around the time you started dating—"

"Samantha."

Sebastian's head throbs. The epiphany is a cannon exploding purple confetti in his brain. It all makes sense. Willie was never comfortable with Sam. That first night, at Val's birthday party, Willie was on edge every time Sebastian danced with Sam. Sebastian figured it was Willie doing the "good brother" bit by being overprotective. That theory has been officially flushed.

How could I not see it?

"She's not the one," Willie would say, over and over, after Sebastian had a fight with Sam or when she ignored his calls. But, hell, Lily said the same thing, so it wasn't anything he hadn't heard before.

But Willie thought *he* was the one.

"Oh, shit," Sebastian says, smacking a hand over his eyes.

Mason says, quickly, "Don't make a big deal of it, okay? Seriously, don't go *Riverdale* on me."

Sebastian's dazed. Guilt has just sucker-punched him. While Mason shrugs, slurping on beer, Sebastian slumps against the tree.

"What I can't figure out," Mason pauses to rub his chin, "is what made him so into you?" With his head bent uncomfortably close to Sebastian's crotch, he says, "Are you hiding something amazing in your jockstrap, Hughes?"

Sebastian sputters and mashes Mason's head back. Mason drunkenly stumbles. Jesus, these are his friends?

Mason says, "I've seen it, bro. In the shower. You've got Thor's hammer down there."

Sebastian goes sunburn-hot from his toes to his hairline. He turns away; his eyes flicker to Willie, whose head is in Hunter's lap. Hunter's smooths Willie's hair back. Willie gives a go at an acoustic version of "Uma Thurman."

"Sorry. I've been trying to do this whole 'be nice' thing, but how the hell do people do it?" Mason groans, hazy eyes glaring at the fire.

"Is Grey influencing you?"

Mason rolls his eyes. Obviously not. Mason chugs the rest of his beer. "She's part of the team or whatever, so I can't be *mad* at her. Sometimes, she says cool stuff. It's weird."

Sebastian's in awe. In what reality does Mason refer to Grey Patrick as cool? Well, "kinda cool."

All of that good karma Mason just earned flies away when someone shouts, "Who invited Coach's daughter?" and, right on cue, Grey smiles nervously while sauntering past the guys hanging by the tree line.

"Holy mother-effin'…" Mason pushes loose locks of brown hair out of his bulging seaweed-blue eyes. Skittish as a goldfish swimming among sharks, Grey collapses next to Hunter. Mason says, "We're officially going to hell. We're all getting kicked off the team."

Sebastian asks, "Do you want me to look after her?"

Mason crunches his empty can. "She's my problem, isn't she?"

He can deny it all he wants, but Mason has a soft spot for her. Being an ass is just his way of showing it.

Mason stomps toward the fire, shouting, "Hey, give the brat some space!" and, "*Grace*, get your hands off that beer!"

"Oh my god, you sound like Coach!"

Mason's shoulders tense. "And I'll kick your ass like him if you drink that." When she flips him off, he gasps as though scandalized. "You're sixteen, you little troublemaker, so come sit over here—no, not next to me!" Mason nearly shrieks.

Sebastian considers joining the mayhem. He could collapse opposite Zach and sing the team's off-key version of "Young Volcanoes," led by Willie's very respectable strumming. The heat from the fire pit reaches him. Stars wink in the clear indigo sky. The sour flavor of cheap beer collects in his throat.

What kind of future captain wouldn't want to sit shoulder to shoulder with his troops? Sebastian's doesn't know. Are all teens this emo and undecided?

Sebastian hangs back, letting his mind cool down before he turns and disappears into the trees.

 18

Sebastian needs somewhere to *think*, and the dock at the lake is the perfect place.

During the day, the lake beyond the trees and grass is still, pale blue under a clear sunny sky. At dusk, it's all indigo slashed with purples and the scent of pine and moss. All the normal noises of camp are muted by the lapping, singing water. It's the one place Sebastian can have to himself tonight.

Life decides to knock Sebastian on his ass by denying him that moment.

Surrounded by a thin reef of smoke, Emir is huddled at the end of the dock. Sebastian's not disappointed; he's floored, but not disappointed. The last rays of sun make Emir's profile fuzzy. His mouth is thoughtfully pouty. Sebastian ignores his fluttery stomach and lets his giddiness carry him all the way to the wood planks.

As he tugs off his sneakers, Sebastian realizes his common sense has died a proud samurai's death. Warnings blare in his head: *You're gonna get caught by the team!*

Emir shoots him a blank face over his shoulder. Sebastian can't get past how unbelievably handsome Emir is.

"Shouldn't you be with the cool kids?" Emir asks when Sebastian sits next to him; their shoulders brush.

Sebastian mimics Emir, dipping his feet in the water. "Not in the mood." His hand swats away smoke. Emir tips his head back and almost smiles when Sebastian says, "Plus, I'm not cool enough for that crowd, anyway."

Emir snorts. His elbow jostles Sebastian's each time he blows out a plume of smoke. The slop-slop of the lake water fills their silence.

Sebastian has absolutely no idea where the memory comes from, but he asks, "Hey, do you still like almond milk?"

Emir's eyes light up. Their feet brush in the water, ankles touching. Emir says, softly, "A bit, yeah, but not as much as I did when your mom made us a mountain of—"

"Biscuits," Sebastian, chin tilted up proudly, does his best impression of Emir's accent.

"You remember?"

"Of course."

Emir flicks his cigarette into the lake, then reclines on his elbows to stare at the sky. He says, "You used to cheat at Mario Kart."

Sebastian gasps, scandalized. "I did not, you just *sucked*." Emir's eyes narrow; his nose is scrunched. "Who picks Yoshi, anyway? Poor choices, Emir, poor choices."

"Whatever." A laugh rumbles out of Emir's chest. It's Sebastian's new favorite sound. "Your mom was always..." Emir's eyebrows drop. He tries again. "She was always so nice to me."

"She liked you." On reflection, Lily was awfully sad when Emir stopped coming around. Maybe she stopped talking about him for a reason? Maybe the reminder made her sad too?

"Do you still stay up all night reading comics?"

Sebastian nods, drumming his hands on his knees.

"Me too."

Nocturnal insects hum around the dock. Emir's ankle skims Sebastian's. "Back in London, I'd leave room on my bed… for you." A blush spreads over Emir's cheeks. Sebastian tries to imagine tiny Emir scrunched against a wall. "You took up so much space."

"I can't help that you're a twig!"

Emir pokes a finger into Sebastian's ribs. "Pretty sad, right, hoping you were gonna come take up all that space in my bed?" He bites his lip. "It was *weird* without you around."

Sebastian shifts an awkward hand to Emir's left knee. "It's not sad."

"Then what is it?"

Sebastian doesn't know. *It's the coolest thing anyone has ever said*, he thinks—not that he tells Emir. But his fingers squeeze around Emir's kneecap, not his best response.

Emir's expression softens.

Okay.

Off in the distance to their left, the team is murdering "We Are Young." Emir's palm slides across the back of Sebastian's hand to twine their fingers. Sebastian's heart mellows out. He never imagined, at the start of summer, that this is where they would be.

The nervous anticipation stirring in Sebastian's body makes him say, "Pretty good night for a swim." He sheepishly pulls his hand from Emir's. Adrenaline vibrates through his cells. He stands and yanks off his sweatshirt. His fingers work to tug off his jeans next.

"What are you doing?"

Sebastian shrugs. He's clueless, but going along with the flare in his belly that moves toward his chest. It's his last summer here, so wasting time isn't an option.

"I never do anything fun."

"And getting naked is fun?" Emir shrinks the second the words leave his mouth.

Hooking his thumbs in the elastic of his boxers, Sebastian pulls, pops them against his skin, and raises his eyebrows suggestively.

Emir says, "Wow. This is really happening."

Sebastian, the living definition of irrational, yanks his boxers down and kicks them away. "So, are you coming or what?"

"Where?" Emir chokes.

Sebastian points to the lake. "Let's go. Skinny-dipping. Right now."

"No."

"Yes."

"This is mental, like… you're naked!"

"It's not like you haven't seen me naked before."

Emir, turning redder than seems possible, says, "That's different."

"Yeah, um, it's not."

Emir's Adam's apple bobs when he swallows. His mouth is a thin white line, but his eyes are black pools, staring unwaveringly.

Sebastian stretches out a hand. "Come on." He almost deflates when Emir hesitates. Then Emir holds out his hand, and Sebastian's shoulders relax. He tugs Emir to his feet. His free hand fiddles with the hem of Emir's hoodie and his eyes are searching.

Emir exhales, then nods.

Together they wrangle Emir out of his hoodie and his T-shirt. Sebastian's uncooperative hands shake when they both reach for the button on Emir's jeans. Sebastian's one big ball of nervous energy, so Emir takes care of it himself.

"Time to live a little, Emi," Sebastian whispers, lips against Emir's ear.

Emir makes an exasperated noise at the back of his throat. Sebastian's into it, but he has a brain freeze when Emir finally shimmies out of his briefs. A fuzzy trail of hair around Emir's navel distracts Sebastian just enough that he mostly succeeds at not drooling.

Sebastian takes a few steps back. Emir has his arms folded defiantly over his chest, but Sebastian ignores the fake attitude. He turns, says over his shoulder, "Meet you in the water," and dives in.

The water is shockingly cold, then warmer as he breaks the surface, still submerged to his shoulders.

Emir paces the dock.

"It gets worse the more you think about it," Sebastian tells him.

"Yeah, well—it's pretty bad right now."

Sebastian shakes out his hair. The team's singing is softer while he's in the water. It's the cheesy soundtrack accompanying this Disney movie moment, but he's okay with that vibe. He says, "Jump, or I'll come get you."

Emir glares as though he's faced with the Darth Vader of lakes.

Sebastian shouts, "Jump!"

Emir cannonballs right over Sebastian's head, creating an epic tidal wave that nearly takes Sebastian under. His dark head emerges. "I'm going to die!" Of course it's an overstatement—the lake's pretty shallow—but Sebastian lets Emir whine as he wades closer.

One laugh turns into a dunking contest. That leads to splashing, and it's all downhill from there. Sebastian swallows lake water while Emir flails.

It's a cool, crisp summer evening with a bruised-purple sky, and Sebastian's gut is warm. He swims to Emir. His hands scoop under Emir's thighs, lifting him. Emir's legs cradle Sebastian's waist. Sebastian kicks to keep them afloat.

Emir warns, "Don't drop me."

"I won't," Sebastian promises.

They don't move much. Emir curls his arms around Sebastian's neck. His chin is lowered, giving Sebastian a good view of Emir's chewed-red bottom lip and his unshaven jaw.

Sebastian's fingers absently rub the tension from the small of Emir's back. A hum escapes Emir. It's Sebastian's cue to start talking. "What's your favorite band?" and, "Do you like museums?" and, "How are your sisters?" fly out of his mouth.

"You ask a lot of questions." Emir's head tips back in laughter, exposing a very enticing landscape of neck. His hand drags through Sebastian's hair.

Sebastian swallows and asks another question. "Is that bad?"

"Sometimes."

"Really?" Sebastian's trying hard not to sound disappointed.

"No." Emir traces the water descending from Sebastian's hairline to his nose with a thumb. "Kendrick Lamar is my favorite. Museums are cool. My sisters are annoying, but too bloody loveable to hate."

"Can I ask some more?"

Emir nods.

They end up in a directionless conversation, ending in how they've never visited New York City, but want to go. "And Sheffield," Sebastian says, squinting against the water dripping from his hair. "To see my dad's family."

"I miss England, a little bit." More softly, Emir adds, "But I like it here."

"*Here?*" Sebastian's fishing and hopeful.

Emir wrinkles his nose, then says, "The States, Bastian, not *here*."

Sebastian can live with that. Besides, it's obvious to him that Emir secretly loves Camp Haven.

Their haphazard conversation continues. Emir wants to study graphic design. He's considering schools overseas. He hasn't found anywhere stateside yet.

"What about New York?" Sebastian offers.

"Thought about it."

"And…" Sebastian isn't trying to hide his smile.

Emir sniffs, shrugging. As much as Sebastian wants to ask him more questions, it's incredibly nice to be around someone else who hasn't mapped out their entire future. He's close to opening up about his own lack of direction.

At the bonfire, "Uptown Funk" breaks out. Sebastian snakes a hand up to curve around the back of Emir's neck. Gradually, their foreheads meet.

Emir's eyes dance. "Are you going to kiss me or what?"

Sebastian's fingers tap out the percussion of the song along Emir's neck. "Um," he says, unable to wrap his head around their dynamic and all the loops, turns, and undefined gray areas where "yes" and "no" never quite mean anything. But Emir's lips part. *Screw it.* Sebastian finally says, "Okay."

"Okay," Emir repeats.

The discomfort in his belly dissolves when Emir tilts his head. Sebastian, trying not to jostle them too much, meets him halfway.

The kiss isn't frantic, but it's feverish. Emir's hands are on his shoulders. Sebastian's mouth parts, gasping, teased by Emir's tongue. It's thrilling and purposeful, and Sebastian's heart is erratic. Emir's lips could convince someone to kill dragons. They're leaning into it, so, so *willing*. His fingers rub the nape of Emir's neck, constant and sure.

Emir sighs; Sebastian's eyes flutter open. Their noses bump as they wade between kissing and breathing. And then Sebastian says, "More," and Emir complies. His choppy breaths are smothered by Sebastian's mouth.

It should be terrifying, drifting in a dark lake with their teammates not that far away. Sebastian can't imagine a time when he was more comfortable.

AFTER AN HOUR OF FLOATING and epic kisses, they rush to pull on their clothes. Skinny-dipping is great until it's time to put clothes back on, Sebastian learns. He nearly falls off the dock yanking stiff denim up his wet legs. The night breeze skims their backs.

When they're mostly finished, Sebastian takes Emir's hand, loosely, in case Emir jerks away now that they're out of the water.

Emir lifts an eyebrow. "Did you think…?"

"I'm not good at that whole thinking thing."

Emir rolls his eyes, then laughs. Sebastian laughs too.

Their hands swing between them as Sebastian navigates through the trees, toward the locker room. He's peeking around. The noise from the bonfire is gone now. Any of the players could be lurking, or the coaches might be patrolling after another *Rocky* marathon. The coast seems clear.

"Do you do this a lot?"

"Actually," Sebastian says, pushing hair off his forehead, "I've *never* done this, ever."

Three summers at camp and friends like Mason and Willie who like to break curfew makes walking around camp after hours second nature. It helps that Sebastian can smell the locker rooms, ripe with sweat and musk, thirty feet away.

His nose wrinkles when they step inside. "Gotta love it." He doesn't know why, but he keeps his back to Emir while he undresses. He tells Emir to grab towels while he starts the shower.

Sebastian hears a throat clear and turns around to quite a sight. Bathed in flickering fluorescent light, Emir shyly hugs his lean body. His hair flops over his forehead.

"Are we getting in or not?" Emir asks.

Sebastian remembers: *Emir, with me, in the shower.* Hesitation flees, and they stumble into the steam.

The spray is hot, pounding noisily against the tiles. It gives Sebastian an excuse to shift closer to Emir. He's scrubbing soap over the hawk tattoo while Emir tells him about his former roommate, a frosh named Connelly, who left the first day of camp. Sebastian doesn't remember him.

"Rooming with a Muslim offended his family," Emir confesses.

"He's a dick," Sebastian says, scowling at Emir's shoulder blades. "And his parents are too."

Emir says, shoulders tight, "He wasn't. You'd do the same thing if you were stuck with someone who went against the things you were raised to believe."

"I would not."

"I'm okay, mate." Emir sighs. "People can have their ignorance."

"It's not cool."

"It's not supposed to be."

Sebastian rests his wrinkled forehead against Emir's spine. "That's bullshit," he whispers.

"People dislike other people for the wrong reasons," Emir says. "Doesn't mean we should act like them."

Sebastian doesn't have an argument for that.

Eyes closed, Emir slicks his hair off his forehead, letting Sebastian's chin hook over his shoulder. "I've dealt with this for a long time, you know. Connelly wasn't the first, and he won't be the last."

The world shouldn't be like that; people shouldn't be irrationally unaccepting. But it's an argument people like Emir have fought through for way longer than Sebastian's been aware of it. He's not blind to his own privilege. He's never faced any prejudice for his skin color, his blondish-brown hair, or his parents' casual relationship with religion. His sexuality is protected by his teammates and coaches. But Sebastian's aware that to blindly hate a race, religion, sexuality, gender, or whatever is the purest form of prejudice.

Sebastian needs a subject change: "Did I ever tell you about how I barely made the team?"

Emir tilts his head to expose a smile.

"Oh, yeah, super boring story, but—"

Emir rests his head on Sebastian's shoulder as Sebastian recounts his first year as a Lion. Drops of water sit on Emir's face, like warm, wet stars. His eyes close; his lashes flutter every few words. Sebastian checks occasionally for Emir's facial reactions, but he's at peace.

"I shouldn't tell you this," says Emir. They're face to face now. He whispers, "I came to a few games, to watch you."

The water's still hot, so that could explain Emir's flushed cheeks, but Sebastian's betting it's a different reason.

"You're amazing. If I could be half the player you are, then I'd impress Abbu."

Sebastian tries to swallow the fact that he's spent his childhood reading about heroes and here he is, a hero to Emir. His nervous hands rest on Emir's hips. "You came to my games?"

Emir nods, sheepishly, but he's not meeting Sebastian's stare. "Emi—"

"I never hated you, but seeing you move on—it was hard."

Words are knotted in Sebastian's throat. He's never going to say the right thing, so he drops a kiss on the tip of Emir's nose.

Emir's eyes go freakishly wide; his eyebrows nearly touch his hairline. "Um, what?"

"What?"

"You just," Emir pauses, choking with laughter. "The nose kiss?"

"What kiss?"

Emir's mouth twists wryly, but he whispers, "Okay, Bastian," in a tone that says he completely accepts Sebastian's loser status, his inability to be smooth about anything.

Sebastian goes for broke, curls a finger under Emir's chin, and angles his face so he can plant a soft peck on Emir's mouth. Emir kisses back. They're learning how to do this without fumbling.

Emir pulls back. "We can't stay here forever," he says.

"According to whom?"

More words almost make it out of Emir's mouth, but Sebastian swoops in for another kiss. The water is turning cold, and Emir might be right.

After their shower, Sebastian is at his locker, unsuccessfully yanking out the things he wants, while Emir towels off. He's been distracted by the hawk inked between the wings of Emir's shoulders. He wants a tattoo. But the little voice in the back of his head screams *permanent*, and he chickens out. And, he's seen a YouTube video called "World's Worst Tattoos," and that led to a dark YouTube-video-vortex he hasn't recovered from.

He finally pulls his team hoodie from his locker. "Here." Sebastian shoves it at Emir. It's wrinkled, but clean, unlike some of the other clothes in his locker.

"For me?"

Sebastian's fingers clench in the soft cotton as he shakes his hoodie at Emir. "Just take it, dude," he says, exasperated. He's not sure if it's an aesthetic kink or simply sentimental, but Sebastian wants to see Emir in *his* hoodie.

Emir slips on the hoodie. "It's kind of big." It's true. The sleeves are too long; extra material puckers around his midsection. But Emir's irresistible while biting his lower lip.

Across the back of the hoodie is HUGHES in blocky gold lettering. Sebastian likes it.

He gathers their smelly lake clothes and towels into his assigned laundry bag before dumping it in the cart near the entrance. Emir pulls on his sneakers, then fiddles with the hoodie's sleeves, tugging them over his knuckles. He disrupts his perfectly messy hairstyle with a hand.

"Ready?" Sebastian asks.

"I guess."

"We can't stay here forever," Sebastian tells him.

Emir rubs at his stubble. He says, "According to whom?" with his tongue caught between his white teeth.

They're still damp from the shower. Sebastian wiggles his fingers at his side. He's having a "should I or shouldn't I" moment. Their hands brush. He sighs.

"Just do it," says Emir. The world outside of the locker rooms is dark, but the sky is gray with moonlight.

Sebastian holds Emir's hand.

 19

SEBASTIAN IS TRYING TO PROCESS his incredibly bad skill in dissolving the awkwardness between them in a poetic or romantic way, proving he learned *nothing* from Sam's insufferable love for *The Notebook*. Their hands swing between them as if this isn't weird, as if they weren't at each other's throats that first morning in Emir's cabin. He's afraid to get too comfortable.

"You're quiet," says Emir.

Crickets chirp their nightly hymns. An owl hoots at the stars. Sebastian is leading them through the dark toward Emir's cabin. He wants to say something impressive.

Emir whispers, "Shit," and, well, that's definitely not a good start, but—

Sebastian squints at a flashlight flickering up ahead. Someone fumbles through the trees and bushes, moving in their direction. He can make out just enough of the man's shape; it's Coach Rivera.

Sebastian's heart is trying to make out with his trachea. He forgets Emir's holding his hand until Emir's fingers squeeze uncomfortably around his own. Emir's having a quiet panic attack, but Sebastian can handle this. It's like being on the pitch, anticipating the other player's next move.

"We're gonna die."

"Emir," Sebastian says.

But Emir's already mumbling, "We're gonna get kicked out of camp, off the team, I can't bloody believe it."

The light is getting closer.

Sebastian whispers, "Look, go behind those trees. You're skinny enough; he won't see you."

"Hey, I'm not—"

"*Dude.*" Sebastian is already turning Emir with one hand and has his other on the small of Emir's back, pushing. "Now is not the time to argue." Rivera's rooting through bushes. He hasn't pinpointed them yet, but Sebastian doesn't like to gamble. "Go," he says with a hiss.

Emir trips over a few rocks on his way to the trees.

Sebastian should be worried about Emir's safety, but he's on the verge of his own mini-avalanche of anxiety. So, he squares his shoulders, shields his eyes against the shine of Rivera's flashlight, and accepts that he's gone from "responsible one" to complete delinquent.

"Hughes?" Rivera pauses mid-step, then shouts, "Hughes!" while stumbling up to him.

Sebastian gives a carefree wave; his other hand is trembling. He smiles his best *I'm innocent* smile for Rivera. "What's up, Coach?" he says around the lump in his throat. "Nice night, isn't it?"

Rivera's thick eyebrows descend. "It's past curfew, Hughes."

"I hadn't noticed."

"What're you doing out this way?" Rivera sniffs, as if he's going to catch alcohol on Sebastian's breath or, worse, a hint of weed. Sebastian isn't offended; he's flattered that Rivera categorizes him as *that guy*. He sticks his chin out proudly when Rivera takes a step back.

"It's late, Hughes."

Sebastian nods.

"Why are you, out of all the chicos, out past curfew?" When Rivera's tired or exasperated, his words drift between English and Spanish.

Sebastian rubs at his abdomen. "Had a big dinner tonight, so I needed a run to burn off the calories." He's amazed at how well he's done keeping his voice casual, especially since his stomach's doing back handsprings.

"Sí," says Rivera, nodding, "Entiendo."

Sebastian slouches, relief giving him a reason to smile genuinely. That is, of course, until Rivera drops a heavy hand on his shoulder and squeezes.

"It's tough, mijo, being as good as you are," he says, gruff and serious, but also kind. "I hate to be the bad guy, but we depend on you. Your teammates, the coaches, all of us. You're our rock."

Sebastian knows. "Yeah." He scuffs one of his Converse on a nearby pebble. A running list of people who depend on Sebastian Hughes exists somewhere. It's made up of Willie, Mason, his sister Carly, Emir, and his teammates.

At least Rivera doesn't sugarcoat it, unlike everyone else. But no pressure, right?

"Hey," Rivera says, still squeezing Sebastian's shoulder, "Have you seen Shah anywhere? We're doing bed checks, making sure you guys aren't getting out of hand."

Sebastian fidgets.

Rivera is shorter than Sebastian but still manages to look down at him. "Give it up, Hughes," he says. "A couple of sophomores were puking in the bushes an hour ago."

Shit. Sebastian doesn't want details on who got caught. He's overwhelmed with guilt. He should have stuck around, made sure all the guys went straight to their cabins after the bonfire.

Instead, he was skinny-dipping, making out, and being reckless.

Rivera waits.

"Maybe he's out on a walk?" Rocking on his heels, Sebastian rubs the side of his neck. "He's the homesick type. I've heard this is his first time away from home. That's always weird for people."

Rivera seems far from convinced. Sebastian doesn't blame him.

"We grew up together," Sebastian explains. "He freaks out in new places. Getting him to chill out during sleepovers was always hell."

"Is he going to be any good for our team?"

Sebastian hates the high-pitched glee in his voice when he says, "He's going to be great, if we can get his attitude in check."

Rivera's laugh is rumbly, like a bear's. He says, "I trust your judgment, Hughes. You'll help us make him into something, right?"

"Yes, sir."

"Good," Rivera says. He aims his flashlight at Sebastian's face so the harsh white blinds him. "Now get to your cabin, and I won't report to Patrick about you breaking curfew."

When Rivera threatens to replace him with Jack if he's caught again, Sebastian nods. *Like hell! Jack couldn't replace me.* He doesn't say it; the ice he's treading is already thin.

"Okay," he says. His heart finally returns to its former position when Rivera walks away.

"Is the coast clear?"

Sebastian peeks around before nodding.

"Were you scared?" asks Emir, picking leaves and twigs from his clothes as he walks up.

"Of being caught?"

"No, of the dark, you chicken shit."

Sebastian chuckles. This whole night has been way too weird for his poor teenage heart. First Mason, then Emir, now Coach Rivera. If anything else happens, they're going to have to airlift him to Bloomington Medical Hospital.

"Whatever," he says, automatically taking Emir's hand in his own.

"I heard you, Bastian," Emir says. His voice is a nice interruption to their silence on their walk to Emir's cabin. "You told Rivera I was homesick. And that you used to look after me."

Sebastian hums. He doesn't regret it, but he says, "Did it make you mad?" because he's not about to be a dick about it.

"Yes," Emir says. Then he shakes his head. "It didn't. It's just…"

Waiting, Sebastian steps over a chunky brown rock. But Emir doesn't finish. He squeezes Sebastian's hand, like Morse code. If Emir doesn't say anything, Sebastian's cool with that. Obviously, they each have their own issues with the whole "right words to say" thing.

THERE'S A VERY AWKWARD MOMENT at Emir's door. Should he hug Emir and leave? Should there be a goodnight kiss? Sebastian has mostly applied these rules and protocol to girls he's dated.

He and Emir aren't dating, haven't done the whole "date" thing, but one thing is certain: letting Emir's hand go isn't high on his priority list.

Sebastian does let go, however, because of clammy palms and the lack of circulation in his fingers. Now his hand is cold. And he hasn't made a move to do anything.

Emir pecks a dry kiss on his cheek. Well, that was pretty simple.

"Thanks," Emir says, his hip angled against the door.

"For what?"

"I don't know." Emir looks at his feet. "But thanks."

Sebastian's chest is rapidly filling with warmth. He hastily says, "Goodnight," and turns away before he makes a complete ass of himself. Then he stumbles on a small rock. The temptation to peek over his shoulder, just in case Emir is watching him, is diluted by his surprisingly strong will—or his utter mortification.

Once he gets to his cabin, Sebastian's smiling so dorkily, he's considering facial reconstruction.

Willie is laid out like a lazy starfish, head tipped back, openmouthed and snoring with dried drool on his chin. Sebastian kicks off his shoes just as Willie mumbles, "You'll always be my favorite, Bastian."

That reminder from the bonfire reemerges—he was such a tool about Willie's crush.

Willie turns away, hugging his pillow. *How did I ignore him?* Willie, the selfless, nonjudgmental idiot, didn't give Sebastian crap about Emir. Willie kept his secret. He never pointed out Sebastian's mistakes. And he did all of that while crushing on Sebastian from afar.

Willie is perfect. Perfect for Hunter, not Sebastian, but that's great, too.

Sebastian whispers, "You'll always be my favorite, too," and something in his chest relaxes when Willie replies, "Mace says we can't pick favorites."

"That's 'cause Mason is nobody's favorite."

"True that."

Willie's voice is dreamy instead of croaky, as if he is sleep-talking. It's a good talk either way. Sebastian strips off his shirt, but leaves his shorts on. He climbs into bed.

It takes him a while to fall asleep, and that's the one thing about tonight that is routine.

 *20*

THE NEXT AFTERNOON ISN'T ONE of Sebastian's better moments. It's not *bad*, but it's not on his top ten either.

Training camp has its benefits. Extra practices produce wickedly defined calves. The sun leaves his skin more deeply tanned: not quite sun-kissed gold, but acceptable. He doesn't have awkward shoulders anymore, either. There are honest, real moments when it seems as if he's becoming someone.

But right now, Sebastian isn't in love with his reflection. His cheeks are still full and round like a toddler's. In the sun's halo, the smudges under his eyes give him the look of a zombie. His jaw isn't square or round, just odd. Oh, and his nose is awkwardly-shaped.

"You're good enough for them."

It's his mantra, along with "You're good enough for the team, for your peers, for him" and "Those days are gone." It's okay to give yourself a pep talk, for the sake of self-esteem. Also, it alleviates just enough pressure in his chest so that Sebastian can breathe.

Until, of course, his eyes spot how soft the skin around his belly is. His shaky hands grab at it. *Christ*. The familiar sting at the corner of his eyes only exacerbates his hyperventilating. A balloon is expanding in his chest.

Every word in his head is "Bastian the Trashcan" in those haunting bullies' voices. *Why?*

"What are you doing?"

Sebastian freezes, mid-breath, with his hands on his belly. He thought he'd locked the door. Emir is staring at Sebastian—no, staring at Sebastian's hands on his bare belly.

Sebastian says, "Nothing," in a tight voice. He has no idea how long Emir has been standing there: what he's seen, what he's *heard*. Sebastian's defenses are up; his body is half-tilted away from Emir's view. "It's nothing."

"Nothing," Emir repeats. He steps inside, shutting the door.

Sweat builds across Sebastian's brow. He's scared. Sebastian is a million things, but *scared* is the only label he can find.

"What's wrong?" Emir steps closer, and Sebastian wants to retreat. But Emir's dilated, concerned eyes force Sebastian to suck in a shaky breath and stay put.

"Don't worry about it, okay?" Sebastian twists a hand in his hair. "I shouldn't have skipped our morning run to let you, um—"

"You mean when I—"

"Yes," Sebastian cuts in, flinching. His eyes are watery, and he doesn't get how Emir is so confident. He's not cocky, but he acts as though he doesn't give a shit. And Sebastian is just—he lacks *that*.

What really sucks is, now he's ruining what happened between them this morning. The sky was still bright pink when he crawled through the window and let Emir drag him to bed for morning kisses. Sebastian's fumbling hands highlighted his lack of sexual experience with boys, but Emir didn't seem to mind. And now he's wrecking it all.

"I'm fine."

Emir presses against Sebastian's back and circles him with his arms. His unblinking eyes stare at Sebastian's in the mirror. "Bastian."

"Let's just drop—"

"*Sebastian William Hughes*," says Emir in a voice eerily like Lily's.

Sebastian winces. He lets Emir move Sebastian's cold, shaky hands away and replace them with his own. Emir's hands are warm and affectionate, smoothing Sebastian's unnerved center.

Sebastian chokes, "I'm not—"

Struggling with this doesn't make it out of his mouth. He doesn't let people see him like this. "I'm okay."

"This isn't okay."

"Yeah, well."

Sebastian's hands are clenched into fists. It's not the end of the world. So why are tears clinging to his eyelashes?

Emir's hand cups his jaw. His thumb nudges Sebastian's chin until their eyes meet. Emir smiles. Sebastian pouts, but he presses into the touch.

"You're beautiful."

Sebastian rolls his eyes. "Guys aren't—"

"Hey," Emir cuts in. "Guys *are* beautiful. And girls are handsome. Words aren't gender-specific. Don't be some jock asshole about this."

Sebastian is caught up in Emir's warm breaths grazing the side of his neck.

Emir says, "Your body is amazing," while his hands rub over Sebastian's ribs.

A protest fizzes at the back of Sebastian's throat.

Emir's lack of height means he has to stand on his toes to rest his chin on Sebastian's shoulder. It also means his arousal nudges the small of Sebastian's back. He's on edge in a very different way.

Emir's whispered, "And you're amazing," and the way he stares at Sebastian as if he's unbreakable vibrates through his whole body.

"We all do it, mate. We all have things about our body we hate."

Sebastian bites back, *Yeah, but you're ridiculously flawless.*

Emir says, "I can't get any definition in my arms, and my ass is flat." He's barely holding back a laugh.

Sebastian's helpless about how fast his mouth curves into a grin.

"It's okay," says Emir, hands smoothing over Sebastian's stomach until he can tolerate the sensation. "We're all imperfect."

Sebastian licks his lips and salty tears hit his taste buds. "Speak for yourself."

"I am, asshole," Emir says, biting Sebastian's shoulder. "And you too. The whole damn team is a mess, but that's the point, right?"

"Yep."

And he's okay. Emir's hands continue mapping his body, and he's okay. He's learning.

"Now," Emir says, "can we go grab some lunch? Riley's being a diva because you're not around."

"He'll get over it."

Sebastian's shoulders slowly lose tension, and his chest inflates freely. At his side, his fingers wiggle. It's as if Emir is at the core of his whole world, pushing the edges wider.

Before Emir can get too far, Sebastian whips around and kisses him.

"You're predictable," Emir says with a hint of smugness.

Sebastian knows that. But just because the kiss wasn't long enough, he slides a hand to Emir's neck, puts his thumb behind Emir's ear, and pulls until their mouths meet again.

"I don't care."

Urged on by uncharacteristic boldness, Sebastian laces their fingers together. Their hands sway when they walk outside. He's never held hands with a boy in the middle of the day. Would he be courageous enough to do this in the halls of Bloomington High? Emir hasn't mentioned whether he's out at school yet. Would he let Sebastian hold his hand? These are serious things that Sebastian has dreamt about, but never counted on.

But he doesn't know if this thing with Emir is going past the summer. Maybe it's like *The Breakfast Club*. Maybe when September hits, they won't acknowledge each other. Sebastian would have absolutely no problem sauntering into prom arm in arm with Emir.

"You're smiling," Emir says as they walk. The sun is high, hitting their eyes. Emir cups his free hand over his brow while he stares at Sebastian.

"Yeah, I guess I am."

Sebastian keeps his other thoughts to himself, for now.

 21

SEBASTIAN IS ALMOST NINETY-EIGHT PERCENT certain that teenagers should be banned from making decisions during the summer, especially teens bored out of their skulls at night, like him. Summer should be a thought-free zone. No school. No extra brain usage. He should be on house arrest, not climbing through Emir's window on a Wednesday night.

Of course, most of this is Willie's fault. They were in their cabin, marathoning *Stranger Things* on Netflix. Free-for-all pizza was for dinner, so Willie conked out after the second episode. The guy can put away some Hawaiian pizza.

Sebastian can also blame some of his bad decision-making on the fact that summer is ticking down. Camp is almost over; less than two weeks are left.

The vault inside is almost perfect, but Sebastian smacks his shoulder on the floor. It doesn't hurt, but it's embarrassing. "So, so," he stutters. Blood rushes to his head. His view of Emir perched on his bed is upside-down. He rolls over, laughing. "You weren't sleeping, right?"

The lamp is still on. An open book sits in Emir's lap. Ink-dark hair falls around his temples instead of standing in its usual sleep-mussed disaster.

"Nope. Just finished my Isha'a."

Sebastian stands. He dusts off his ripped jeans, fixes his checkered flannel shirt. "Ish- what, now?"

"Isha'a," Emir repeats. "It's the last of the salats, daily prayers we do as Muslims."

These reminders about Emir's religion and his life at home light memories that flicker through Sebastian's brain like tiny paper lanterns in the wind. He remembers the adults in Emir's family fasting during Ramadan and a small backyard gathering to celebrate a feast day Sebastian can't remember the name of, but he recalls the beautiful clothing, the music, and Emir's parents passing out gifts to the children. And he remembers the giant, toothy smile Emir wore while pressed to Sebastian's side on a sticky June evening.

"Is this a bad time? Should I go?"

"No." Emir closes the book, carefully placing it on the desk by his bed. "It's okay."

"Okay."

Sebastian's snuck in here every evening lately. After dinner, he crawls in to find a space left for him on Emir's bed. Sebastian talks nonstop with his head on Emir's chest. His fingers trace the shape of Emir's mouth. Sometimes, Emir talks, shedding his shyness. Eventually boring conversations turn into making out.

"Hey!" Tonight Sebastian came with a plan. He tosses Mason's keys in the air, then catches them. He didn't steal them; Mason always hands them over during the week so he doesn't lose them. Being the token "good guy" has its advantages. "You wanna get out of here?"

"Are we allowed to leave?" Emir asks.

"Didn't bother checking the rule book."

Emir runs a hand through his hair; his fingers catch on the tangles. He says, "You *wrote* the rule book."

It's not an attack on Sebastian, but he still flips Emir off. He blames his lack of a solid comeback on the way the bridge of Emir's nose crinkles when he snorts.

"What's wrong?"

"Nothing," Sebastian says. His mind has been drifting lately, more than usual, wondering what this thing with Emir is or isn't. "I dunno, I just want to get out of here. Just me and you."

"Okay."

"You're sure?" Sebastian squeaks in an unnaturally high voice.

Emir shrugs and stands. "Yes, Bastian," he says. He grabs his beanie, pulls on a pair of slightly wrinkled black skinnies, grips a hoodie—

The sight of Sebastian's last name in blocky gold letters across Emir's back is mesmerizing.

Emir stalks up to him, poking a finger at the middle of Sebastian's chest. Brow furrowed, he says, "And if I get kicked off the team, you're doing all the talking to Abbu about why his precious only son is no longer going pro."

"Pro?"

"Semi-pro." With a crooked grin, Emir says, "Okay, after high school, I won't ever play again. But he doesn't need to know that. Besides, it'll sound better coming from a genuine guy like you."

"Obviously." Sebastian rolls his eyes. He circles Emir's thin wrist with his fingers. Emir turns his hand and twines their fingers. It helps to untie the knot in Sebastian's stomach. "Now, let's get out of here before you change your mind."

"And miss an opportunity to watch you *try* to break the rules? I wouldn't dare."

"Whatever."

MASON LEFT HIS IPOD HOOKED up to the aux cord, and The 1975 hums through the speakers when Sebastian revs up the car. He cuts the volume. "Mason's addicted to them," he explains.

"Huh." Emir's has his feet on the dash, slouched in the seat with a half-impressed expression. "Didn't think this was Riley's thing."

"Mace would totally suck face with Matt Healy if he could."

"Makes sense."

Sebastian bites the inside of his lip. Mason is one of those Urban Outfitters, coffee-drinking, I'm-not-but-I-am hipsters. Sebastian doesn't have a problem with those guys, but it's hilarious considering Mason used to wear sweater vests and Keds when they were in middle school.

Emir asks, "Where to?"

"To the land of Oz," Sebastian says. Or simply boring old Oakville. Going too far from camp is risky. Around them, a cloudless night showcases the indigo-black sky and giant stars hung like diamonds. Sebastian could stare at it for hours.

Emir taps his hands on his knees. "Cool."

Yeah, it is.

No one's in sight when Sebastian pulls off toward the main road. His nerves are still wonky; his fingers are white-knuckled around the steering wheel as the tires drag over dirt and rock. He's subtly observing Emir in his peripheral vision.

Emir drops a hand on Sebastian's thigh, squeezing. Sebastian doesn't flinch. *Sweet.* At least his body knows how to act around Emir.

Emir says, "It's just you and me, right? So just drive."

So Sebastian drives to the melody, and Matt Healy singing about how his car smells like chocolate.

AT THE EDGE OF TOWN, an old cornfield has been mowed, stripped, and turned into a drive-in named Oakville '76, the year it was built. This town lives and breathes creativity. A massive space has been cleared for cars to park; a colossal screen plays outdated movies. At least they run a different film nightly. During the week, no one shows up except the slackers, elderly folks, and horny parents searching for somewhere to, *well*.

It's mostly empty tonight. Sebastian quietly geeks out about the feature presentation: the first *Iron Man*. The movie is just a backdrop for a small line of cars with fogged windows, jiggling back and forth. Occasional streams of profanity can be heard.

"Sorry," Sebastian says over his shoulder to Emir.

They're slowly walking to the concession stand. It's staffed by college kids home for summer or townies with nothing better to do. The selection sucks: over-buttered popcorn, Red Vines, and M&M's.

Emir falls in step next to him. "It's not so bad."

A man older than Sebastian's dad emerges from a rusty Cadillac. He grins smugly with a hand firmly pressed to his wife's ass. Sebastian *hopes* that's his wife.

"No," says Emir between chuckles, "It's definitely cool."

"Cool," Sebastian repeats.

"It's pretty empty."

"Yeah," says Sebastian, noting the suggestion in Emir's voice. Then it hits him. Emir *likes* that this place is deserted. As in, he's all on board for a night, just the two of them, with no one watching. "Cool, right?"

Emir snorts, bobbing his head.

If Sebastian were bolder, he might kiss Emir in public. It's new, uncharted territory, though. This whole "first time for everything" is a lot more pressure than people make it sound. It doesn't stop his mind from doing pathetic loops around the idea of holding Emir's hand all forty steps to the concessions stand.

They part ways when they reach the line. Emir stands off to the side, thumbing through apps on his phone. Sebastian gradually inches closer to the front of the counter. He ponders what to order. What would impress Emir? Sebastian is trying to prove he isn't lame but failing to find examples to support this theory.

"We've gotta stop meeting like this."

Sebastian is thankful, when he turns, to find Val behind him.

She's mega-preppy tonight: cardigan over a white shirt, khaki shorts, hair tied in a loose ponytail. But she gives a middle finger salute to private school with a shiny Marilyn Manson button on her sweater.

Sebastian raises an eyebrow. "What're you doing here?"

"I'm here with Maggie." Val points to a few feet away. "You remember her, right?"

Though the concession stand is just a gutted shack painted in ugly pastels, it has supreme fluorescent lighting. Sebastian has a prime view of a short girl brushing manicured nails up Emir's forearm. Her jeans are on the obscene side of tight. Her tilted head reveals a crooked but attractive smile. Sebastian recalls her flirting aggressively with Zach at the ice cream shop last summer. He zones in on her freckles and her scrunched nose when she giggles at Emir. Sebastian isn't sweating it, doesn't have clenched fists at his sides or a heart rattling like a snare drum in his chest—much.

"She's nice," he says tightly.

Val flicks up an eyebrow. "And she's single." Val's having way too much fun teasing him.

"Yeah, well. Single guys are everywhere, right?"

Single guys who are not Emir. Plus, Emir's gay. Gay and whispering something to Maggie with a wry smile.

Whatever is happening in Sebastian's chest is new. He's not calling it jealousy. Sebastian was used to guys checking out Sam. It happened a lot; it was something he was proud of. He had this beautiful girl on his arm, and she only had eyes for him.

Of course, that story doesn't include a happy ending. But he's not harboring ill feelings over it. *Anymore*, not anymore.

Val whispers, "Who is that?"

"Emir," Sebastian says. "My teammate." He almost says *friend*, but that's presumptuous. He's definitely not going to call Emir his boyfriend. The word sits weirdly in his mouth. He's okay with dating a guy, but he hasn't worked up to referring to him as his "boyfriend," not that he has anything to worry about, since they're not even close to using that term.

Yet, he tells himself.

"Cute," says Val, hooking an arm through Sebastian's. "Single?"

Maggie leans close as Emir backs off, laughing. "Yeah," Sebastian says, biting back *and gay!*

"I don't think he's interested. Maybe someone else has his attention?"

Sebastian's staring a hole through Maggie's pretty, dimpled smile. She's quirky-cute. He'd date her, if he wasn't completely into—

His mouth drops open, and Val winks. *She knows!*

Sure, the team and coaches are aware of Sebastian's sexuality, but that's his second family. He has no reason to hide it from them. He never told Sam, though. And he trusts Mason with his secrets, so Val definitely didn't know. At least, he *thought* she didn't.

"You look at him like… " Val pauses, scratching her cheek. "Like I used to look at Mace, that's all." She smiles sadly.

Maggie is ogling Emir as if she might eat him. She's licking her lip gloss-stained lips. An intensely green monster is devouring Sebastian's insides. He's not ashamed. It's taken a while, but he's starting to own his bisexuality.

"It's not… It's okay, right?" Sebastian admires his Chuck Taylors instead of meeting Val's eyes. "That I'm bi?"

Val pinches Sebastian's forearm. "Totally."

It crosses Sebastian's mind that Val could've known about Mason too. Did he tell her he was curious? Maybe she just *knew*, like a sixth sense.

Emir cackles. Maggie is very pleased about something. She's sly, and Emir's nervy: signs of a bad first date. Sebastian doesn't like it.

"I think he likes you, too."

Sebastian says, "How can you tell?" Emir's face is hidden behind Maggie's as he whispers in her ear. Her face falls, and Emir shrugs.

Val whispers, "A girl knows," and leaves it at that.

Maggie stomps up to them. "He's gay," she tells Val, ignoring Sebastian. She makes a face, not as if she's offended by Emir's sexuality, but by his rejection.

Internally, Sebastian's having a dance party for one. The song in his head is, "He's mine, pint-sized!"

"I'm sorry," Val says, but she doesn't look it.

Maggie tosses her curly brown hair over one shoulder. Nearby is a lanky guy, thin like a basketball player, with a buzz cut and a goatee. Just like that, she's over it.

Sebastian doesn't understand people at all.

"So, like." The guy behind the counter's limp blond hair hangs into his bloodshot eyes. His nametag reads *Capt. Mary Jane*. "I've got half a joint out back that I'm dying to finish. Can you guys order already?"

Val snorts into her hand. Maggie rolls her eyes. Sebastian's unsure what to make of this guy. The lights overhead buzz like electric bug catchers. It's warm tonight, but the heat along Sebastian's back is Emir.

"We're gonna miss the beginning," he says, chin hooked over Sebastian's shoulder, fingers twisted in the belt loops of Sebastian's jeans.

Sebastian turns his head. Emir's amused at Maggie's wide-eyed look. *Screw it.* Even in small-minded Oakville, Sebastian can be a tiny bit out of the closet. He replies, "Okay." He's addicted to Emir's thumbs tracing his hipbones.

"So, um, popcorn?" Capt. Mary Jane asks.

Sebastian doesn't exactly *growl* at him, but he mumbles their order as Emir pulls away. Val's still giggling as if she can't believe what just happened. Sebastian can't either. He does, however, pay for their snacks and sodas, giving Val a "what can you do?" shrug before strolling over to Emir.

"Defiant Sebastian Hughes," Val calls. Her smirk edges on proud. She shouts, "I like it," raising her hand to give him devil horns, the universal sign for "Rock on."

Sebastian snorts.

"Don't stay out too late or you'll get benched, Captain Hughes!"

Sebastian gives her a one-finger salute. He's wound up. The "casual" brush of Emir's hand as they walk is far from accidental, and this whole "screw the system" thing is too good to be true.

In the car, Emir says, "I still can't believe you remembered."

His feet are back on the dashboard. He's slouched in his seat. His chin is tucked to his chest, and the blue glow of the big screen shines on his cheeks. He pops a handful of peanut butter M&M's into his mouth.

The Mustang's top is peeled back. It's past ten, but the summer night is still heady with warmth. Sebastian smiles at his hands. His chest boils with a confident fire. He's done another thing to wipe that recurrent, beginning-of-the-summer scowl off Emir's face.

Emir says, "Didn't your mom used to keep a bowl of these…" He shakes the bag of candy. "…in the kitchen?"

"And didn't you used to pocket a handful before you went home?"

Emir wiggles his eyebrows, unashamed. In the background, Tony Stark is building an iron suit from scrap metal; the dialogue is muted by the wall of sound Mason's iPod provides.

"Anna Sun" comes on, and Emir props himself sideways against Sebastian. "Is this a date?"

Sebastian tips his head in Emir's direction. An old Ford pickup next to them rocks to and fro. On the radio, the lead singer moans about a house falling apart. Sebastian bought them Dr. Peppers and he guzzles some of his to buy time.

Is it a date?

"I don't know," he says. Sebastian wanted to get away from camp. But being alone with Emir at a drive-in while he licks melted chocolate from his fingers is plain awesome. A fuzzy ache starts below his navel. "I've never been on a date," he says, swallowing, "with a boy, officially."

Emir drums his fingers on his knees.

"Wait, have you been on a date with a guy?"

"There was this guy." Emir picks at a loose thread on the knee of his jeans. "We met at an art show. He wasn't from Bloomington. On the weekends he would take me to this tacky pizza place outside of the city."

Sebastian controls his face. But jealousy bubbles at the back of his mind. What the hell, *of course* Emir was attracted to other guys.

Emir says, "It didn't work out because he didn't want anyone to know about us. At the time, I didn't want to come out either, but he was a certified dick about it."

His head tilts away, so Sebastian can't see his expression. But his jaw tenses. Sebastian suspects he's more hurt than angry. "Sounds complicated."

Emir laughs, but it sounds melancholy. "I was sixteen, Bastian, so I wanted a boyfriend. But the whole thing made me uncomfortable with my sexuality, with being out."

"He isn't still, um…" Sebastian stares at the explosions on the screen. "Is he still around?" He doesn't ask because he's intimidated, *that much*, but the guy's an asshole for making Emir hesitate about being open with himself and others. Lack of support, especially from someone you're interested in, is destructive.

"Nope," Emir replies. "Would you be jealous?"

"Nope," Sebastian says, like the biggest liar to ever open his mouth.

Emir's gray eyes reflect light from the big screen.

Sebastian chugs Dr. Pepper; carbonation tickles his nose. It's a good thing he's seen this movie a dozen times, because he's staring at Emir, mesmerized. He considers pulling the "yawn, stretch, put an arm around your date's shoulder" trick, but he's not quite that smooth. Mason could pull it off. Sebastian imagines Mason *has* pulled it off.

Biting his lip, Emir says, "You never answered my first question."

"Huh." Sebastian taps his index finger on his chin. Their lips are just a breath apart, but Emir doesn't close the gap. Sebastian whispers, "Okay, yeah, a date. Sure."

Emir's eyes flick down to Sebastian's mouth. He says, "I've watched this movie a hundred times," and his hand ghosts from the side of Sebastian's neck into his hair.

"Me too."

They're almost kissing.

"Um—" Sebastian cuts himself off and surges forward. Their noses bump. He adjusts the angle. Emir's mouth tastes like Dr. Pepper and peanut butter and summer. His kisses taste like the very thing Sebastian didn't know he was missing.

Tickled by stubble, Sebastian's fingers spread along Emir's cheek. He feels more than hears Emir suck in a breath. He can't tell who makes the first move, but Sebastian gets a hand on Emir's thigh and Emir crawls—*climbs* into Sebastian's lap with the steering wheel digging into the small of his back.

"Emir," Sebastian gasps, his hands palming denim.

"Shut up."

Sebastian most certainly does not let out a dreamy gasp when Emir's teeth nip at his lower lip. He is not a teen-romance cliché.

Emir is balanced on knees that pin Sebastian's hips. His left hand cradles the back of Sebastian's head. A soft sigh breaks his lips, inches from Sebastian's, as he lowers his hips.

And Sebastian is doing his best to ignore the flare spreading like a supernova in his belly. He has one warm hand under Emir's hoodie and another teasing a button on his jeans.

Emir laughs into his mouth. "Curious?"

Sebastian's a teenager, a virgin with guys, and stuck at summer camp for thirty days with very little alone time. Curious is an understatement. All their fooling around has never quite gone *there*.

"Sometimes."

Panic rams into Sebastian's chest when Emir goes quiet. He's prepared to retreat, but then Emir says, "Me too. Just not here, okay?"

"Okay."

Sebastian is still on edge, though. He's not freaking out, but the pressure is real. It's not like trying to figure out a math problem, but he wants to get it right. This isn't just sex. Sebastian's not tossing this in the "summer fling" pile. This is a bigger deal than being with Sam or with anyone else.

They kiss again, and Sebastian relishes Emir's shiver when he pulls away.

"Wow." Emir exhales.

Sebastian stares at Emir's eyes. They're dark, hidden by shadows, and that makes it slightly easier for Sebastian to ask, "Have you ever...?"

"Yes."

Sebastian's picturing a faceless, but very attractive, guy touching Emir. His stomach churns with acid. He says, "Cool."

"We'll figure it out," Emir says, as if he can read Sebastian's every thought.

Sebastian's lips are raw. He licks them as his fingers trace patterns on Emir's skin. Tony Stark is blowing things up behind Emir's shoulders.

"We'll figure it out," Sebastian says, because tonight isn't the end of camp or the end of the world. He stretches his neck for another kiss.

22

Last summer, Mason Riley was on top of the world. He's been the undisputed best attacker on the Lions' squad since sophomore year; he started every game. His grades were passing, students adored him, and scouts lined up with pamphlets on why their schools are the best fit for him. His thing with Val was normal; normal for *them*. Also, he wasn't hurting for hookups during the school year. Mason was never lonely.

Something has changed.

Mason whispers, "She broke up with me."

It's an especially quiet Saturday evening, so Sebastian doesn't have to strain to hear him. They're hip to hip on a bench outside the ice cream shop. Mason wasn't in the mood for burgers with the guys, and Sebastian had no interest in catching the Will Smith flick playing at the drive-in. It's moments like this he misses during the school year.

Mason works a part-time job at the mall in the off-season. Most of his money goes to helping his mom with bills. A slacker during the soccer season, Sebastian spends his downtime catching up on classes. They share Saturdays at Starbucks and the occasional Hughes family barbeque; Lily Hughes is a good PTA, bake-sale, life-of-the-party kind of mom.

Evenings like this, shooting the shit and talking about soccer, music, whatever, under a bright pink and blue sky, are important to Sebastian.

Sebastian nudges his sneaker on the pavement. "She did?"

Mason glares at Val, who's near the diner with her friends and a handful of visiting college guys. "I haven't told anyone," he says. His hands are clenched in his lap.

"Yeah, okay."

An unspoken rule exists between bros: No questions about love-life-shit unless prompted. Sebastian respects the rule, but he's curious about what the hell went down between Mason and Val. He's been letting Mason deflect for weeks, but now the cracks in his armor of silence are discernible.

"She ended things after last season." Mason's mouth goes tight. "She thought it was time for her to be serious about life, and that I'm never serious about *anything*. It was kinda rank."

Sebastian scratches his temple, giving Mason space to talk.

"She's right, though." Mason winces, and Sebastian does too. He's about to protest, but Mason laughs, dryly. "It's cool; I can take it. I should've been serious about her, but I wasn't."

Sebastian met Mason a month before he met Willie, a week after Emir left, and that has created a sense of loyalty. But he still says, "She's a damn good girl, Mace," because he believes it, because she deserved more than Mason gave.

Mason nods. "Part of me is over it," he says, frowning now. "But it messes with my head, bro, like full-on brain damage."

Sebastian's afraid Mason will shut down if he hugs him. He punches Mason's arm.

"I'm not as good as I want to be," Mason says, slouching. "Mom keeps telling me she'll be fine, whenever I go away for college, she'll be fine. But I *can't*."

"Join the club," says Sebastian, slumping forward. His elbows dig into his knees. "We're a mess."

Mason elbows him and says, "You'll do fine, dude. You're built of awesomeness."

If you only knew...

"I'm mostly okay with that, being a mess," Mason says. Sebastian believes him, mostly.

In the line at the ice cream shop, Willie and Grey argue like a married couple about flavors. Sebastian's grateful those two have become inseparable over the summer. Grey has been a crucial distraction, keeping Willie's mind off the fact that he's sidelined by his knee.

What truly trips Sebastian up is how soft Mason has gone for Grey. He doesn't kick her from their table every day; he says a few polite words between mocking or talking over her, and he *smiles*. Like right now, when he says, "Who invited The Brat?"

The sky is changing from cotton candy colors to indigo. The wind is light against their faces. Sebastian whispers, "Willster to the rescue."

Mason says, "He loves to watch me suffer," and glares at Willie, as if he's trying set him on fire with his mind.

"Still don't like her?"

"She's tolerable." Mason Riley is such a poser. One side of his mouth twitches. "She talks too much. And she looks at me, like—" Mason waves a hand, and Sebastian says, "Like she's drunk in love with you."

Sebastian's familiarity with Mason's expressions tell him one thing: Mason is smitten. He hangs an arm around Mason's shoulders and pulls him in. "It's not so bad," he insists. "You two are kinda friends now, right?"

"About as much as you and Shah are," Mason says, casual as can be.

Sebastian might spew chunks all over his favorite sneakers. He chokes out, "He's okay." Mason is the one guy Sebastian knows who does irrational, stupid things, and lives life as if regret is a foreign word. Sebastian shouldn't hide Emir and their confusing *whatever* from him.

"Uh huh."

"Things are," Sebastian pauses, "*interesting*."

Mason raises his eyebrows but doesn't interrogate Sebastian. He respects the bro code.

Good, because Sebastian didn't want to have to hire assassins to put Mason out of his misery. Then who would he soak up the last dregs of summer with?

The ice cream shop has old-school megaphone speakers attached to the sides that play music Sebastian's parents danced to. They're blaring a crackled Elvis Bishop tune. Sebastian flashes on that one scene in *Guardians of the Galaxy*. He loves that movie. He loves the nostalgia the music evokes, the way it fits this perfectly weird little town. Next to him, Mason hums, tapping a foot.

This distraction keeps them from noticing Grey. She's a ninja, suddenly thrusting a cone at Mason. Her big green eyes reflect the last hints of sunset. "Peppermint." She waggles the cone in Mason's face. "Your favorite, right?"

"*Jesus*," Mason says, almost in a squeal.

Willie hooks his chin over Grey's shoulder. He says, mockingly, "She *knew*, dude, how awesome is that?"

"As awesome as someone shoving that plastic spoon up your—"

"Is that a thank you?" Grey cuts Mason off. She has one eyebrow raised.

Mason grumbles, shifting until his thigh is pressed firmly against Sebastian's. "Just sit, Patrick." Eyebrows lowering, he growls, "Quietly."

Grey flops on the bench. She hands Mason the cone. A satisfied curl appears on her lips when he licks viciously at melting ice cream.

"Small victories," Willie whispers to her.

Mason flips him off.

Sebastian folds his hands behind his head, doing his best to stretch out while squashed four-deep on the bench. He hums "Blister in the Sun" while Mason and Willie continue their brotherly bickering. Grey tries to get a word in. She's not annoyed. Maybe it's because Mason doesn't shut her down each time she opens her mouth.

Around them, the team fills the streets: having water gun fights, window-shopping, parading around like a bunch of teens drunk on good weather and freedom.

Sebastian should get in on that.

"Isn't that Shah?" Mason points at the ice cream shop.

Sebastian's breath stalls. He peeks through his eyelashes, pretending Mason's wrong. It's simply a random skinny guy with tense shoulders who's severely shy in public settings and has Permanent Scowl Syndrome. This guy just *might* look like

Emir, if a person squints. Sebastian's delusion lasts five seconds, until the guy begins to turn around—

"Yep," Grey says, lips smacking on strawberry ice cream. "It's him." She is now the enemy to Sebastian.

"Huh." Willie is careful not to meet Sebastian's eyes, but he smirks as if he has a secret. "He never comes to town with us."

All of Sebastian's friends are now dead to him. He'll begin his search for new ones tomorrow, but first—

Grey asks, "Should we invite him over?"

Sebastian studies his shoes. His cheeks are hot. He refuses to make eye contact or say the wrong thing.

"He doesn't like us," Mason says.

"He doesn't like *you*," Willie and Grey say together, cracking up.

Mason fakes a laugh while giving them a two-finger salute. "That's not humanly possible. I'm *very* likeable." His chest is puffed up and his chin juts out. "Isn't that right, Patrick?"

Grey punches him in the thigh. Panic butts into Sebastian's life when Grey says, "I'll get him to come over."

He manages a "No" that's both strangled and anxious.

Three heads turn slowly in his direction.

Sighing, Sebastian wriggles off the bench. He dusts off his jeans. He's fighting off a frown. "I'll go get him." His friends' narrowed eyes confirm that they're putting it all together.

If he told them, would it be so bad? Mason and Willie have never judged Sebastian, not when he didn't stop a goal during a game, or when he cried over Sam. Having a *thing* with Emir should be harmless.

Clearing his throat, Sebastian says, "Maybe he'll be a little less anxious if I'm the one who invites him over. We're, um, friends.

Again." He leaves out *and I think I'm falling for him* because that is a moment of pure boxed-macaroni-and-processed-cheese-cheesiness he can't live out loud.

"Okay," Mason says. Grey's smiling eyes affirm Mason's words. Willie looks skeptical.

Sebastian turns on his heels. He takes a deep breath, stuffs his hands into his pockets, and strides over to the shop.

"Can I have a—?"

"Vanilla and chocolate swirl, right?" Sebastian props his hip against the order window counter like a smooth criminal. Emir sizes him up. Sebastian licks his lips. Emir raises his eyebrow.

"Uh..."

"Still your favorite, right?" Sebastian's trying not to seem too hopeful.

"No." Emir turns back to Barb and says, "Actually, can I have a scoop of butter pecan?"

Barb, along with her husband Shea, owns Clovers and Sprinkles. They have an agreement: Barb, with her sweet, kind, wrinkled face, mans the till while Shea, who has a penchant for mumbling four-letter words in his Irish brogue, scoops the ice cream. Sebastian's pretty sure Barb wears the pants in their relationship, though.

Sebastian's an absolute idiot. After all these years, Emir couldn't possibly like the same ice cream flavors. He almost misses it when Barb asks, "Anything for you, Bastian?"

"He'll have two scoops of cookie dough ice cream in a waffle bowl," says Emir before Sebastian's tongue remembers motor skills. Emir wiggles two fingers confidently. "My treat."

Sebastian does a double take. Of course Sebastian's still the same, boring guy he was when they were kids, while Emir, who doesn't like the same ice cream flavors, who's semi-dated a guy, *who has had sex with a guy*, has changed.

Emir asks, "Hey, are you okay?"

No. Sebastian wipes at the tingling sweat at his hairline. Eventually, he remembers why he's standing in line with Emir. "You don't usually come to town."

Emir shrugs, an apple-red blush blooming through his cheeks. "Yeah, my mom says I need to try harder to socialize," he says. "And I thought, well, it was time to be around. To *try*, like Zach said."

Sebastian nods like a happy stoner. He likes that every moment with Emir is like being on a rollercoaster for the first time, minus the wanting to throw up bit. "Cool," he says.

Ten feet away, Grey clears her throat.

"Um, my friends," Sebastian jerks his head to where Grey is waving like a crazed Nick Jonas fan, "would like you to join us."

Emir pales.

Reality sinks in. Sebastian's heart does a trip-skip-flatline. "Hey," he says, fingers catching Emir's elbow, "It'll be fine, okay? They're harmless."

Emir's mouth twists skeptically.

"Okay, Mason is a bit much. But Willie and Grey are cool. And—" Sebastian pauses, aware his next few words will be too gooey-pathetic. "I'd love it if you came over."

10cc is singing about not being in love over the speakers as Emir whispers, "Okay."

"Okay," Sebastian repeats. He might be brain-dead. His fingers skim the meat of Emir's palm. He almost grabs Emir's hand.

"Thanks," says Emir. He takes their ice creams from Barb. His eyebrows silently direct Sebastian to lead the way.

Sebastian does, fingers tingling the entire time.

"Shah, you walk amongst the living." Mason greets them with spread arms and a teasing grin.

Eyes lowered, Emir stands close to Sebastian. Sebastian sneaks a hand behind him and rubs circles into the small of Emir's back.

Willie eyes them. "Welcome to the pits of hell, Emir."

Sebastian says, "Better known as the geeks of the team," as his friends shuffle and squeeze to make space on the bench for them.

"Speak for yourself!" cries Mason. "I'm the top of the food chain around here."

Grey sighs. "Face it, you're a bottom-dweller now that you hang with me."

Mason mocks her, sticking his tongue out. She chucks rainbow sprinkles in his hair. Willie hefts his legs up; the backs of his knees cross Grey's lap and his Vans rest on Mason's thighs, while Mason and Grey bicker.

Sebastian considers disowning all of them.

But then Emir says, "Well, I obviously bring the group's loser level up five points for having better hair than Riley." Grey nearly spills her ice cream giggling.

Squinting, Mason points his spoon at Emir. He grins. "You can stay. I like you."

Emir relaxes against Sebastian's side.

Well, it's decided then. This isn't the worst idea Grey's come up with.

It's a hard fit, five teens stuffing their faces with ice cream on one bench, but they make it work, mostly. It takes some Cirque du Soleil maneuvers, with Willie spread out in Grey's lap and Sebastian smooshed in the middle, Emir's thigh pressed tightly to his, but Sebastian's not complaining.

He's overwhelmed with laughter.

It's Willie's fault. For a half hour, he's been telling grand tales of their adventures, each more embarrassing than the last. Sebastian could do without remembering that time he drank too many wine coolers and took a dare to do keepie-uppies naked. But Grey's face is streaked with fat tears. Mason is choking. Emir is guffawing, his face pressed to Sebastian's shoulder. Sebastian can deal.

Mason and Willie argue over their respective teams. Willie stalks FC Dallas and Mason has had a man-crush on Beckham since puberty, so things get heated quickly.

"You're both wrong," Grey says. "It's all about Kansas City."

Willie scoffs at her. "Who made you the authority?"

Grey says, like a badass, "I just *am*."

"Shut up," Mason says, no heat in his voice. He nudges her, and she quickly turns pink. Mason rolls his eyes when he notices.

Sebastian leans on Emir as Willie continues with another story.

"—and then, like Charlie Brown going to kick a football, the douchebag misses a free kick. It was epic." Willie's doubled over, wheezing as he talks. "*He* went flying but the ball didn't move."

Sebastian never gets tired hearing about Mason's first game, especially not the way Willie tells it.

"Didn't Coach bench you?" Grey asks.

"Twice!" Willie howls. "I don't know why Coach kept putting him back in."

Mason says, smugly, "He knew I was an all-star even back then."

"Or," Willie drags out the 'r' as he elbows Mason's side, "we had three players out with mono thanks to the lovely Cara Beckman."

Sebastian and Mason both make a face. Cara Beckman was a junior cheerleader with excessively teased hair and a thing for athletes. She tried flirting with Sebastian a few times, something he found amusing.

It's sticky-warm. Mason flicks sweaty dark locks out of his eyes. He says, barely annoyed, "Okay, enough of that, William."

Willie's face is scandalized. "Uncool, Riley."

The moon is out. A fistful of stars accompanies it, but there's hardly enough light for Sebastian to truly enjoy Emir's face as he laughs. He likes the crow's feet around Emir's eyes. Dark stubble makes the pink of his mouth stand out.

"Um, *staring*," Emir whispers. His tongue has a dollop of ice cream on it when he sticks it out at Sebastian.

"Sorry."

Emir says, "I didn't say I had a problem with it," and Sebastian sags with—he doesn't know. He still hasn't figured it out. They're friends, from what he can tell, but there's also more. Possibly. Sebastian *wants* more.

Sam made the first move on him. Sam told him she was his girlfriend. Sam said, "I love you" first, words she didn't mean. Sam broke up with him. First by text and then in person. His reference points when it comes to dating are pretty messed up, so he's not sure how to approach discussing this with Emir.

Now isn't the time, though. Not with Emir amused at something Willie's animatedly explaining, laughing at Mason's jokes, or putting a hand over Grey's knee. This is Emir, as himself. Sebastian's scared of ruining that.

He waits for his moment to direct Emir's attention toward him. It happens when his friends talk college, a conversation Sebastian's avoiding like bird flu. Sebastian scoops up a spoonful of ice cream and knocks his knee against Emir's. When Emir looks at him, Sebastian holds out the spoon. Emir smiles slowly.

"Hey," Sebastian says, softly, as he feeds Emir, "They like you."

Emir mashes ice cream around with his tongue. "How can you tell?"

"I just *can*."

It's a good enough reason. He scoops more ice cream. Humming and nodding, Emir pops his mouth open. Sebastian has better reasons, like how Mason hasn't once been unnecessarily snarky with Emir, or how Willie's yapping like there's a fire sale on all their top-priority secrets, but he's enjoying the glow that radiates from Emir.

Acceptance has an amazing effect on people who pretend they don't need it.

Emir says, "They're pretty cool."

"Yeah?"

Emir shrugs, then nods.

"Oh shit, Shah, did you ever hear about the time our boy Hughes was so nervous dancing with this girl that he blew chunks all over her dress, at her *birthday party*?"

Correction: Sebastian's friends are the worst.

 23

SEBASTIAN IS SPRAWLED ON HIS back, in bed, tossing a soccer ball in the air, then catching it. It's their last Sunday at camp, but he's been spaced out since dinner. Something about a good meal and a heap of anxiety puts him under. Only a week of camp remains, then school starts in two weeks. Sebastian isn't ready for camp to end.

He's not ready to face his future, whatever that looks like.

The window is cracked open. It's muggy tonight, and the inside of their cabin smells like Willie's filthy socks. They're his "lucky" socks, so Sebastian's making an exception, but they're rank. He tolerates so much in the name of friendship.

Outside, Willie and Hunter lead a charge toward the lake; their howls are louder than the chirping symphony of crickets and creepy owl hoots.

"No skinny-dipping!" yells Hunter.

"Boo, Hunter, you're such an asswipe about nudity," Jack complains.

"Actually," Hunter says, breathless, "I just don't want to see your pale, flat ass anymore. I get enough of it in the showers."

Willie's laugh is echoed by the others before their voices drift out of earshot.

Their last traditional bonfire night will be Friday, the day before they head home. It'll be monumental, but it also means Sebastian still has time for camaraderie. It's why he's not pressuring himself to drag his ass out of bed and join the cavalry.

He takes deep breaths. Tosses the ball up. Catch and repeat.

Sebastian refuses to call this this sulking, despite humming Bon Iver and Crowded House, the music of the sulk people. It's introspection. A bit of reflection is good, in doses. Besides, Sebastian figures the longer he does this, the faster he'll fall asleep. Practices are grueling this close to the end, and he could use the extra rest.

"Son of a—!"

Sebastian's head snaps toward the window, where Emir is crawling in—and then crashing to the floor.

Emir's a pile of upside-down, skinny limbs, grumbling "Stupid window, stupid camp" as he rolls to his stomach. He stands and dusts off his shorts. At least Emir's scowl isn't directed at Sebastian. *This time*, he reminds himself.

Emir stops straightening out his jersey with a sheepish smile. "Well, hey."

Sebastian's brow rises. "What's up?" He's transfixed by Emir's fluffy hair. The lamp sweeps honeyed light over Emir's brown skin and softens the tense line of his shoulders. Sebastian turns the soccer ball like a globe between his hands. "Everything okay?"

"You mean besides your window trying to kill me?" Emir waves an arm behind himself. "Yeah, I just…"

When Emir's voice drifts off, Sebastian squints at the jersey that's too big for Emir's slight frame, and then reality smacks him. Emir's wearing *Sebastian's* jersey, the one he keeps hung up in his locker. Nothing has ever been so poorly-fitting and arousing at the same time.

"I borrowed it," Emir says, one finger hooked in the collar, pulling.

Sebastian resists saying *You stole it* because his chest is tight, half with pride, the rest with confusing fondness. "Cool." His mouth turns up happily. "People might talk if they see you in it."

"I'm used to people talking about me."

Sebastian snorts. Emir isn't rejecting the idea of people assuming something's going on between them. That threatens to make Sebastian get on one knee for more than one reason.

Emir rocks on his heels and pulls on the jersey's hem. He's fidgeting like a child who needs to use the bathroom. He *looks* the way Sebastian *feels*. "So. Are you busy?"

"Pretty un-busy," Sebastian says. He drops the ball to make a grand sweep of the room with his arms.

Emir's eyes are blown black with a hint of gray remaining. He gives Sebastian a loaded look, one of those "we need to talk" expressions.

Sebastian's chest tightens. Maybe this is it. Maybe Emir isn't comfortable with how Grey seems to be catching on. Or how Sebastian got a little too bold the other night after ice cream, blatantly ditching his friends to walk Emir back to his cabin.

Is Emir calling it quits on their non-relationship, or whatever this is?

"What is it?"

Emir stares at his hands. His eyes gradually lift. The pinched corners of his mouth relax. He says, "I was thinking about something." Artificial light dances over his softly dilated eyes.

"Yeah, sure." Sebastian waits, holding his breath.

Emir stuffs a hand in his pocket. He yanks out something; his white-knuckled fist is closed. He tosses an object on the bed near Sebastian's hip.

An ache spreads through Sebastian's belly, but it's not panic, not when he identifies the object as a condom. He's on autopilot, trading glances between the crinkled foil and Emir's eyes. He believed Emir wanted to cut things off, but Emir's jumpy about approaching the topic of sex with Sebastian. Go figure.

Shyly, Emir says, "So what do you think?"

"Like, right now?"

Emir shrugs, not making a fuss. But it's a pretty big deal to Sebastian. He's nearly choking on his own spit.

Emir says, "If you're interested."

Sebastian is seventeen, perpetually horny, and this is *Emir*, of course he's interested! Voicing that intelligently is a completely different matter, though. He nods and chews hard enough on his lower lip to draw blood. He pats an empty spot on the bed. "Now is good."

Heat flashes across Emir's cheeks. It's the first time Emir has been this shy around him in forever. He squirms, thumbs hooked into the waistband of his shorts, and—*Okay, this is happening.*

Sebastian's keyed up. His brain is fried. His fingers wrap around Emir's wrist and give a small tug until Emir falls forward.

"Whoa." Emir has his palms flat on either side of Sebastian's head, half straddling him, and his eyebrows touch Sebastian's hairline.

"Sorry."

"No, you're not," Emir accuses, amused.

"You're right."

Sebastian doesn't know where to put his hands. Great. He's every bit the virgin Mason teases him about being. A frustrated wrinkle appears between Emir's eyebrows before he's inclining until they're chest to chest, their noses almost touching. Sebastian goes for his hips, a safe bet.

"I can't stop thinking about you. All the bloody time," whispers Emir huskily. He gets a hand under the collar of Sebastian's shirt; his thumb ghosts the curve of Sebastian's collarbone. "It's proper annoying."

"Is that a compliment or an insult?"

"Both," Emir rasps. He shivers when Sebastian's fingers curl into the waistband of his shorts.

"Good." Sebastian pulls. "I'd hate to think you were losing your touch."

Something dark and hungry glazes Emir's eyes. "How did this bloody happen?"

"Not sure."

Emir's lips part. Sebastian palms his cheek; the stubble is scratchy and rough against his skin. Emir turns his head enough for Sebastian's thumb to nudge his lips. His eyes flicker shut.

Sebastian whispers, "Are you mad it did?"

"Yes. No. How the hell am I supposed to know?"

Sebastian has no clue himself. But he figured Emir has more common sense than he does. Maybe they're both two extremely lost teenagers? Maybe, when they're older, they still won't have it all figured out. It's not something Sebastian needs to dwell on because he's in bed, with a guy.

This isn't about reflection. This is scratching an itch. It's sex, and Sebastian doesn't need to overthink it.

They kiss. It takes them a moment to find a rhythm between mouths and bodies. Emir's hand is flat against Sebastian's chest. Sebastian has fingers in Emir's hair. Their foreheads thump at a wrong angle. Emir hisses "Ouch," but then Sebastian attacks his mouth, and they're good again.

Not perfect, but imperfectly amazing.

Sebastian is wasted on bliss. His legs get caught in his stupid jeans. Emir reclines, biting his lip, and shoves the condom into Sebastian's open palm.

No turning back.

He gazes into Emir's glassy eyes, which are bright like stars. Emir's right. Girls can be handsome and boys—*boys like Emir*—can be beautiful too.

Sebastian gets his shirt off and goes for Emir's—nope, *his*—jersey next, but Emir swats his hands away. "Can I—" Emir pauses, inhaling. "I want to keep it on."

Sebastian blinks so hard fizzy dots cloud his vision. His fingers release the hem of the jersey; his hands drop onto his belly. Emir's hunched over; the lamp casts pale light across his features. His breaths come in short bursts. Sebastian nods. "Yeah, that's—that's hot."

Fluttering eyelashes and crooked lips are Emir's only response.

"I've never done this," says Sebastian. Leaving that out was an option but, if he's bad at this, he at least owes Emir the truth. "Not with a guy or a girl, so this has major chances of sucking." Sebastian winces at his own words.

Emir's eyes are amused.

Perfect, Sebastian *is* a joke.

Inching closer, Emir says into Sebastian's mouth, "You won't." Before Sebastian can protest, he whispers, "Trust me; it's not hard to figure out."

Sebastian's calmer, something he never imagined after his last admission. But that's Emir's fault. He *hates* Emir Shah for making him this hungry for anyone, ever. He's going to write a list of all the ways Emir has screwed up his life, starting with this moment.

Sebastian slept through Sex Ed his sophomore year. He tenses trying to figure out the condom. Emir doesn't comment.

"Ready?"

Emir rolls his eyes like he can't *believe* Sebastian. Sebastian doesn't mind. This is all he's ever wanted.

⚽

SEBASTIAN IS HARDCORE SMILING.

It's an amazing feat, since he's breathing so hard he sounds asthmatic. Emir's laughing into a pillow next to him. Fortunately, considering Sebastian already lacks an ego, Emir isn't laughing *at* him. His blush is only an aftereffect of what just happened. The incredible, toe-curling thing that just happened. And, no, he isn't going to tell anyone he thought that, ever.

Sebastian is sprawled on his back. Emir's flat on his stomach. Sebastian's arm is still caught under him, and there's a searing line of heat where their thighs touch under the sheets. The open window provides minimal circulation without the usual nightly draft. His nose wrinkles at the cabin's new scent: sweat and an earthy, boyish smell.

"Are you okay?"

Emir turns enough for Sebastian to have a nice view of his elated eyes.

Yeah, Sebastian feels like that too. Like someone just cracked open his whole world, poured a mountain of candy at his feet, and told him to have at it. He's *stoned* on how great the last twenty minutes of his life were. He withholds that from Emir, though.

"Stay here?"

"Are you sure?" Emir's eyes are hesitant.

Sebastian clears his throat. "Positive." When Emir's lips open to protest, Sebastian says, firmer, "Emi, *stay here.*"

Emir nods; his eyes begin to crinkle. He tentatively shifts closer. Sebastian yanks him the rest of the way. Emir's face smooshes in his neck. Sebastian ignores his slight embarrassment and presses a kiss to the top of Emir's head.

It takes all of five minutes for Emir's breaths to even out. Sebastian grins, smug; Emir has no problem falling asleep when he's in Sebastian's arms.

A roaring yawn escapes Sebastian. Sleep doesn't follow. His eyes follow the haunting shadows tree limbs create on his ceiling. Emir's breath tickles his jaw. His mind is currently involved in a high-speed, Olympic-level ping pong game. How long has he wanted this: a guy to make his heart race and move slow tempo at the same time? Sex with Emir was—well, he just went with it. No overthinking involved. It's a missing piece of himself finally shoved into place.

Emir's hazy in Sebastian's peripheral vision: a mix of sepia skin and dark hair. Sebastian strains to get a better view. Emir's eyelashes flutter every few breaths, but he's mostly still and content. Obviously, Emir isn't affected by the fact that they just had sex. So why is Sebastian sweating the small stuff?

And just like that, apprehension subsides, and Sebastian's okay. He's more than okay. Emir is still here, in his arms. Sebastian might not be an authority on great acts of intimacy, but they did something pretty amazing tonight. So what if a tiny bit of vulnerability is scratching at his skin? He's fine with panicking a little. Emir, who is major-league stubborn and a hair shy of being an asshole, panics sometimes too.

It's okay. He tightens his arms around Emir. It's cool that *everyone* has their moments of overthinking.

⚽

SEBASTIAN STARTLES OUT OF A dream about soccer balls and cookies having a dance-off to the music of *Grease*, sits up, and peers at the cabin doorway. Specifically, at Willie leaning there.

The moon is barely a crescent tonight. Willie's silhouette is bathed in silver starlight. Sebastian swallows; his mouth is cottony, and his throat is tight. Crossing his arms, he pulls his knees to his chest.

Willie cocks his head just enough to highlight his blank expression. His curious blue eyes settle on Emir. He's still unconscious, curled around one of Sebastian's pillows.

"I, uh…"

Sebastian's a tool. His face is hot; nerves prickle up his arms. Willie, his best friend who would fight an alien invasion for him, is staring at a mostly naked boy in Sebastian's bed. Willie, who is much more level-headed than Mason, isn't going to freak out. He's just going to blink his eyes and stare.

"Will—" Sebastian chokes on the rest. What's he going to say? That he wishes Mason had never blurted out Willie's "thing" for him? That he just wants things to go back to normal? Sebastian has no clue what "normal" is supposed to be anymore.

Whatever is happening between Hunter and Willie now doesn't eliminate what Willie felt for Sebastian, does it? Do people simply get over crushes on their best friends by snapping their fingers? It can't be that easy.

Willie obliterates most of Sebastian's anxiety by smiling. He says, "I'm gonna go stay at Hunter's tonight. If that's cool?"

Sebastian nods.

"Looks like you could use some privacy, bro."

Next to Sebastian, Emir's mouth is parted; little breaths come out. His fingers are curled against the sheets. Sebastian lifts his eyes. "Is that okay?"

"Definitely."

Willie treads quietly around the room. He takes his laptop, leaves his iPod.

"So." Sebastian's being an idiot. He's about to open a big, ugly book of topics they've been dancing around. "Are we good?" slips out of his mouth before he can stop himself.

Willie rotates on his heels. He strides to Sebastian's bed. Dread wrecks Sebastian's stomach. This is when Willie finally goes Incredible Hulk.

Instead, he ruffles Sebastian's hair and says, "Absolutely, bro. I'm happy for you."

Fighting off a need to puke, Sebastian whispers, "Good."

Before he walks away, Willie flicks Sebastian's forehead. "But next time, put a sock on the door. You know the rules, man." He waves a hand at Emir. "Seriously, things could've gotten *really* weird if I walked in on that."

Sebastian smiles so wide his vision goes blurry. Willie doesn't hate him. They're friends. No matter what outrageous decisions he makes in life, there are still people who will always accept him: ones that'll punch him, hug him, and tell him corny jokes.

Willie salutes him at the door, then shrugs his bag higher on his shoulder.

The door shuts, and Sebastian whispers, "Thanks, Willster," to the shadows.

 24

SEBASTIAN LEARNED FRESHMAN YEAR THAT all the best trash talk doesn't actually happen on the pitch.

It happens in the locker room.

The greatest shit-talking, towel-snapping, pranks, stories about getting laid, and bad jokes about a guy's junk all go down around shower stalls and slamming lockers. Occasionally, one cerebral player gets in another player's head, using words to knock him off his game in order to steal his starting spot. It's a team sport, but everyone wants to be the star sometime.

Sebastian accepts this. But today, for whatever reason, he's just not in the mood.

He yanks off his shirt. It's soiled with grass, dirt, and sweat, a very rank combo. He pulls a new one from his locker and sniffs the underarm. Clean. He's between practices, so he doesn't bother with a shower. Coach Patrick is making them sleep, eat, and drink grass through their last days at camp.

"If you want to win a championship, you've got to sacrifice a nap or two," Coach shouts every morning during laps. After lunch, it's the same thing. He's no Alex Fergusson, but he inspires most of the guys to power through drills.

Willie's passing out chilled bottles of water. Sebastian snatches one with a nod of appreciation. Willie's expression is easygoing.

He says, "Don't choke," when Sebastian cracks the top and guzzles as if he's been in the desert. He adds a rude gesture that Sebastian supposes is a reference to oral sex. Sebastian's too zoned out to give a decent comeback, but Willie waves this off with disappointed eyes.

Sebastian can't help it; he sucked today. He couldn't block any of Mason's shots. The freshmen are a bunch of uncoordinated minions and Gio's passing is garbage. Sebastian's blowing this whole "future captain" thing. He's not bothered by that; nausea gurgles up any time he puts too much thought into it. Sebastian's not ready.

To his left, the defenders are huddled around one of the benches. Sebastian sips his water. Carl, hard features accented by his crewcut, is leading the talk.

"With Will out for the season because of his knee, we're screwed," says Carl, hunched forward. He's sweaty and sunburned on his nose.

"Shit." Gio leans on a locker.

Rollins, a freshman winger, asks, "He can't tough it out a few games?" He pushes damp black hair behind his ear.

"No way." Carl's face is more pinched than usual. "Dude's toast. Done for. The body's gone cold, my brother." The guy likes his hyperbole, something Sebastian learned in freshman gym when he nailed Carl during a friendly baseball game. Carl rolled around the field for half an hour, claiming a dislocated shoulder.

Rollins sighs. "Damn."

That's the thing about Willie; he's loved by the newbies, too.

Pressing his brow on his forearm, Sebastian rests against a closed locker. Coach Rivera was the one who told him, not Willie.

Sebastian doesn't blame Willie, though. Being told your high school sports career and any future plans to play have gone up in smoke is pretty heavy. Sebastian would be in far worse shape; he commends Willie's upbeat attitude.

Hunter walks up, towel hanging from his neck. "We've got a good replacement," he says.

Carl growls under his breath. "You're effin' brain-dead."

"Who?"

Hunter turns to Gio. "Emir."

"Shah," Carl says, incredulous. "Can you believe that shit? You can't replace Will with *that guy*."

"Why not? He's got the skill."

Sebastian peeks over his shoulder. Carl's upper lip is curled. He wants to put his fist through Carl's face, but he's staying out of it. Carl's a jerk. At least the whole squad isn't on his side.

"I dunno," Rollins says. "I saw him keeping up with Zach. He's cool."

Carl points a thick finger in Rollins' face. "No one asked you, frosh." He turns to Hunter. "He's a *flake*. Most of us don't hang with him at school, anyway."

Sebastian's left hand clenches into a fist. Carl's still mouthing off, and Hunter is arguing back, but with less heat. Carl needs to shut his stupid mouth. And then it hits Sebastian: Carl's second string, and the next in line for Willie's position. Emir on the team means less playing time for him. And that's so ugly, because they're a team. One for all, and all that shit.

"What about you, Hughes?" Carl sniffs; his face looks warped when Sebastian turns around. "We can survive without Shah, right?"

Sebastian's eyes narrow.

And it's as if Carl's aware he hit a nerve, because he says, "Shah's not *my* teammate," with a venomous smirk.

Heart hammering in his ears, Sebastian stalks up to Carl. He spits, "I think you should shut the hell up and quit badmouthing him."

"Why?" Carl's not as tall as Sebastian. He has to tilt his chin up to stare Sebastian in the eyes. "Shah got you sweet on him or something?"

"No, I stick up for *my team*. He's one of us."

"Sounds like he's got a stick up you."

It's hard for Sebastian to ignore the catcalls around them. His nails are digging into his palm. He imagines his knuckles bloody and Carl laid out on the cement.

Do it.

Carl shows his teeth. "He's *not* one of us, Hughes." He takes one small step closer to Sebastian. "He's never been like us."

To Lily's utter delight, Sebastian's never been in a real fight, just a few scuffs and scrapes like all kids, nothing serious. He's willing to break her poor heart to fracture Carl's jaw.

"What's that mean?"

"He doesn't get us, and we don't get him. Two totally different sides of the world."

"So, being different isn't allowed on this team anymore?" Sebastian says, glowering. "Because Hunter is black. Gio is Hispanic. Oh, and Emir is Pakistani." He steps forward, leaning into Carl's face. "And Willie is gay, if that's a problem."

"Nope."

Sebastian nods, once. "Then shut the hell up, because this is a family. We're not douchebags or superior to anyone, got it?"

"I don't want *him* in this family."

That voice in the back of Sebastian's head grows louder: *Do it.* His hands are numb, white-knuckled. A few other players join the crowd around them. Mason's pushing through the mass of bodies. To his right, Emir is rigid; his eyes are dark slits.

Sebastian turns his glare back on Carl. "Screw you, Tiller," he says, seething. "You don't know him."

"What, you want us all to have a group hug and pretend this isn't how it goes? Team sports doesn't mean everyone makes it at the end of the day. So now we're playing rookies as starters just because? I'm not down with that, Hughes."

Beating Carl up would be a mercy deal. The guy doesn't have too many allies, and Sebastian can't be the only one fed up with his tireless complaining. He has no sympathy for Carl, or his inability to lock down a starting position. That's no excuse to be a dick.

Not all of Sebastian's anger is directed toward Carl or is about Emir. This is for all the guys who shoved Sebastian around. For the ones who made him dislike his appearance. The kids chanting "Bastian the Trashcan." For every asshole who sneered self-righteously at him, at his friends.

"Your *friend*," Carl says, grinning, "can ride the bench by himself like he does during lunch."

The room's attention falls on Emir now. He looks away. Sebastian's rage finally hits a new peak.

"Fuck you."

Sebastian doesn't know where that came from. His chest cracks open with pride. It's as if he spat those two words at everyone who's a douche like Carl.

"Yeah, fuck you too, Hughes. You're not the captain," Carl barks.

Sebastian's fists shake at his sides. Coach Patrick doesn't tolerate violence, not unless it's on the field. All's fair on the green. Sebastian just needs something to put his fist to. A wall, a door, whatever.

He's giving in to the chant in his head: *Do it, do it, do it…*

"Move!" Coach Patrick barks like a rabid dog. Players are shoved around. His hand presses flat against Sebastian's chest. His other hand grabs Carl's shirt. He shoots Sebastian a glare. "Since you half-wits want to forget we have a game in a few weeks, we'll skip lunch for another round on the pitch! You want to fight? Fight exhaustion, because I'm going to wear your asses thin for this." When no one moves, Coach barks, "Now! Gear up."

A mass exodus breaks out. Sebastian can't identify who's glaring at him and who's looking at him with compassion. Breathing roughly, he slumps into a locker.

Coach seethes. "I expect more, Hughes, a lot more." He stalks off, and Sebastian nearly crumbles under the weight of that last glare.

Sebastian drags a hand down his face. He tilts his head until fluorescent lights blur in his wet eyes. Coach hasn't been this pissed in forever. Sebastian hasn't let a guy get in his head like that since childhood. Dealing with bullies was easier back when he was undersized. He couldn't fight back.

Today, Sebastian was ready to *crush* Carl. What kind of candidate for captain is he?

"Dude," says Zach, patting Sebastian's shoulder. Sebastian can't look at him, but he sounds shocked. *Join the club.*

"C'mon, Bastian," Mason whispers. "Shake it off."

The scuff of cleats on the ground signals Mason's exit. One by one, Sebastian's failing his friends. When he finally raises his eyes, Emir is in front of him. His arms are folded and he's not saying a word.

"What?"

Emir's mouth parts, but he only sighs. His eyes are drained of brightness. Without a word, he stomps out of the locker room.

Yeah, I had that one coming, too.

When the room is empty, Sebastian pushes off his locker. He turns, rolls his shoulders, and then slams his fist into a locker door. His knuckles throb, but at least his anger is centered on the pain. It's a shame, though. Relief doesn't come.

"Is this who you are?"

Nope.

"Is this the type of player or person you want to be?"

Not at all.

"I don't understand. Where's the real Sebastian Hughes?"

I have no idea.

Sebastian's not actually answering Coach O'Brien. He's been letting O'Brien chew him out for ten minutes now. It's hot, day-old vomit looks better than he does, and, to top it off, they had another scrimmage. It was a repeat of Team Drews versus Team Hughes, but this time they lost epically. Hell, he let Robbie make two goals on him. *Robbie*. He never lets Robbie sink one in. Sebastian has no explanation.

Their hard work over the summer is circling the drain.

His brain can't come up with a damn thing to say to O'Brien or Rivera to make himself look better.

O'Brien sighs. "We can't beat the Spartans like this." He squeezes Sebastian's shoulder, then says, carefully, "And you're just—this isn't good for you."

Obviously. Sebastian hardens the line of his mouth and stares at the pitch. He doesn't want to have this conversation. "I'm sorry," he whispers.

"Okay." O'Brien stares at him. "You've got this, Sebastian. You do."

Sebastian doesn't agree. He feigns a smile and skulks off. Cement is in his shoes as he climbs the bleachers. Willie passes him a water. Sebastian collapses and tries to absorb Willie's genuine positivity as their shoulders knock.

"Feeling the burn yet?"

Choking on his first gulp of water, Sebastian flips him off. Willie's humor could cure the zombie plague. Sebastian wipes his mouth with his wrist. "How about you?" His eyes drop to Willie's knee.

"Best I can be."

Sebastian's not going to pry, because it's Willie's business and because Sebastian hasn't been the best at telling people his own secrets.

Willie's spine is curved on the empty bleachers behind him. "It's bullshit, but I'm okay." Oakville's cloudless sky means the sun embellishes the blueness of his eyes, like the petals of forget-me-nots. "Coach says I can still suit up every game, cheer you guys on from the bench."

Sebastian squeezes Willie's good knee.

"It sucks," Willie says, "but it's not the end of the world."

Sebastian envies Willie's confidence. It *is* the end of the world, to have something you love taken from you. Sebastian's suffocating all the time, trying to get his head around what'll happen in a couple of months when soccer's over. He has no idea *who* he is without this sport.

It takes some effort, but Sebastian manages not to frown. Willie's mind-reading talent has probably already figured him out. He asks, "When?"

"Mom's gonna try to schedule the operation before school starts."

Sebastian is ripe with sweat, but he doesn't care; he drops an arm around Willie's shoulders. "We'll figure it out."

"You'll bring my homework while I recover?"

"Yep. As long as you don't ask me to help you with Shakespeare."

"Because you suck at Shakespeare."

"We *both* suck at Shakespeare, Willster."

Willie's smile tucks into his eyes, creasing the corners. "True story."

Sebastian rests his chin on the top of Willie's hair so Willie is half folded in a brotherly embrace. Leave it to Willie to take Sebastian's mind off a shitty day.

⚽

"Mason Riley, front and center!"

Grey stands at the center of the pitch. She's wearing a poorly-fitting team uniform, soft curls in a messy ponytail, cleats, and a warrior's face. It's very badass.

Most of the team's spread out on the bleachers, still licking their wounds from practice. They lift their heads as soon as she barks. Gio whispers, "¡Qué mierda!" and Rivera points a warning finger at him with slit eyes.

Grey doesn't budge. Her hands are on her hips, and a soccer ball is cradled in the crook of her arm.

"She looks scary." Willie's in awe.

"She *is* scary," Sebastian whispers.

Mason's sitting cross-legged on the grass with his back to Sebastian, but he's bug-eyed, slack-jawed, and pale. At least, that's how Sebastian imagines him.

Grey's eyes shrink until Sebastian can't find the green in them.

"Sweet baby Jesus, Mother Mary, and all the freakin' saints," says Mason. He chucks his water bottle and scrambles to his feet. His head snaps in Zach's direction when he and a few others hum "Build Me Up, Buttercup," and they quickly go quiet. If his iron-stiff shoulders tell anything, Sebastian would conclude that Mason's pissed, and a little afraid too.

"What's she gonna do?"

"I don't know," Sebastian says to Willie. "But I'm gonna like it."

"What the hell…" Mason stops short of Grey. "…are you *doing?*"

Grey's lips twitch. She's not fazed by Mason's hissing or flailing arms. She has reached hardcore, superhero levels of greatness.

"*Grace*—"

"I'm done with your bullshit, Riley."

"Uh, language." Kyle chortles from three levels below Sebastian, who flings his empty water bottle at the back of Kyle's head. He's pleased when Willie chuckles.

"Okay, okay." Mason raises his hands, palms facing out as if he's surrendering. "Point taken. You're a big girl, and I'm—"

"Going to have a scrimmage game with me, right here and now. One-on-one." Grey spins the soccer on one finger. "First goal wins, and winner calls their prize."

Mason tosses his arms up like a Muppet and shouts incredulously, "You're so weird!"

"If I win, we go on a date."

A couple of catcalls and some wolfish yells of "You go girl" break out from the players. Willie cheers, spirit fingers and all. Yep, this is going to be awesome and bad.

"Have you lost your mind? Your father is—" Mason waves a hand behind him. Leaning forward, elbows on his knees, Coach Patrick is on the bottom bleacher.

Grey clears her throat. "Coach—my *dad* has been nothing but supportive of me since I was a kid." Her voice start to rise. "He's always made sure I had what I needed, and he tells me all the time to go after what I want, no matter the cost."

Coach squares his shoulders.

"Guess what I want?"

Mason mumbles, "A lobotomy."

His bitchiness slides right off her back. *She's evolved into Grey two-point-oh.* Sebastian tries not to groan at his own geekiness.

"A date, Riley."

"Oh, wow, isn't that romantic," Mason sneers. He snatches the ball from her. His head tips closer. "But when you lose, you back off. For good. No more heart-eyes, flirting, being all weird. I get the same treatment as the other guys, got it?"

Grey flinches. Then she tightens her mouth, nods, and backs away. She's actually going for it.

"Fifty bucks says he makes her cry." Jack chuckles.

Gio rolls his eyes. "Twenty says Coach murders him and dumps the body in the lake."

Mason and Grey stomp away from each other. Coach O'Brien charges onto the field, blowing his whistle. He lays down the rules. "Keep it clean," he says, glaring at Mason. Grey's mouth is drawn in a thin line; her eyes are still narrowed at Mason.

Sebastian bets she'll kick Mason in the junk. He *might* laugh at that. In fact, he's leaning in favor of it.

O'Brien clears out of the way. Mason moves like he's playing a practice squad. He's lazy. He tries to fake her out by going left, then right. "Come get it, Patrick."

Grey bites her lip, watching him.

"Silly girl," teases Mason. "This is the big leagues."

Grey growls, then goes after him.

Mason has sick tricks and amazing footwork. He's top in the conference for a reason. But Grey counters everything. She's on him like a cougar chasing its prey. The team *oohs* when Mason can't get around her, and Mason says, "You're not that great."

Grey slides a foot between them, tripping him up. It's legal, so O'Brien doesn't call her on it. But Mason's unprepared.

"No shit," says Smith, whistling.

Before Mason can react, Grey hooks a foot on the ball and sprints in the opposite direction.

Zach cups his hands around his mouth. "Down goes Riley!"

Sebastian bites his knuckles. Okay, he's a dick for silently rooting for Grey and not for his best friend, but Sebastian's a sucker for the underdog. Grey's making him a believer.

"You little brat!" Mason yells, trailing behind Grey, but it's too late. He's beat, and Grey is going, going, gone.

The guys are half-stunned as Grey celebrates. They give her a standing ovation. Leave it to Grey to unify this team again.

Sebastian says, "Grey Patrick is a legend." Today's a day for the record books. He mentally dubs it *The Day Mason Riley Had His Ass Handed to Him by Grey Patrick*. It's long, but catchy.

By the time Mason catches her, he's wheezing. He collapses in the grass, sprawled like a paralyzed starfish. His hair is sweat-flat across his brow; his cheeks are flushed. The clouds circle over Mason, mocking him.

"So that's what defeat looks like." Cracking up, Willie elbows Sebastian's ribs.

Grey saunters up, hands on her hips, towering over Mason. "I've watched you play for years, Riley." Curls slip from her ponytail, framing her cheeks. "I know you better than you know yourself as a player."

Mason scuffs the grass with his shoe.

"You're weak on your left side and way too confident."

"Shut up."

"You're amazing, just not perfect."

On the bleacher below Sebastian, Rollins and Mikey sit a little taller. Not many people have successfully put Mason Riley in his place. By the start of the season, Sebastian bets the freshmen will be wearing T-shirts with Grey's face on them.

Mason's slight head-turn reveals a mouth twitching into a smile. He twists, getting his elbows under him for leverage. "So, what time do you want me to pick you up?"

"Never." Grey ignores his melodramatic collapse on the green. "For years, I've let you be a jerkface because I'm younger. And because I've got a crush on you." Her voice hardens. "It sucks to be me sometimes, so I don't need you to rub my face in it."

Mason's sputtering.

Grey lifts her foot and presses it lightly against Mason's chest. "I don't want a date, Mason. I just want you to know that I accept that I'm young and I'm a weird girl." Then, she hovers closer. "Also, you just got *owned* because I'm young and a weird girl."

Mason thumps his head against the grass. "Wait, what?"

Grey's already stepping over him. She scoops up the ball and turns it between her hands. A true badass. After all, Grey just flushed Mason's reputation down the toilet. Her eyes meet Sebastian's, and she mouths "*Grey freaking Patrick.*"

Sebastian's lips split into a smile.

"That's it boys, hit the showers! Dinner's in a few." Coach's voice is stern. Grey sidles up to him. Coach hooks a big arm around her small shoulders. He whispers to her, and Grey shakes with laughter as they leave the pitch. The team follows.

"Epic," Willie says, standing carefully.

"A classic!" Hunter swoops in out of nowhere to help Willie.

Sebastian starts down the bleachers. His feet slow when his eyes find Emir, waiting: tightly-wound frame, shoulders hunched, hands shoved in the pockets of his shorts. The pinch of his mouth pulls his cheeks inward. His chin is lowered defiantly, but their eyes still meet.

"What's wrong?"

"Don't do that again," Emir says, voice scratchy, angry. "I don't need anyone saving me."

"I didn't—"

Emir cuts Sebastian off. "I've dealt with this for years, okay? Who cares if people don't like me or want to be around me?"

Sebastian's not expecting this. He still doesn't know what to expect with him. Will it be a scowling Emir or maybe a laughs-at-all-of-Sebastian's-stupid-jokes Emir?

"I'm not here to make friends," Emir says gruffly; the edges of his mouth are tight. Obviously, Sebastian's done nothing but piss Emir off since day one. "I'm here for my dad, that's it. If you're guilty over what happened a long time ago, don't drag me into it. We stopped being friends, and I *survived*."

Trying to lower his anger to a simmer, Sebastian flexes his fingers.

"Don't be a hero."

And that's what makes his blood boil. This isn't all his fault. Doesn't Emir get that? It's Sebastian's *job* to play peacemaker. He's been doing this since way before Emir decided to try out. It hasn't changed. *Sebastian hasn't changed.*

"Fine." An ache throbs from Sebastian's temples to his eye sockets. "Do whatever, *mate*, 'cause I just—I don't know what the hell I was doing. It's not like I'm your—" Sebastian can't man up enough to say the word he's supposed to.

Emir lifts his chin. "Yeah, you're *not*."

Clouds swarm overhead, hiding some of the sunlight. This is the part where Sebastian's supposed to tell Emir he expects them to still be friends when camp's over and school starts. That he hopes they'll be a lot more, too. That this isn't a summer fling, a casual hookup, and that he's tired of Emir being blasé, so unreadable that Sebastian's confused and desperate. But he's so exhausted, he can't figure out where to start.

Emir's hand sweeps over his face into his hair. When it drops away, his face is blank. He walks away without a word.

 25

THE DAYS ARE STILL HUMID and warm, but the sky turns plush pink, then deep blue-gray sooner. Sunsets bring a comfortable chill, a sure sign of an early autumn. Camp's over but for the bonfire tonight. Sebastian's managed to survive the past few days solely on routine, something he's good at. Tomorrow afternoon, they'll pile in Mason's car to go back to Bloomington.

Then it's school and a lengthy countdown to graduation.

Sebastian's been avoiding anxiety-driven thoughts about life after high school. He takes in the low sun, orange like the top of a Dum-Dum lollipop, and appreciates the steady warmth.

Classic Oakville. Next summer, who knows where he'll be, how nice the weather will be, if he'll ever feel like this again.

Sebastian wants to get wasted, not on cheap beer, but on the buzz of summer. Maybe he can get so blitzed he won't have to wake up tomorrow hungover by reality.

The pitch is green and prickly under Sebastian's hands. "What a world," he says softly. Earthy scents and dank heat fill his nose. Damp with sweat, his shirt sticks to his chest. He's bumming away the hours until dinner.

Practice today was long and grueling, but it didn't suck. The team was in sync. Sebastian thanks Grey for that.

He pulls his knees close to his chest. Absently, his fingers run a short length across the inside of his forearm. He'll have a nasty bruise tomorrow after blocking an attack from Robbie, but, whatever. It was worth it. In fact, the whole day was sweet.

"I thought you played with balls in your spare time? You suck!"

Willie says, breathlessly, "Whatever, Riley. I get no complaints about the way I *handle* balls, thank you."

Mason and Willie are having their annual keepie-uppies challenge. The contest is an excuse for Mason to show off and for Willie to prove himself. He's been saving whatever strength he has left in his knee for this day. Sebastian always wipes the green with both of them, but today he doesn't have it in him. Instead, he observes fondly.

He would've never made it on the team without them. He wouldn't have made it through *high school* without them. Maybe if he and Emir had stayed friends…

Sebastian groans. He's gone three days—*three whole days*—avoiding Emir. It's easiest during meals, since Emir never sat with them anyway, but the solo morning jogs, evenings spent in his own bed, and especially practices are all tedious and draining.

What troubles Sebastian is, he thinks he should apologize. Will it matter? Were things going to continue once the season was over and Emir wasn't out to impress his dad? Sebastian doesn't know.

And here he is again, unsure of what happens to his life after soccer. Sebastian just needs someone to give him an answer.

A clipboard thwacks on the grass next to Sebastian, followed by a groaning, disgruntled Coach Patrick. "Too old for this," says Coach, hairy legs stretched out in front of him, brim of his snapback pulled low to shade the sun.

Sebastian lifts an inquisitive eyebrow.

"I can't figure out why you always do this." Coach leans back on his hands. "What seventeen-year-old has so many moments of self-reflection?"

Coach reminds Sebastian of a TV dad, all deep speeches, then a bear hug. He goes from vicious wolverine on the pitch to Mr. Rogers without blinking an eye.

"Uh, I—"

Coach holds up a finger. "It's not bad, Sebastian, except it only happens after a bad practice or a tough game." Coach's smile deepens his crow's feet. "Remember when we played that amazing school from Chicago?"

Sebastian will never forget.

After the disastrous loss the Lions suffered, Sebastian spent an hour coughing up his guts in the stalls. Then he staked out a spot in the stadium's empty bleachers and sat for hours with his headphones, sulking. He didn't say a word for twenty-four hours.

"You're good at beating yourself up, kid." Coach drops a meaty arm around Sebastian's shoulders. "But enough is enough."

Sebastian nods, blowing out a breath to get the hair off his forehead.

"The other coaches and I have been talking." Coach pauses, staring at Mason. Sebastian's stomach clenches. Coach shakes his head, and says, "You've grown, kid. There's a bullseye on you across the conference; everyone's talking about the goalie from BHS."

Sebastian's throat is dry. He gets out, "Wow!" but it's hoarse.

"You're better than Riley," Coach says without levity. "We weren't expecting that after freshman year."

Sebastian says, "I'm not," by instinct, but Coach *tsks* at him, so he shuts his mouth.

"It was a unanimous vote. You're captain."

It doesn't sink in immediately. *Captain.* Then, the goosebumps break out like a bad rash. Numbness and relief hit Sebastian at once. He scratches his temple, trying to piece together a "thank you," but Coach beats him to it.

"They follow you," he says, nodding toward Mason and Willie. "You're the only leader they want."

Carl definitely wouldn't agree.

Coach considers him. "College scouts want you, Bastian. Treat this season right, and you can have a scholarship wherever you want."

Sebastian breaks eye contact to gaze at the sinking sun. The sky is edging toward pink. His fingers curl around prickly grass. The waning warmth cools against his neck.

Bloomington High's soccer team has a new captain. *Captain Hughes.*

A whooshing breath finally escapes him. "Thanks, Coach."

Coach grunts; his arm goes lax on Sebastian's shoulders. He's rough around the edges, intimidating, but Coach considers every one of the players his son, including pranksters like Mason. Sebastian is proud to be part of that.

Coach changes the subject. "So." Sebastian's neck hairs stand up at Coach's insightful look. "Shah, huh? Never suspected him as your type."

This moment would be much funnier if Sebastian wasn't positive he's a second away from a heart attack. He's damned, flinching at his pathetic "me neither" laugh and Coach's speculative, but amused, glare. He doesn't know what's worse, being caught by his mom making out with a girl or Coach's awareness about his pining for the guy who hates his guts. Both?

And *pining*? Jesus, Sebastian hates how his brain works.

"He's my," Sebastian chokes, tries again. "He's my friend." *And he's my type, too.* Maybe it wasn't apparent when he first realized he was into guys, but those childhood memories make Sebastian think something was there, lying dormant.

Coach hums.

Sebastian says, urgently, "I care about him, but nothing's going on." *Anymore.* He shovels a pound of regret on top of that word.

Coach rocks in place, jarring Sebastian. He says, "O'Brien is convinced he's gonna make a mean sweeper if he can keep his cool." Emir's biggest flaw. "Keep him in line."

Sebastian sputters. His hands scrabble on the grass. He can barely keep his own feelings in check. What is Coach thinking? He squeaks, "Okay." Coach peers at him, and the next few words nearly rip Sebastian's jaw off trying to get out. "But what if—what if I'm kind of in love?"

"Kind of?"

Sebastian clenches his eyes shut. He's lightheaded and obviously about to make a huge mistake. "I think I am."

It's the first time Sebastian's said it out loud to anyone, including himself. He's still figuring out his own definition of love. Shouldn't you wake up wanting nothing more than your partner's smile or affectionate eyes or fond voice? For such a sought-after emotion, love sure comes with a lot of answerless questions.

Sebastian hangs his head. "I'm supposed to lead this team, but I can't even convince them to *like* Emir. I can't tell them that *I* like Emir." He glares at the smooshed grass near his cleats. "We talk about acceptance, but it's different when you're in the position of telling these guys how to be men."

"You're not teaching anyone about manhood," Coach says. Then, in a calm, firm voice, "And you're sure as hell more than just your sexuality to them."

Sebastian ignores his irregular heartbeat. He focuses on Coach's words and on the serene but serious expression on his face.

This is more than a speech.

"When Xander was kicked off—" Coach takes a long pause. He never talks about his nephew. "Xander's so smart and a Patrick, which makes him a handsome squirt."

Sebastian's laugh vibrates deep in his chest.

Coach eyes the sunset. He always has a monologue or at least a quote in his back pocket for any occasion. But now he's searching for something. "Things don't rattle Xander. He knows who he is, always has. When he decides something, he does it because it's in every bit of his soul."

Prickly grass slips between Sebastian's fingers as his hands roam the pitch. He'd kill for some of that certainty.

"He knew he was gay. It wasn't a question or a decision," says Coach. "And he didn't hide it from my brother, his mom, or me."

"Wow."

Coach chuckles, wistful, and then he's serious again. "He questioned himself when he was kicked off the team. He hid away. He didn't want to be out and proud or even acknowledge his sexuality." Coach sniffs, and Sebastian gives him privacy by not meeting his gaze. "For the first time, my nephew was unsure *who* he was."

A familiar queasiness clenches Sebastian's stomach. It's warm, but a cold sweat is looming. He doesn't know how Coach carries on.

"I should tell all of you more often why I make this team a safe place for anyone who's considered different."

"We know."

Coach shakes his head. He's talking about more than just Sebastian, more than Willie and Mason. It's anyone who gets stamped with a label, who's predicted to fail because of society's rules, because of a stereotype.

"It isn't easy being the one coach in the district who stands up for guys like Xander," says Coach, chin lifted. "I don't let one kid walk away from my team without a chance to be himself, whether it's gay or bi or trans or whatever. I get shit too."

Sebastian's heard of the coaches who refuse to look Coach Patrick in the eye and the parents and faculty who call Coach "a supporter of sinners who'll burn in hell."

"I made a change, kid," says Coach, sighing. "I wasn't doing enough to make sure my nephew, or anyone, knows this life isn't defined by who you fall in love with."

Sebastian wants to fall on his back, stare at the darkening sky, and digest all this. *You are not defined by who you love*. It's a slogan for a poster or a T-shirt, but, holy shit, it says so much. Sebastian can see, in vibrant Technicolor, the one thing that's missing for him: *respect*. Not acceptance. Because that would mean Sebastian wants people to *approve* of him. Of his affection for Emir. He's not searching for that brand of recognition.

He wants people to respect him regardless of who he falls for.

"I do this for Xander. It's the right thing to do." Coach's arm drops from around Sebastian's shoulders. He reclines, hands supporting him, and says, "I'm not searching for sainthood. This is about people like you who need to know you're much more than you realize."

Sebastian rests his chin on his forearms. Coach is right. He doesn't tell them often enough why he does this.

"How is Xander now?"

Coach smiles widely. "He has a boyfriend and is in public school. Top of his class, on the basketball team." He chuckles. "I couldn't get him to transfer to BHS, though."

"Of course."

Coach groans, sits properly, and grabs his clipboard. "You've earned their respect and support; that's the least of your worries." He gets to his knees, then his feet. "But if you're not honest with them and honest with yourself about Shah, then you'll lose their respect."

Sebastian tenses.

"I don't condone romantic relationships on the team." Coach has that firm, "I'm the adult" expression again. Then it softens as he says, "But if you care about someone, go with your gut."

Sebastian chews on an awkward smile. Okay, talking about Emir with Coach is mostly awkward, but it doesn't beat being caught by his mom. *Nothing* beats being caught by your parents doing anything.

"Okay, Coach."

Coach dusts grass from his shorts and walks off. When he's out of sight, Sebastian's shoulders drop and he blows out a long breath.

"Okay, spill."

Sebastian rubs a hand across his face. Willie and Mason loom over him, giddy as kids at Christmas. Sebastian doesn't know whether to crack up or put them out of their misery. He opts for the latter.

"I'm captain," he says, and he can't do it without goosebumps racing up his arms.

"Bullshit," Mason says, accusingly. "Captain Hughes?"

Sebastian nods, and then yelps with laughter when they dogpile him. Mason's elbow jams his ribs. Willie knees him in the thigh. Breathless and sweaty from wrestling, they lie in the itchy grass.

"Ouch."

"You guys suck," complains Willie. "Worst friends ever."

The sky is on fire, all crimson and orange. Their breathing isn't synchronized, but it might as well be. Mason's on his left, Willie on his right. Finally drunk on summer, Sebastian tucks his hands behind his head.

After too much quiet, random conversations happen, starting with Willie's gross admission about his crush on Hunter. Okay, it's disgustingly cute. And it's the world's worst kept secret, now.

"Duh." Mason rolls his eyes. "Gonna ask him to be your *boyfriend?*"

Willie turns red, but he's already sunburned, so it's barely noticeable. He whispers, "Maybe."

Sebastian can picture Willie and Hunter being *that couple* at homecoming: matching campaign posters, kissy-faces for the coronation, a spotlit, last-dance moment at the end of the night. He says, "Will's gonna have a high school sweetheart."

"Whatever," Willie says, giggling as if he's lovesick. He changes the subject: life after graduation, Sebastian's favorite! Mason's still on the Michigan boat, possibly deferring his MLS dreams for a few years. Willie's leaning toward a technical school.

Sebastian gazes at the fading clouds. He *can* tell them, he just doesn't.

"I think," Mason stops, scratching his nose. "I want to ask Patrick out."

"Patrick Wiggins, from the track team?" asks Sebastian.

Willie gasps, "Wait, Coach Patrick?"

Mason smacks his palm on the grass. "No dumbass, *Grace*."

Willie's jaw drops, and Sebastian has to elbow him before Willie pulls it together to say, "Oh, yes. Right. Grey Patrick... the girl you hate?"

"I don't *hate* her."

"Um, hate to break it to you, dude, but—"

Mason cuts him off. "I like her, and I'm an ass, okay?"

"*Like*-like her?" asks Sebastian, for confirmation.

Mason turns his head, glaring. He might punch Sebastian, but not before he says, "I messed up. Mom would murder me if she knew I acted that way toward a sweet girl." He lowers his eyes. "Guess I'm just like my dad."

"You're not," Sebastian says. Mason's shoulder relaxes against his. "We've all screwed up, but you're not him."

"Sage words from Sebastian the Great."

Cool nicknames aside, Sebastian doesn't hesitate to punch Mason's shoulder. He's a dick, but he's improving. Maybe Grey will do him some good?

Willie, on the other hand, is a traitor to his kind. Sebastian senses the next topic coming like the killer in a horror movie. Willie opens his big mouth. "So, what's up with you and Shah?"

Sebastian squints so hard, he can shoot lasers.

"Yeah," Mason says, devious grin on his face, "are you two hooking up? Don't lie to me, man."

Sebastian angles his head to face the sky. He can't lie to them. Willie's witnessed a half naked Emir in his bed. Mason's been around so long that he's become more perceptive about Sebastian's bullshit than his own. They're his brothers, and this weight he's been carrying around just exhausts him. The clouds start to dissolve, leaving the sky an open book, and Sebastian thinks, *Why not?*

"Yeah. No." Sebastian shakes his head; his thoughts are like a derailed train. "We *were*. I fucked it up, badly. I just—" He sucks in a noisy breath. "I dunno, but I'm pretty sure it's not going to end the way I wanted."

Mason says, "Do you want me to rough him up?"

Sebastian chokes on his own spit before laughing. Tears bite at his eyes. He's not sure if they're because of Mason's offer or from relief. Telling his friends about Emir is like coming out. How did it become *that* heavy? Why do people let things so precious to them turn into dark, unbearable secrets?

Willie's fingers are simultaneously cold and perfect when they squeeze Sebastian's elbow. "Do you want us to help? We can talk to Emir, or Hunter can."

"Nope." It's an accident when the tears drip off Sebastian's eyelashes. When did he become such a drama queen? "I can handle it."

"Check you out." Mason whistles. "You came to camp a loser and you're leaving a man. Take notes, Will."

Willie stretches all the way across Sebastian to punch Mason's shoulder. They squabble like toddlers fighting over a toy, and Sebastian sighs. Part of him is submerged in guilt. Both of his best friends are willing to kidnap and torture Emir for him. What has he done for them? He hasn't been much of a friend while they've been dealing with their own romantic lives.

But then Willie says, "If you say so. But we've got your back, Bastian," and reality sinks its teeth into Sebastian's brain. Sometimes it's okay not to be the perfect best friend. Sometimes it's okay for your friends to take care of you.

Whatever vicious spring has been tightening in his chest finally uncoils. Then his eyes get a little bleary, but he doesn't wipe away the tears. These are happy ones, so it's okay. He doesn't care if crying's not considered manly. Who writes these stupid definitions of manly, feminine, beautiful, or handsome, anyway?

"Bastian, dude," Mason says, as if he's been hit with an epiphany. "You like Emir."

"Shut up, Mace."

"Skinny, quiet, uncoordinated Emir Shah."

"Okay. Point made."

"Holy shit! I didn't see that one coming."

Mason is doomed to be friendless before he graduates.

The bonfire is in a couple of hours, and then they'll pack for the ride home tomorrow. Sebastian doesn't want to move, and his friends make no effort to move either.

"We're missing dinner, fellas," says Mason in a slow, lazy drawl.

"Yeah," Willie whispers. He points upward. The sky stretches toward infinity, a tapestry of every shade of purple and blue, dotted by dim stars. "But we're not missing this."

Sebastian's cheeks press right into his eyes.

Fondly, Mason says, "Damn you, Will, and your poetic mouth."

 26

August unofficially dies after a few days of lazing around the house. Sebastian creates a comfortable dent in the living room sofa and mindlessly flips through TV shows while his parents come and go. Lily makes Sebastian help in the garden or bake cookies, anything to spend extra time with him. Oliver pats Sebastian's shoulder, talks about the trades going on in the Premier League, and catches him up on the things he missed while at camp.

Carly calls him a bum and shoves his legs off the couch to make room for herself. She always scrubs a hand through his hair before stealing the remote. Tonight, the Food Network drones. Carly asks, "All right, pup?"

Sebastian shrugs.

"How is counseling going?"

Sebastian blinks, then says, "Pretty good."

After the Carl incident and Coach's speech, Sebastian knew it was time to talk to his parents. Maybe not about *everything*, but some of his ghosts. It wasn't easy. When is telling your parents about your insecurities easy? But they were patient, understanding; that helped. Carly's calls helped. And the counseling helps, too.

"It's good. Real good," he repeats.

"Anything else?"

During their phone calls, Sebastian's considered telling her about being bi, about Emir, about totally freaking out over graduation and the foreseeable end of all his happiness. Carly isn't brilliant with advice, but she's levelheaded. Then, too, she'll call Sebastian a dumbass in the most loveable way. They've always been close.

"Last year of school," he says with a grunt, and she nods knowingly.

Carly passes him the bowl of popcorn and the remote. "Is that it?"

Sebastian hesitates. His phone vibrates in his pocket, but he doesn't answer. It'll be Mason or Willie. Carly stares at him with soft eyes and a crooked smile like their dad's. Sebastian's breaths stutter. Since he got home, he's been walking around like a zombie from *Warm Bodies*, and now he's finally awake.

"Is this about a boy?" Carly says it as though it's nothing, as though she's been waiting.

And Sebastian just shudders and nods.

Carly nods too. She squeezes the bottom of his foot and grabs a handful of popcorn with her other hand. "Yeah, that sucks," she says, turning back to the TV. "If you ever want to talk, you know. Call me, pup."

She leaves it at that. No lectures, no scary sister stink-eye for being bi, or for being a total idiot about a boy who hasn't called or texted since camp ended. Emir doesn't even have Sebastian's cell number. He never asked, and Sebastian never gave.

"Do Mom and Dad—?" Sebastian stops, barely able to get a word out.

"Nope. But let me know when you're gonna tell them." Carly angles her head, exposing her devious expression. "I want to record and post it on Snapchat."

Sebastian tosses a throw pillow at her head. He slouches, feet propped on the coffee table, and pretends he's not thinking about Emir.

It's all he thinks about.

⚽

ON THE FIRST MONDAY OF school, Willie has his surgery. Sebastian's last class is an elective course. His teacher, an elderly gym instructor, doesn't bother with roll call, so he ditches to hop into Hunter's beat-up Honda Accord. They burn down the freeway toward the hospital, jamming to Hunter's random playlists.

Hunter wears a shaky smile; he's too shy to admit he's wound up over how Willie's doing. Sebastian feels the same way. But he cracks jokes and Hunter laughs. His hands beat on the dashboard to the Fugees track Hunter's iPod cranks out.

"Nice selection, bro," he says, awed.

Hunter's fingers eventually relax on the steering wheel, creating a weird butterfly effect on Sebastian until he's mellow, too. Why haven't he and Hunter hung out before now?

"Mind if I go in first?"

They're in the main lobby, with their backs to the grumpy desk nurse who gave them shit about not being "immediate family." Hunter's a charmer when it comes to adults. And Sebastian, in his Bloomington track suit, can pull off a great Boy Scout smile.

"Nope." He smacks Hunter's arm, jostling him but earning a grin. "He's all yours."

Hunter's skin is slightly darker thanks to summer, but the faint blush blossoming on his cheeks stands out. "Okay," he says, rubbing the back of his neck. "I won't be long."

Sebastian wiggles his eyebrows suggestively, says, "Take your time," and gets reprimanded by the nurse for laughing too loudly when Hunter trips while getting away.

Comfy pumpkin-orange chairs are parked in one corner of the waiting room. Sebastian kicks his feet up on a table cluttered with boring celeb magazines. He pulls his laptop and headphones from his backpack and watches YouTube videos.

According to a very timid confession in the elevator, Hunter and Willie are boyfriends now. Sebastian can't hide his pride.

Willie's happy coasting on a wave through life. His self-confidence shows in the way he ignores anyone who gives him a sideways glare for being a too-blond white kid dating a very cute black guy. Willie doesn't give a shit. He has a middle finger for anyone demanding that he do it their way. Maybe he can tutor Sebastian on how to be a boss like that?

"He's ready to see you," Hunter says. He's mashing a text on his cell, eyebrows scrunched. He pockets his phone. "Sorry. My parents don't know everything about Willie yet."

"Ah."

"I'm gonna tell them," Hunter says quickly.

Sebastian holds his hands up, eyebrows raised. "It's cool." Actually, it's a relief that he's not the only one carrying secrets around. Sebastian stands and packs up his things. "I'll keep it short and sweet," he says, patting Hunter's shoulder.

Hunter sags, but grins. He grabs Sebastian's elbow before he can get too far. "Listen," he says, serious. "I have some classes with Emir, and…" Hunter's stalling. "I know what it's like to fall for someone, and it's all confusing."

Sebastian deflates. Did Willie tell Hunter about his crush on Sebastian? Is this something else? Maybe Hunter's always waited around for Willie to notice him.

Hunter's phone buzzes, and Sebastian's heart beats to its noisiness. He says, "I don't know what it's like, Hunter, being in love."

"You know it's not easy to figure out, right? It's not overnight. And it doesn't happen just because you've been with someone for years. It's just this feeling. I don't think love knows how it works." Hunter's thumb rubs the crook of Sebastian's elbow.

"What is it, then?"

Hunter's eyes brighten. "If you're watching *Scooby Doo* and think of someone because it's their favorite cartoon. If you're allergic to flour but still eat someone's burnt pancakes. Or if you hate the color green but you wear it because it reminds you of a person's eyes just before you kiss them—well, it might be love."

Sebastian smiles helplessly. Is Hunter even a seventeen-year-old?

"And if you ever tell Will about this, I'm gonna use your testicles for keepie-uppies practice," warns Hunter. He gives Sebastian's arm a friendly squeeze.

"Got it."

Sebastian walks away with one thought: *Willie and Hunter are perfect for each other.*

❀

"Well, this captain thing suits you pretty well," Zach says after another grueling practice.

Sebastian can barely keep his eyes open. "You think so?"

Zach collapses next to Sebastian in the penalty box and hands him a water before cracking open his own.

Sebastian drags the bottle across his face. The relief that comes from cold condensation mixing with sticky sweat is great.

"You're certainly making an impression," says Zach. "Rollins has a man-crush on you."

Sebastian practically chokes on his first gulp of water. "He does not!" He *hopes* Rollins doesn't. Rollins is a freshman, and all over the place when it comes time to hold a conversation.

Zach shrugs. "Maybe not." He sips more water, then says, "Either way, we're looking good."

And they are. It's their final practice before Friday's big game and, though it's three weeks into the school year, the team's acing everything Coach Patrick throws at them. The defense still has a few holes—their wing-backs have opportunities—but nothing Sebastian can't live with. Their synergy is on point.

"We're passable," Sebastian says, dryly. Zach shoves him. Sebastian tips, catches himself with an elbow, and then laughs.

"Check this guy out," says Zach, nodding toward the sidelines where Willie, on crutches, practiced scowl and all, is reaming out the offense. "He's recovering nicely."

Sebastian's certain that's mostly because of Hunter. But also it's because Coach has been encouraging Willie's involvement from the sidelines. He's not letting Willie drown in self-pity, not the way he did those first few days. They call it *post-operative depression*, and Willie had it bad. He shut down, closed off the world, and wouldn't look Sebastian in the eye when he visited.

Now he's back, and all the coaches treat him like he's part of the staff instead of a player riding the bench. It's obvious the team respects him. And he's got this coaching thing down.

"It better not go to his head."

"It will." Suppressing a chuckle, Sebastian shakes up his water. Mason's going to be the first one to burst Willie's bubble. Sebastian's looking forward to it.

"Dude." Zach nudges Sebastian with an elbow. "Emir is a *beast*."

Sebastian crosses his ankles and lays his hands in his lap. He whispers, "Yeah."

Emir has become a monster on the pitch. He's every attacker's, including Mason's, worst nightmare. He outruns everyone and has a good read on a player's next move. He protects the penalty box as if it's his, as if he's determined to keep people away from Sebastian. It'd be flattering, but they're still not talking.

Zach knocks their shoulders. "They're crediting you for his turnaround. Mad respect, Bastian."

Sebastian lifts his eyebrows. Did he do *anything* for Emir? These days, all he does is give Emir a thumbs-up every time he makes a good play on the pitch. Sebastian's a coward. He should be shouting "I love you" as a good '80s movie demands. Sebastian is no Jake Ryan.

Even now, Sebastian's got it bad, staring at Emir in his practice uniform while Emir leans on Hunter or talks with Gio. His eyes scan Emir's toned calves, his narrow waist, his broad shoulders, and that skinny, long neck.

What a lovesick loser! All he has to do is stop being so sulky and say all of this to Emir. He finishes his water.

"We've got this in the bag, man," says Zach, offering Sebastian a fist bump. He reciprocates and focuses on what's ahead.

The Spartans are dust.

 **27**

Sebastian's not hiding.

He's calling this meditating, huddled in his old Lions hoodie, which now smells like Emir, with his knees pulled to his chest. His ass is numb from sitting on the stadium's cold stone bleachers.

John P. McKee Stadium, across from Bloomington High, belongs to the local community college. It's a coliseum built for gladiators. And because BHS's football team sucks, the college rents out the stadium for the soccer team's home games. It has a collegiate-level playing field, renovated locker rooms, and enough space to fit the whole city in the stands.

It's cool enough that Sebastian's breath is visible when he exhales. He studies the pitch. A lot of dreams come true on that stretch of green and white. Last year, a lot of dreams were crushed there too.

Sebastian fishes out his phone, keys in the code, and then glares at it. His wallpaper is a profile photo of his sworn enemy: St. Catherine's star attacker, Dawson. The guy is set for the pros; he's that good. "Asshole," Sebastian whispers. He keeps his photo as a reminder. He will not be beat by Dawson this year.

Friday, everyone will remember his name.

"Wow, this place sure is weird when it's not packed with people cheering you on." Lily settles next to him. Sighing wistfully, she drops her purse in her lap.

Sebastian pockets his phone. Usually, after practice, he hitches a ride with Mason. Today, Sebastian needed to be alone.

Lily pokes his cheek and asks, "Okay, what's got you down, Bumble Bee?"

No one's around to hear her, but Sebastian's still slightly embarrassed. She won't hesitate to use the nickname publicly. Parents say the worst things when a crowd's around, as if they earn extra parenting points for humiliating their children.

"Well," Sebastian starts, but Lily is wearing her *means business* face, so he bites his tongue.

Her superpower is seeing through his bullshit.

He says, shyly, "I'm scared, Mom. When the season's over, I have no clue what to do." His unexpected fearlessness outweighs the sweat breaking out across his hairline. "I don't know if I want to go to college, let alone where. All I have is this sport and the guys. After that, I'm lost."

Lily hums, and here it comes: The Talk about how important college is and that life goes on after sports. But Lily is an unpredictable force of nature. She asks, "What's wrong with being lost?"

Sebastian laughs. Behind his eyelashes is a needling burn. "It's wrong, Mom. I should be looking forward to college, to playing on a professional team."

"But why?"

"Because—"

Lily holds up a hand, and Sebastian's mouth snaps shut. She says, "Bastian, you can do whatever you want, when you want. The only thing in life you *have to do* is live it." Her hand covers his, squeezing. "Go to college, chase your dreams of being a pro athlete. Or take some time off, find yourself, and be an 'adult' later."

Sebastian blinks hard.

"Just because people create rules doesn't mean those are *your* rules. I don't follow those rules; neither does your dad."

Sebastian sniffs. A tear escapes, forcing him to slant his chin.

Lily clucks at him. "Do you honestly believe Mason and William won't hunt you down to get into trouble after graduation?" He shrugs, and she frowns as if she can't believe him. "Those boys are ruthless. Thank the heavens we stopped having children after you, because now I have three sons when I only asked for one."

Sebastian knows she's right. Mason will find some way to get him arrested, and Willie will bail them out.

"This is your senior year." Lily has a finger under his chin; her thumb wipes at a tear. "Let life happen. All the plans we make are not guaranteed."

"But—"

She cuts in. "High school is just like the night sky. It's beautiful. Some moments, you're just in awe of it. But it's dark and endless, which can be scary, too. When the stars fall away, what's left?"

Sebastian shrugs, his vision blurred.

"The sun," she says, giggling. "Darkness goes away, but the sun shows up and you start over again. So let high school happen, and eventually *you* light up the rest of your life. Burn as bright as you want. The wonderful thing about the sun is, it's always there. People don't have to see you to believe you'll be there."

Sebastian's heartbeat slows. He scrubs his sleeve over his wet eyes. His mom is pretty awesome. The future's foggy, but that's okay. He can take life wherever he wants, and his parents, Willie, and Mason will support him.

"I was thinking New York." New York City is huge and nothing like Bloomington. "Coach says a few schools are interested in me, and, if that doesn't work out, I can get a job until I sort it out." He pauses, waiting for her disapproval.

Lily smacks his shoulder. "Perfect, you can take me shopping, and Dad will love the coffee shops. I'm in." Her eyes scrunch; she's happy. "And take your sister with you. She's driving me nuts."

Sebastian can imagine it: a cheap apartment with big windows overlooking the city. Maybe he'll try out for the Red Bulls, or he could play for the Ramblers. He's read brochures. Playing for the International Gay and Lesbian Football Association, being involved in a team from the LGBTQ community, sounds pretty sweet. Coach Patrick would approve.

It doesn't escape him that Emir wants to go to New York too. So maybe he's daydreamed about them living together, sharing M&M's while studying in bed. That's just a pipe dream now.

"So," Lily, who is also part psychic, says, "was that Raj Shah's son I saw in the parking lot on the way in?"

Oh, God. Sebastian's body tenses so much his jaw clicks. Lily's mouth twists into a very curious smile, a sign she's calling his bluff, so he says sheepishly, "He's on the team this year."

Lily lights up. She claps. Her eyes are crinkled, the way Sebastian's get when he's over the moon about something. "Oh,

I love that boy!" she cheers. Then, in a careful voice, she says, "I always thought it was such a shame you two stopped seeing each other when you were younger."

Me too.

"Do you two talk?"

"Yeah, sort of. We're friends."

"And?"

"About that," Sebastian pauses, blinking so hard he might cry. He's trying to cough up a little bravery, just say the words, and not freak out.

"Bastian?"

He sucks in a breath. All he has to do is come out to his mom. Tell her how much his heart *aches* over a guy. He knows Emir's come out to his parents. They've talked about how supportive Emir's family is, and how Emir worried his religion would get in the way, but it hasn't. He's still a Shah, still as important to them as ever.

Sebastian's nerves hang on his tonsils, but he manages, "Emir is all I think about." *Almost there.* "Not as a friend, Mom, but… We started something, over the summer, and it didn't work out."

His shaking body wants to curl in on itself. Lily rests a hand on the nape of his neck and says, "You can't do anything to fix that?"

Sebastian's heart kicks like a wild animal. She's not disappointed or angry. She's worried. Her son admitting he's bisexual isn't the apocalypse; no, it's her son being without the person, *the boy* he loves that saddens her.

"Maybe." He shrugs wearily. "I hope. I don't know, Mom, but I love him."

And there it is. He's said it out loud, and he means it.

Sebastian's stomach backflips. Lily's eyes are huge, as if all she wants is to help Sebastian get Emir back, as though she'll love him no matter whom he loves.

"Oh, Bumble Bee, you're too perfect." Her fingers swipe away his tears. "I knew what you two had was special. As kids, you were inseparable. Whatever it is, things have a way of working themselves out."

Sebastian's against having a Taylor Swift oh-my-god moment. He scrubs the back of his hand over his eyes and sits taller. "You think so?"

"Honey, the universe is a bizarre place. Back then, Emir gazed at you like you were a solar system. So much to see! It's fate."

Sebastian laughs. None of this is funny, but holy hell, it's *hilarious*. He's just come out to his *mom*. He's got tear tracks on his cheeks and wants a giant root beer float. It's as if the whole damn world knew before Sebastian that he was lonely without his best friend, that he's in love with Emir.

"Well." Lily nudges his side, asks, "Does he know?"

"I don't think so."

"Tell him!"

It sounds easy. How hard can it be to say three words when he's already royally screwed things up by not saying *anything?*

"Thanks, Mom."

She squeezes him. "I love you, Bastian, and I truly love that boy too. Get your act together, because when I visit you in New York, I expect him to sit right next to me at all of your games."

 28

Pure, seconds-from-puking panic hits Sebastian an hour before Friday's game. The stadium is packed end to end. Bloomington soccer is the real draw for locals. No one misses a home game.

"We're ready," he whispers to himself, pacing the tunnel outside the locker rooms. He can't sit. He's too jumpy and anxious and delirious. This is his pregame ritual, and no one disturbs him, no one except Grey. She keeps poking her head out of Coach's office. Her big, reef-green eyes stare at him; her mouth is puckered as if she *might* say something.

"I'm fine."

She nods once, then disappears.

Sebastian unclenches his hands, shakes out his fingers, and returns to pacing. He didn't bring his headphones, so he can't crank The Killers and give himself something to transfer all his restlessness into. He scuffs his cleats on the cement and prays his stomach gets off the Tilt-a-Whirl it's been on all day.

"Dude, I can't believe you didn't know the answer to that one."

"I can't believe *you* didn't warn me about the quiz today."

Sebastian flinches at the voices. It's Hunter and Emir. Their laughter precedes their slow walk into the corridor. Shadows created by the poor lighting make it easy for Sebastian to hang back, plastering himself to the wall. He's been working toward saying *something* to Emir. He's just not there yet. And rehearsing "Hello" and "I love you" in the bathroom every morning isn't helping.

Hunter tousles Emir's hair. "Something distracting you lately, Shah?"

"Yeah, making you look like a loser on the pitch!"

Sebastian thumps his head on the wall. Damn it, he's missed Emir's raspy chuckle. It's a shame his balls aren't big enough that he can just *tell* him that.

Farther up, a door swings open and out barrel three of St. Catherine's defensemen. Sebastian only recognizes one: Mason's biggest rival, Cole Henry. Two bruisers flank him. One has shaggy gold-brown hair and an ugly smirk, and the other, a lean guy, has dark stubble and eyes green as spring grass. His jersey reads MICHAELSON, but his scowl says "Chief D-bag."

They stride up, blocking Emir and Hunter.

"Looky what we have, fellas," says Cole. "If it isn't Bloomington's sissy squad."

The hall echoes with their guffaws. Sebastian tenses. His sweaty fingers curl into fists. He's used to teams giving each other crap. It's all strategy, like any other sport. Hell, Carl or Zach do it to players frequently. If you can get in an enemy's head, the advantage is all yours. But these assholes are intent on something else.

Michaelson says, "The rainbow rebels, right?"

Shaggy punches his shoulder. He leers at Emir, then Hunter. "Careful, they might call their unicorn-riding coach on us."

They all howl, and Hunter's jaw tenses. Emir, on the other hand, stands tall, eyes black with thin gray rims. Sebastian's certain Emir is going to deck one of them, and then he'll be out of the game, dissolving any chances they'll have on defense. Of course, Sebastian will be benched, too, if any one of these idiots lifts a finger against Emir.

"Lay off," Hunter says, gruffly.

Cole steps into his space. "Or what? Did you know you play for a team of homos? Does your momma know that when you come home covered in—?"

"Piss off," Emir snarls. His shoulders are wire-tight; his nostrils flare.

Michaelson and Shaggy slant forward, but Cole spreads his arms, keeping them back. He chuckles. "Oh, you've got a mouth on you." His head cocks. "Bet you put it to good use, right?"

"What a lovely accent," teases Michaelson.

Cole licks his teeth. "Yeah, he does. London boy?" He's in front of Emir now. "Do you like playing with a team full of fairies?"

The skin around Emir's eyes tightens. He lets out a long breath, but he doesn't back down.

Sebastian's heart is rabbiting. He could take Cole. Maybe the other two, also. They're all talk, a St. Catherine's trademark. He just needs to get close enough to—

Another door bangs open, from Bloomington's locker room, and out marches Zach. He stops, sizing up the situation. Then, he grins wolfishly. "Well, St. Catherine's School for the Poor and Shameless," he says, and, in two strides, he's between Cole and Emir. After a beat, Cole steps back.

Sebastian's still wound up, ready to swing.

"Is this a pregame pep talk?" Zach asks. He slants his eyes at Cole. "You need some advice from our new star sweeper on how to tighten up your shitty defense?"

Cole scowls. "You're going down, Keating."

"Hmm, those fighting words or are you flirting?"

Cole's hands ball into fists. Michaelson and Shaggy snarl behind him. Zach rocks on his heels while Cole turns red, huffing.

"For a school full of preppy assholes, you're sure concerned with my team's sex lives." Zach's posturing is at an all-time high. "Want in on the action?"

"You pack of faggots better—"

That's it. It's all Zach needs before he's in Cole's face, chest to chest, noses nearly touching. He growls, "Say it a little louder, dickhead." His grin is leaning toward psychotic. "That's right, some of my bros are gay or bi, and they can kick your ass blindfolded."

Cole flinches while Michaelson and Shaggy blanch and lean away.

Zach says, "Next time you want to talk shit to my brothers, do it with confidence." He points behind himself. "Shah and Hunter? They're family, and I'll whale on any of you prep pussies that messes with 'em, okay?"

Cole's mouth is thin, trembling. He slowly steps backward. He signals to Michaelson and Shaggy with a jerk of his head; their grumbles are tinny in the corridor as they stomp off.

Zach turns around, eyes lit up. He's still feasting on their cowardice. He is so menacing. "Douchebags." He points his chin at Hunter and Emir. "Hey, next time you guys head out, let me know."

"I could've handled them," protests Emir.

Zach cuffs the back of Emir's neck with a big hand and pulls him forward. "I know, Shah." His grin twitches. "But I've been dying to deck one of those shitheads since I was a frosh. They called me a bastard because my mom left my dad. It got in my head, so I owe them."

Sebastian's mouth is dry. Zach just full-on opened up to someone other than Sebastian, to Emir, of all people. Zach never talks about his mom.

"Thanks, Keating."

"Anytime, Shah."

Zach drags Emir into a headlock. Emir playfully fights back, though Zach's size overpowers him. Hunter joins them, jumping on Zach's back. They all stumble into the locker room with a thud.

Sebastian sags against the wall. The concrete is cold against his ass. He pulls his knees to his chest. "Dude," he says, quietly, "is this my life?"

No one answers, of course.

Sebastian's heart finally slows to a lethargic thud, and he laughs. It's one of those movie-villain-cackles, reverberating off the walls. Grey peeks her head out, but he doesn't care. He's just witnessed a freaking *miracle*.

"Okay," says Grey, slowly. "Game time in twenty."

Sebastian whacks his head on the wall to make sure it's not a dream. Then he nods at her. He hums "Eye of the Tiger," because *Rocky* movies really are magical.

The Lions are about to kick the Spartans' asses.

THE LOCKER ROOM IS FRANTIC. Guys are hopped up on adrenaline, roughhousing, shoving each other, snapping towels. A few players are being taped up to protect soreness or mild injuries. Gio and Jack are engaged in a furious game of bloody knuckles. Rollins is pale, huddled in a corner, saying Hail Marys.

Warm-up gear is shed; uniforms are pulled on. It's noisy and smelly and just the kind of atmosphere Sebastian craves before a game. He still might vomit, but in a good way, like he would stepping off the world's fastest rollercoaster.

"Delson! Get out of that mirror and suit up," Willie shouts, moving swifter than any boy on crutches should.

Kyle flips him off and returns to his reflection, fixing his hair. "Coach Willie's more of a hard-ass than Rivera."

"And don't you forget it," Willie says over his shoulder.

Mason is hunched over, forearms on his thighs, head bobbing, with the chord of his Beatz wound around a finger. He's got a bench to himself. No one bothers him thirty minutes before a game. He doesn't meet eyes with anyone; he's slipped into a zone.

Sebastian gets it. Everything about today is exciting. It's terrifying and so big that they all need a way to escape for just a few minutes. That's the thing about life: The biggest, most thrilling moments can make you wish they wouldn't happen at all.

Coach barrels in, with Grey following, then Rivera and O'Brien. He says, voice booming, "Okay, gather 'round, Lions," before he slips into his usual pregame speech. It's profanity-filled and meaningful.

Sebastian rests against his locker.

Freshman eyes are saucer-wide. Guys elbow to get closer. Coach doesn't talk for the hell of it. If he isn't going to inspire you, he's silent. He's not going to quote dead legends. He spouts rap lyrics, spinning them to fit his brand of motivation. Sebastian's never heard LL Cool J used so poetically.

Coach pins Sebastian with his eyes. "Now, let's hear from Captain Hughes."

Sebastian doesn't shrink, though his heart has claimed residence in his throat. He's not expecting the applause or the back-claps as he nudges his way to the front. They amp up his nerves. He smiles shakily for Willie, then avoids eye contact with Carl as he passes. Carl's still shit on the bottoms of his shoes.

When Sebastian climbs up on a bench, towering over his peers, things shift. It hits him like electric shock. Last Saturday, he ate cold pizza for breakfast, binged an entire season of *American Horror Story* from the couch, had waffles for dinner, and it was just another day. Today, he's playing one of his biggest games, witnessed his friends come together, and is staring the boy he loves right in the eyes.

And that's the thing, life is sometimes just another day, and sometimes it's moment after moment after moment that only paralyzes you if you let it.

Sebastian's not letting it.

Mason says, grinning, "C'mon Hughes, inspire us."

Sebastian rubs the back of his neck. "I suck at speeches." He pauses; a teacher once told him that pointing out your weaknesses leaves you vulnerable to your audience. "We all know what this season is about, right?"

"Winning the championship!"

"Well, yes, *that*." Sebastian winks at Gio. "Also, it's about proving ourselves, proving life isn't only about what you accomplish." His eyes find Zach, then Willie. "It's about proving to yourself you can make the best of what you've been given."

Zach tips his chin up.

"We're not those guys from camp anymore. That's our past. Last season is our past too. It doesn't define who we are right now." Goosebumps break out on his arms; his eyes well up. This isn't just for Zach; it's for Sebastian too. He's not his past, his youth. He's *not* Bastian the Trashcan anymore. That's a lesson he's learned from counseling and talks with his family. "*We* decide our futures. No one can stop us, especially not some pathetic Spartans.

"We don't need to beat any team, 'cause we beat ourselves. 'Cause we're better than all of them." His hands are shaky. He clears his throat. The lump of anxiety melts, and he says, "Now who are we?"

"Lions!"

Willie is the loudest. He hobbles forward and leans into Grey.

"And what are we gonna do?"

"Kill the Spartans!"

Coach clears his throat gruffly and drags a finger across it.

Sebastian holds in a chuckle. "Okay, maybe not *kill*, but you will protect your brother. If someone hurts your family, take them down—" Again, Coach clears his throat, and Sebastian says, with a wry smile, "—*legally*, please."

A cacophony of laughter breaks out. The roughhousing resumes, and Sebastian hops to the ground. Willie ruffles his hair, and Mason's at his side. He's breathing too fast, but the rush is awesome. He peeks over his shoulder.

In the corner, Emir's watching blankly. Then he nods. Sebastian bites his tongue before he says something outrageous.

THE STADIUM IS ROARING WHEN the team runs onto the pitch. In the bleachers, a giant sea of black and gold is only blemished by the occasional blots of St. Catherine's crimson and yellow team colors. Sebastian's goosebumps return. The fans get louder with every step.

His parents and Carly are in their usual seats just behind the home bench. Lily is whooping with black paint smudged across her nose. Sebastian flushes, then waves. He expects that from her. What he's not ready for are, two rows behind his clan, Raj Shah and Emir's entire family. Emir's sisters are holding up a massive white sheet with "WE LOVE YOU BHAI!!!" painted on it in black and gold.

Emir's cheeks are burning, and he covers his eyes with a hand. When the hand drops, Sebastian mouths "Bhai" and Emir's lips form *Brother*.

Raj's face looks proud, ecstatic. Emir hasn't played a single second yet, and already Raj is over the moon.

The stakes have reached a new height.

 *29*

SEBASTIAN LOVES GREEK MYTHOLOGY, ALL the stories about heroes and legends, monsters and tragedy, romance and death. He wrote an epic paper about Jason and the Argonauts. It's the only reason he passed Mr. Gentry's lit class sophomore year. He knows this game is a clash between Titans and Olympic gods from the first coin toss.

Three minutes into the first period, a Spartan takes Kyle out with a brutal, illegal tackle. Kyle is carried off, and the other guy, Jeffries, takes a red card and gets a high-five from Cole on his way to the bench. The Spartans aren't going down without taking half the Lions with them.

Cain, a frosh, comes in for Kyle, but Sebastian's hopes slip. Kyle was one of their best offensive threats.

The game continues with a little less enthusiasm. Then Carl takes out two Spartans with a shove when the refs are following Mason around the pitch. He shoots Sebastian a wry grin. "Oops, I didn't see them."

Sebastian bites his lip to maintain a straight face. He still hardcore hates Carl's guts, but St. Catherine's coach losing his shit on the sidelines is pretty damn funny.

It's a scoreless game halfway into the first period. Sebastian's giddy over blocking five of St. Catherine's attempts. Mason may not have nailed a shot yet, but their offense is running great passes. It's all good.

Sebastian doesn't let a single free kick get past him. Between these stripes and posts is his house. Dawson and all his flunkies aren't faster than his hands.

Willie is animated on the sidelines. Smacking his hands on a clipboard, he barks, "Run a forty-two." When Cain trips over his own feet, Willie swears at the clouds. Hunter's hands smooth Willie's shoulder from behind. He leans back, and Sebastian *almost* chastises them for PDA in the middle of a very important game.

The whistle blows, and Sebastian drops into his zone. Ten seconds in, Dawson's bulleting toward him. Sebastian hunches into position. But a black-and-gold blur steals the ball. Emir passes it up to Gio with a "Go, Gio, go" before Sebastian's caught his breath.

It's the tenth time Emir's done that. Yes, Sebastian's keeping count.

O'Brien shouts, "Nice play, Shah!" and Emir barely reacts. He maintains the same face: furrowed brow, thinned lips, steely eyes. But Sebastian has this *synergy* with Emir, something that began somewhere in the middle of Camp Haven's pitch under a stormy-gray sky. It's only the start of the season. Sebastian can't imagine how good they'll be together in a month.

Over his shoulder, sweaty hair pushed back, Emir shouts, "Am I still a rookie?"

Sebastian smiles with his eyes.

By the time the ref blows the whistle for halftime, Sebastian doesn't remember the last five minutes. He's developed an obsession with the gold SHAH on the back of Emir's jersey.

"They're afraid of us." Coach Patrick paces the locker room. The team is gathered around him, mopping up sweat, chugging from paper cups spilling Gatorade. "Last year, we were down two goals in the first half." His eyes center on Sebastian. "Now they can't get around our defense."

"And they won't," says Zach, softly patting Emir's cheek.

"Yeah," agrees Coach. "So, now—"

"They're weak on the left side."

Coach mutters, "Yes, I'm aware, Grace." She grouses back. Coach points at Mason. "That's the plan, Riley. Concentrate on getting the ball toward the left. Rivera says their goalie is tracking you, so we might use Robbie as a decoy."

Mason scrunches his face, indignant. Then, with as much modesty as he can muster, he mumbles, "Yeah, sure. Go Lions." He gives Robbie a thumbs-up.

Robbie's white as a sheet when Sebastian palms his back. He says, encouragingly, "Come on, rookie," and leads the charge back through the tunnel.

The second half brings a new buzz to the stadium. The crowd's loud enough to drown out any calls on the field. Sebastian's hunched over, scouting. He has his eye on one thing. The Spartans have also changed their lineup. Michaelson and Cole have switched, putting a giant obstacle right in Mason's path.

Shit.

The whistle blows, and Sebastian makes a last-second decision. He shouts, "Em! Emi!"

Emir's head snaps around, and Sebastian cringes at his scowl. Maybe calling him Emi wasn't his brightest moment, but whatever. If they're going to win, he needs Emir on his side.

"If they get through, get the ball to Smith."

Emir's eyebrows slide inward. It's possible he'll ignore Sebastian's advice. But then Emir nods eagerly. And, no, Sebastian's stupid heart isn't so far up his throat that it might break out in Charlie Puth songs.

He's right, though. Cole is all over Mason, and Robbie isn't faring any better. Shaggy passes up to a Spartan winger, and Sebastian anticipates the coming attack.

Emir, like a strike of lightning, picks off the attacker. He snags the ball; the other guy is too winded to chase after him.

Rivera is barking, "Give it to Robbie; Robbie is open!" Willie bites his nails. Grey hangs her head between her knees.

It all happens in action movie slow motion. Ignoring Rivera, Emir passes the ball up to a shell-shocked Smith. No one's covering him, so he runs. A Spartan clips Smith, but he scoops the ball to Zach before eating grass.

Zach takes a rip at the ball.

The whistle blows, fifteen minutes on the clock, and Sebastian stares at the jumbo scoreboard: SPARTANS — 0, LIONS — 1

The crowd loses their shit. The Spartans' sideline is sick. Rivera lights into Emir for making such a risky play, but Emir keeps his chin up the entire time.

Rivera, eyes narrowed, says, "Get back out there, kid," and Sebastian catches him smiling as Emir jogs back onto the field.

"If I get benched next game," Emir pauses, catching his breath, "I'm never speaking to you again."

"Does that mean we're speaking now? Like, we're cool?"

Whatever Emir's about to say, he's too flustered, so he flips Sebastian off as he treks back into position. And, okay. Sebastian will take that. These days "I hate you" sounds a lot like "I love you" coming from Emir.

Mason scores another goal at the four-minute mark, but it's pretty much academic after Zach's goal. Sebastian shuts out Dawson five more times, and the Spartans never recover. It's a clean sweep, two to zero. Sebastian can't hear himself breathe over the roaring crowd.

The sky's broken up with gold and maroon. Sweat chills Sebastian's brow. It's the middle of September, so the air is nippy when the game ends at sunset. Heads hanging, St. Catherine's boys stomp out of the stadium. Cole trails, scowling, and Sebastian hopes they meet again in the state tournament so he can make that face permanent.

"Fellas, fellas," shouts Zach in the locker room. His voice carries over the chorus of "Immortals" coming from the showers and all the laughter as guys strip out of dank uniforms. Willie's on his shoulders, smiling from ear to ear, when Zach says, "Sergio's Pizzeria for a couple of pies. It's a team tradition."

Sebastian's huddled on a bench, squished between Hunter and Mason. Soaked, limp hair sticks to his forehead. He twists around to get a better view of all the action.

"First round," says Zach, pointing at Sebastian, "is on our beloved captain."

Hunter whoops happily.

Sebastian sags when a chant of "Captain Hughes" breaks out. Winning has never been so draining. But the exhaustion from war and relief and joy is incredible, and a night of pizza means fewer chances of the guys doing something arrest-worthy.

"You coming?"

Mason's eyeing him, observant as a hawk, so Sebastian says, "Maybe, but there's something I kinda want to do first."

He has plans. He's not sure if they'll work out. Maybe this is his worst idea yet, including setting fire to a neighbor's garbage with Mason when they were thirteen, or playing drunk Scrabble in a cemetery. Might as well, right?

Sebastian whispers, "Could use your help, actually."

Mason flicks up an eyebrow. His silence only elevates the ridiculous thump of Sebastian's heartbeat. But a glint shines in Mason's eyes. "Anything you need, Captain."

 30

Iᴛ'ꜱ ᴇꜱᴘᴇᴄɪᴀʟʟʏ ᴅᴀʀᴋ ᴡɪᴛʜ ᴛʜᴇ stadium's floodlights off. The sky's an inky blue over the deserted pitch. It's been thirty minutes since Sebastian sent his parents a text saying he'd meet them later and twenty-five minutes since he sent the team off with promises of dropping by Sergio's. It's been twenty-two minutes since he hijacked Grey, whispered his idea in her ear while slipping her some money for supplies, and pried her hands from around his forearm as she leapt around ecstatically.

Sebastian grimaces at his surroundings.

Two dozen lit candles are spread around the pitch. Grey helped, cracking jokes about the grass catching on fire. Yeah, exactly what he needs. But as cheesy as it is, those flickering lights add to the whole grand-romantic-gesture crap he was aiming for.

Sebastian hugs himself against the dry, chilly air. He paid Clark, the stadium's tech guy, to create an atmosphere. None of that One Republic or The Fray lameness. No Coldplay. Sebastian's cheesy, but he can't do corny.

In his head, the soundtrack to Sebastian's life with Emir is vibrant and loud, like electric indigo. It's thunderstorms over a city. It's neon-bright, like summer fireflies.

The crappy PA system is playing M83, and it's perfect.

Sebastian fishes out his phone and checks the time. He paces in a circle. He's trying not to get too far into his own head. Lily's words echo: "When the stars fall away…" They prevent him from having a panic attack. That is, until Emir says, "What the bloody hell is this?"

Sebastian winces, then turns slowly. Sweat prickles against his scalp. It only takes him five seconds to realize he's not going to have a panic attack. No, this was worth the wait and the small bursts of anxiety.

Emir is staring at Sebastian, motionless. It's discomfiting, but whatever, right? It's not Emir's first time using the "what the hell?" glare.

"Bastian?"

Sebastian beams, unashamed.

A line of candles separates them. Sebastian stretches a hand toward Emir. After a long pause, Emir's palm slides over Sebastian's. He steps forward, angling right into Sebastian's body, hesitation be damned.

Sebastian says, "I'm sorry."

"Okay."

"For a lot of things," Sebastian quickly adds. Emir laces their fingers together and it steadies him. "For years and years of being a total idiot, and for those last days at camp." He didn't plan what he'd say. He whispers, "Also, for not telling you a bunch of things."

"Like?"

"I've missed you, forever. When you went to England, when I first saw you at camp, the last few days." His throat tightens. "Before and after today's game."

Sebastian never had to express himself to Sam. With her lack of investment, she didn't need it. Or maybe she did, but he's chalking up to youth his failure to recognize such things. Now, with Emir, he's learning to get his thoughts and emotions and nameless-whatever out of his system.

Emir says, "Me too."

"Yeah?"

"Yeah, reckon so," says Emir, smiling. "You bloody well know that."

Sebastian doesn't know a lot of things, but he's discovering them. He's tired of being a coward. But things like this take time. He says, clearly and openly, "I love you. I didn't know it years ago, but I don't think you understand those things when you're ten."

"Me neither."

Sebastian didn't know how much he wanted to hear those words until now.

Emir says, "You don't realize how much you've done for me. Abbu was so proud of me today." Tiny flames make Emir's eyes translucent gray. He's meets Sebastian's eyes. "It was so hard being around you at first. I wanted to walk away."

Sebastian's fingers squeeze Emir's. Emir twitches, but doesn't pull away. And Sebastian, full of calm and understanding, threads fingers into Emir's damp hair to keep loose strands off his face.

"You're losing your touch."

"Your face is insufferable."

"Weak," teases Sebastian.

"And I want your bloody hoodie back. It's mine," Emir says. And scowls.

It's the opposite of romantic, and Sebastian laughs, sudden and bright, until his stomach coils into a knot. "Better," he says between breaths.

Amused lines form around Emir's eyes.

"So, this is, um, me and you?" Sebastian pauses. "I'm allowed to call you my..."

It's just one word. His brain isn't used to referring to someone as his boyfriend. Maybe he wants to be okay with it. He's already done the hard part, coming out to his family, defining what love is to him.

He can do this.

But Emir must sense his intent, because he brushes his mouth over Sebastian's. He whispers, "Just call me Emi, okay?"

Lips still resting near Emir's, Sebastian says, "Emi."

His heart does acrobatics. Emir flashes this toothy smile that has been all for Sebastian since forever. So, he kisses Emir.

Five minutes later, slightly out of breath, Sebastian says, "I have no idea what I want to do after graduation." If he's going to do it, he might as well shed all his secrets.

Emir circles his arms around Sebastian's neck. "College? Pros? Stripper?"

Sebastian snorts. He wiggles his eyebrows, and Emir quickly protests, "I'm not sharing you with anybody."

"That's good to know."

The low-burning candles shine light across their faces. Sebastian slides a hand up Emir's spine. "What about New York?" he asks. "I don't have a plan, but if the pros don't work out, maybe coaching?"

"Good idea. You're getting better at that."

"I've got a lot of practice with a stubborn player."

"New York sounds good."

"Yeah?"

Emir's cold fingertips press Sebastian's nape. His warm breath brushes Sebastian's cheek. "We could make do."

Sebastian almost loses focus. Emir's thumb rubs that soft spot behind his ear, and Sebastian cranes his head back. *We.* Emir said "we," and Sebastian has to be sure. Emir's shy expression is confirmation enough.

"I've applied for a scholarship, and my parents have found some good deals on apartments," Emir says. "The Village?"

It takes a second before Sebastian comprehends: Emir is asking *him.* "Yes" slips from his mouth. And then he kisses Emir, again. It's not perfect. Sebastian doesn't care, because nothing about them has ever been perfect. But it's soft, and he settles into the shape of Emir's mouth, slow-building toward incredible.

"Finally!"

It's Willie hollering, followed by wolf-whistles and laughter. In the bleachers, the whole team is either making dramatic kissy faces or gagging like total assholes.

Sebastian loves them. He loves that Emir hides his face in the crook of Sebastian's neck, earning them a few more catcalls, before Emir owns his abashment. Sebastian loves that Zach is arm in arm with Jack.

Charlie screams, "Get it, Hughes!"

"I got it all on video," yells Grey, shaking her cell in the air. She's hip to hip with Willie, and Mason is leaning into her. Huh. That might work out.

A quiet coolness settles in Sebastian. He hasn't figured it all out yet. But an entire season is ahead of him. And then graduation.

There's still time.

The future is only grim because people see it that way. It's unpredictable. Life is a summer storm of insecure thoughts. There's an umbrella of precautions to prevent insecurity, but it doesn't always keep the rain out of your face.

Besides, over the summer, Sebastian's learned that he doesn't mind the rain. Good things happen in the rain. It's great for scrimmages and sleeping in and accidental kisses with the one person you think hates you most.

Right now, the future can kiss Sebastian's ass.

He's under a blue-purple sky. The air smells of burnt wax, ground spices, and chilled cider; his favorite autumn scents. And his team—nope, his *family*—is cheering him on. The future looms, and it isn't promising him a chance to watch Mason make the pros, to see Zach get the hell out of Bloomington, to crash in Willie and Hunter's dorm. And that's okay. He doesn't let it ruin the moment.

Sebastian is sometimes directionless. The old scars from bullies are still healing. And, yeah, he can be dull and boring, but he's okay with that. His family and friends are okay with it. His boyfriend, which sounds weird but awesome, is okay with it too. It doesn't need to get better than this. It *can*; he hopes it does; but maybe that's for another summer.

"Hey," Sebastian says, his thumb rubbing Emir's cold, dry lips. "Are you gonna get up early and go running with me tomorrow?"

"Shut up, Bastian," Emir says. He grins. "Of course I am."

ACKNOWLEDGMENTS

THIS BOOK HAS BEEN A journey from the first word but it's a journey I would've never taken had it not been for quite a few amazing people.

Thank you S.A. McAuley for pushing me to finally write a book instead of hiding in a corner. You saw the first draft, the first synopsis, and the first rejection. You never let me quit. You are my hero, my writing guru, but, most of all, you are my friend. I love you.

Thank you to everyone at Duet Books and Interlude Press for believing in Sebastian's story and in me. Annie, you've been one of my biggest cheerleaders since the beginning. Sebastian is as much yours as he is mine. Candy, you're a rock-star. I am still unsure how you do everything you do, but I am grateful you're always the first to jump in and get your hands "dirty" for every author. C.B. Messer, you're a magician. You pulled the book cover concept out of thin air! It's beautiful and everything I didn't know I wanted but am thankful to have. To quote Willie, your talent is "Epic."

Forever grateful to my editors Annie Harper, Nicki Harper, and Zoë Bird. Each of you embraced the story I wanted to tell. I went through loops and challenges and a few teary-eyed moments, but it was well worth it. Thank you for taking my lump of clay and carving it into something beautiful.

To my beta readers: Caroline, Gaby, Daniela, Lincoln, and Tiffany—the things each of you did to help me fine-tune this book cannot be repaid in simple "thank you's." I love the bond we've made over the Lions.

Special thanks to my sensitivity reader, Fadwa. You helped to craft who Emir is and helped me to understand him in a new light. I hope Muslim teens everywhere see a part of him in themselves.

Jude Sierra, Pene Henson, and Ben Monopoli—thanks for encouraging me to submit this book! Also, thanks for dealing with my moments of self-doubt and pure panic over it, too. C.B. Lee, you're awe-inspiring; I can't begin to thank you for all you've done for me. Rebecca Bratton, you told me to quit my job and pursue this dream. You wouldn't take "no" for an answer. I am forever indebted to your bravery, your words of wisdom, and your friendship.

To every fandom reader and writer who has messaged me through the years: a heap of gratitude and love for always standing by me. You sparked a fire in me that I hope never goes out. Special thanks to Eszter, Lynn, Jazz, Avery, Rayza, Ashley, and Ducky—your "you can do this" messages have been incredible.

My wonderful family and friends—Wow! This really happened. Thanks Mom for taking me out of a dark place and telling me I can pursue this dream. Thanks Dad, Sonya, Tamir, Lindsay, and everyone who cheered me on. Tamica, Jason, Ahmad, Angela, and Tony, thanks for always letting me be me.

Finally, to all the LGBTQIA+ teens everywhere—you're my inspiration. You're the leaders. You're the star players. You're the true heroes. The future is yours whenever you're ready to take hold of it. Until then, burn as bright as you want!

ABOUT THE AUTHOR

JULIAN WINTERS IS A FORMER management trainer who lives in the outskirts of Atlanta, Georgia and has been crafting fiction since he was a child, creating communities around his hand-drawn "paper people." He began writing LGBTQ character-driven stories as a teen and has developed a devoted fan fiction following. When he isn't writing or using his sense of humor to entertain his young nephews, Julian enjoys reading, experimental cooking in the kitchen, and watching the only sports he can keep up with: volleyball and soccer. *Running with Lions* is his first novel.

🌐 julianwinters.tumblr.com
🐦 @julianw_writes
📷 wintersjulian

Q&A WITH JULIAN

Q: How did your love of team sports, culture, and dynamics inspire and influence your writing?

At the heart of any team sport is one underlying theme: family. I believe we have two families in life—the one you're given and the one you create. That's the culture you witness while watching team sports. It's very inspiring. In the soccer world, there are so many moving parts—so many cogs in this fantastic machine, and every piece is important. But what I also love are those moments of players laughing and teasing each other and bonding. They're the first ones to stand in defense for one of their own. I wanted those dynamics reflected in *Running with Lions*. Every character is an important piece of the machine. At the end of the day, this sport created a second family for them.

Q: Was diverse representation something you set out to achieve?

Yes and no. We live in a time when it's rare to go through everyday life without interacting with people from diverse backgrounds. It's one of the most beautiful aspects of life: building those connections with people unlike ourselves. A lot of the characters, their backgrounds, were organic for me. I didn't set out to feature characters from different races, religious beliefs, or social backgrounds in order for my book to reach a diversity benchmark. It'd be unrealistic for me to write a story that didn't feature characters who weren't from different backgrounds when, for most of my life, my friends and coworkers and classmates have all been from diverse backgrounds.

It's time we normalize diversity in books, films, and TV. It needs to be the standard rather than the unique occasion.

Q: What drew you to writing a Young Adult novel? Are there particular themes of YA that you felt were important for *Running with Lions*?

I want to write books that inspire or comfort young adults because I didn't have those things growing up. A lot of who I became as an adult were manifested in those years. I didn't always have places to look for encouragement or understanding. It's an opportunity to use my voice and reach queer teens, to tell them I understand, to let them know life's not perfect but it truly does get to a better place.

One theme that was very important to me was Sebastian's indecision about his future. It's a topic I wish was explored more in YA. Not every teen walks into the first day of high school with their future planned out. Some aren't even sure what they'll do the day of graduation. Those young adults need to know it's okay. They need to see their fears or concerns or indecision represented on the page. The speech Lily, Sebastian's mom, gives at the end of the novel was my way of telling those teens that life will happen when you're ready for it to happen. Until then, carry on the best way you can.

Q: What books did you love when you were growing up?

I'm old school. I loved *The Outsiders*. The family aspect of that novel really resonates. Another favorite was *The Catcher in the Rye*. Unfortunately, there weren't many LGBTQ+ novels accessible to me, but I'm thrilled there are so many choices now.

Q: What books have you read lately that you wish were available when you were a teenager?

As a certified comic book geek, I wish C.B. Lee's *Not Your Sidekick* was around when I was a teen—not just the superhero aspects, but the storytelling, the setting, and the diverse characters. It's nice to see myself in so many aspects of that book. *Aristotle and Dante Discover the Secrets of the Universe* by Benjamin Alire Sáenz is a book that would've helped me come to terms with my emotions and my sexuality in a much healthier way. I would've also loved books like *Noah Can't Even* by Simon James Green, *Simon vs. the Homo Sapiens Agenda* by Becky Albertalli, *Whatever* by S.J. Goslee, and *The Rules and Regulations for Mediating Myths & Magic* by F.T. Lukens because they're fun books with clumsy, comical, and earnestly confused main characters, which perfectly describes me as a teen!

For a reader's guide to **Running with Lions**
and book club prompts, please visit duetbooks.com.

an imprint of interlude**press**

 duetbooks.com
 @duetbooks
 duetbooks
 store.interludepress.com